A GAME OF TWO HEARTS

A TOUCHLINE SAPPHIC ROMANCE

IONA KANE

IONA KANE

A Game of Two Hearts

Copyright © 2022 by Iona Kane

Cover design: Cath Grace Designs

Editor: Global Wordsmiths

Visit my website: ionakane.com

Follow me on Instagram, Facebook and Twitter: @ionakanewriter

For Vix
I miss your bone-crushing hugs

ONE

Tess stripped off her overalls and looked around at her handiwork with a deep sense of satisfaction. The room was never going to be pretty. Her newly reclaimed home was an unlovable nineteen-seventies town house, but she had just finished painting the rooms in a variety of deep and pale greens, and it felt calm and fresh, and most importantly, all hers. It wasn't until she'd begun to look at paint colours that she realised she'd never made a decision about decor in her life. She'd had ideas, but Pete had always overruled them.

Now here she was, with her sole name on the deeds of a house, choosing how to decorate and furnish it. It had taken her long enough to get to this point of independence, and she planned to savour every moment. To be more accurate, her foreseeable future contained a lot of rushing about and trying to make ends meet, so savour might be a bit optimistic. But without a doubt, she would appreciate her freedom.

Tess pulled up a garden chair. The furniture she'd ordered would be a few more weeks. She'd had to shop around for the best deals, and she couldn't afford to be fussy about quick delivery. But she'd got the kids' beds delivered and assembled. This house had its memories and a lot of them weren't great, so she wanted it to look and feel completely different, as far as she could within her tiny budget. She groaned, knowing there really wasn't time to be sitting around. She dragged herself out of the chair and swung the French doors open wide. It was a glorious September afternoon, and she shouldn't be cooped up inside. She wandered into the garden and tipped her face to the sky. That way she could enjoy feeling the warm sun on her skin without taking in the devastation around her. When she'd left eleven years ago, the garden had been an oasis of bedding plants and shrubs, providing colour and escape. Gardening had kept her sane, the kids playing happily on the lawn, while Pete was left in peace to play his video games or whatever his obsession was at the time. They'd only lived in this house for a couple of years, but she'd inherited the garden in good condition, and it hadn't taken her long to get it perfect. It had broken her heart to leave it and start all over again.

Now, after more than a decade of renting the house out, the garden looked like a rugby pitch at the end of a hard season. Not all the tenants had neglected it, but the most recent had done the bare minimum. After an unusually dry summer, there wasn't much life in the beds, and the lawn was patchy and brown.

She pulled at some weeds for a while, but when she stood back up, it was hard to see where she'd made a difference. She ran her hands through her hair as she surveyed the mess, mentally prioritising what had to be done now and what could wait until later. She'd orchestrated a long weekend without the kids, and she wanted their new home to be welcoming. Elsie had wanted to come with her to help, but Tess had insisted she make the most of her last few days of the summer holidays before she started her A-level year. It was going to be stressful enough with the long commutes each day.

Tess wondered again if she'd made the right decision coming back here. It had seemed an easy solution to getting her financial independence and cutting ties with Pete as quickly as possible, but her commitment to keep the kids at their schools in what was such a critical year for them both, now seemed like a tall order. And this miserable village was miles from anywhere. She'd hated the feeling of isolation when she'd lived here before, but she was going to have to put up with it, at least for now. She shrugged her shoulders to loosen them and returned her attention to the job in front of her.

"C'mon, Mum, I don't want to be late," Elsie said.

She tossed the car keys to Tess, who was attempting to throw on her jacket and load the dishwasher at the same time. Tess bent to kiss the top of Archie's bowed head as she passed. "An hour of gaming and no more, promise? And only after you've done that English homework."

Archie looked up from his comic book. "I hate English."

"All the more reason to get your homework out of the way. I *will* check in the morning so don't let me down, Archie."

He shrugged and returned his attention to his comic.

"I'm sorry we're leaving you on your own. We should be back by bedtime. Promise me you'll be okay?"

"I'm not a baby, Mum." He didn't look up.

She ruffled his auburn hair. "I know you're not. Be

good, and we'll be home soon. In bed by ten, remember, if we're not back by then. With these early starts, we all need to be tucked up at a reasonable time."

He shrugged again. "Yeah, bye."

"Mum!" Elsie's voice was impatient now.

Tess leaned in for another peck. "See you later."

Elsie slouched against the car, looking at her watch. Tess unlocked the doors quickly, and they got in. "Sorry, sweetheart. I don't like leaving him."

"He's in his element. You could put him in a town surrounded by all his friends, and he'd still prefer to be on his own in his room. I don't know why you worry about him so much, Mum. He's fine." She waved her wrist in Tess's direction. "I, on the other hand, am going to be late."

Tess turned the key, silently rejoicing when the engine started first try. She wished she'd insisted on buying a newer car, but the old Volvo had always been reliable for the shopping and school runs, and she'd never felt the need to upgrade. Now she was doing so many miles a week, the old wreck didn't fill her with as much confidence. She pulled out of the drive and headed for the main road to town. "We'll be there in no time. At least I know the roads."

"How does it feel to be back, Mum? It must bring back some weird memories." Elsie watched her closely.

"It is a bit strange, I admit." She wanted to say the feeling of relief to finally be free of Pete outweighed any other concerns, but she tried to shield her kids from the hostility of the breakup and never badmouthed Pete in front of them. Pete, unfortunately, hadn't done the same.

"Why don't you sell up and move closer to town? You won't meet many people living out in the sticks. You've got a chance to live your own life, finally. You might find someone who makes you happy."

Tess glanced at her before returning her attention to the road. Did Elsie really think that was a priority for her? To get trapped in another relationship. "Oh, I don't think so, Elsie. I'm very happy being on my own. And what the two of you need comes before anything else. The last thing you deserve is even more disruption."

"If I get into Haresby Uni, I won't want to be living out here, so you'd be doing me a massive favour."

Elsie laughed, and Tess laughed along with her. But she'd been having similar thoughts herself since they'd moved back into the village. Another house move so soon seemed out of her reach though. Moving cost money, and a similar-sized house in a nice part of town would be much more expensive. She could barely afford to keep things going as it was. "So, are you looking forward to your big return to Haresby Rugby Club?"

Elsie snorted. "I'm not sure I'll be remembered for my short spell as the star try-scorer of the minis team. I used to make the boys cry if I ran past them and scored."

"You were so much better than any of them, and all the dads ever did was complain."

"I didn't mind. I just loved running around with the ball. And even when we moved on, you made sure I didn't miss out. I know you had to call in so many favours to get people to take me to training." She leaned across and squeezed Tess's knee. "I do appreciate all you do for me, Mum."

Tess cleared her throat. "Well, it looks like the women's team still has a good setup, and they had some success in the league last year, so you should do well there."

"You enjoyed it, didn't you? The time you were there? You always talked about that season with affection, even though it ended so badly."

5

"Maybe part of it was because it was the last place I ever played, but yes, I did. From the first night I arrived, I loved that club." She allowed herself the rare indulgence of drifting into that memory.

August, twelve years ago.

Tess stood, half-listening to the women's captain, Emily, and Steve, the coach, giving her a potted history of the club. Pete's parting shot as she left the house was to assure her that she'd make a fool of herself, so she was full of nervous energy to get out on the pitch and prove—to herself if no one else—that she hadn't lost all her skills. In truth, not only had she not played for almost eight years, she'd also barely even touched a ball. but now everyone she'd met at the club so far had brought up her playing history, and she feeling the pressure.

Distracted by an engine noise, she looked over Emily's shoulder towards the pitch and saw a ride-on mower approaching. Rather than the usual grizzled groundsman-type, a young woman in her early twenties was steering the mower skilfully towards a trailer hitched to a nearby van. Her short, blond hair was styled in the kind of sleek crop Tess had always wished she could tame her own thick, wavy hair into. Emily looked over her shoulder and waved as she heard the mower approaching. The girl nodded before she manoeuvred skilfully onto the trailer and killed the engine. She jumped off and began to attach the straps to secure it to the trailer.

"Jack! Get over here and say hello to our newest recruit."

The coach seemed like a nice guy, but Tess wondered if all new players received this level of attentiveness. The blond woman gave another brief nod and finished securing the mower before she jogged over to join them. She was tall, much taller than Tess's five foot three, but most players were. She was used to being towered over.

"Jack, meet Tess Kennedy." Emily's smile was wide. "Tess, this is Jack Russell. As well as being one of our best players, she and her dad do a lot to keep this club going."

The young woman looked down and scuffed her feet in the gravel of the car park.

"I was admiring the state of the pitch when I arrived," Tess said. "That's bloody good maintenance. You and your dad are doing a grand job, Jack."

The girl looked up and gave her a small smile. She rubbed her hand on her jeans and held it out. "It's Rowan. Thank you. Dad is the genius with the grass. I just do the donkey work. Welcome to the club," she said quietly.

Emily laughed. "Jack doesn't really like her rugby name, but once you get one, it's with you for life."

Tess felt for her. Rugby banter could be harsh, and you only made it worse if you showed you were bothered by it. She winked at Rowan. "Lucky for me I never had a nickname. I was always just Tess."

Steve led the way to the clubhouse. "Right, Tess, let's show you around inside, and leave Jack to get back to loading her mower."

"I've loaded it," Tess heard Rowan mutter as they walked away. "In one go, but none of you noticed."

Elsie was still chatting about her hopes for this new rugby team, and she didn't seem to notice that Tess had drifted off. Tess wasn't surprised her most vivid memories were of Rowan. She'd felt an instant connection to the quiet young woman, although any hopes of an easy friendship were cut short the moment Steve introduced her to the team as an ex-international fullback. She'd insisted she was a utility player and was happy in whatever position suited the team best, but she saw Rowan's eyes narrow as she looked across at her. That was just the beginning of their problems. But when she left so suddenly—first the club, and then shortly afterwards, the area—it was Rowan she'd regretted being unable to say goodbye to.

She'd met her good friend Jules that night too. They'd stayed close over the years, and Tess valued their friendship dearly. In the early days after she left the area, she'd often asked about Rowan, and Jules would laugh and give her an update. But then Jules had stopped playing, and her friendship with Rowan had gone downhill. Finally, she'd told Tess in her own direct way that she didn't want to talk about Rowan or "bloody Haresby RFC." Tess had accepted that even the closest friendships have some no-go zones and left it alone.

She questioned her own enthusiasm for renewing her relationship with a club that had seen the sudden and brutal end to her playing career. But she'd been fleetingly happy here for a season, somehow managing to juggle childcare commitments with her return to the game. There had been a supportive, inclusive culture among the members of the club, and it was a good environment for Elsie to experience her first rugby club as an adult.

She smiled to herself as she turned into the car park. *As an adult. When did that happen? One moment she's climbing onto my knee for a cuddle, and the next she's making big decisions about her future and asking me if I'm doing okay.* Elsie was the most caring child any parent could hope for, but Tess was wary of depending on her for companionship. She was meant to support her children, not the other way around.

"Just drop me here, Mum, please. I'll walk in." Elsie grabbed her kitbag, gave Tess a kiss on the cheek and was out of the door before Tess had fully stopped.

That was so very Elsie. Independent to the core. "Good luck. See you at nine?" She leaned out of the window and was rewarded with a quick wave as Elsie shouldered her bag and went to meet her new team. Tess wound up the window slowly and turned the car around. She headed for the local pub to spend the next hour and a half looking for jobs on her laptop. She was pleased Elsie was keen to join her old club, and she hoped she and sixteen-year-old Archie would find it as easy to settle. She seriously doubted it.

TWO

Rowan groaned loudly as she poked her head into the changing room. Once again, it hadn't been cleaned. On the hunt for a broom, she swung all the doors open as she went, trying to rid the rooms of their musty, damp smell. Her stomach rumbled as if to echo her groan. She'd forgotten to pick up a sandwich on the way, which she'd promised her dad she'd do. But she'd been running late and had correctly anticipated the cleaning that would be needed before the girls arrived. She'd have to wait to eat till she got home.

Tonight, they were welcoming a potential young recruit. Their under-eighteens team had folded a few years ago after her dad had become ill again, and no one else was prepared to take it on. Now they relied on the local university to feed them new players, as well as those who occasionally moved into the area. This week, the team secretary had called her to say a young woman was interested in playing senior rugby after relocating, but that was all the information she had.

She swept up the worst of the mud and dropped an armload of old bits of tape and discarded water bottles into the rubbish bins, making a mental note to speak to the committee again about the cleaning rota. Car tyres crunched the gravel outside, and she headed back out to greet her teammates.

She waved to the mostly younger players drifting across the car park. Not many of the women she'd started out playing with remained with the team. Sue Day, their veteran hooker at forty-three, was still beating off opponents half her age, but everyone agreed she was a freak of nature. Most of Rowan's peers had given up playing when they started a family or moved away. The worst had been when her best friend Becca had stopped because she couldn't fit it in with her caring commitments for her brother and her busy career. Rowan had only ever had her dad to factor in, and he was as rugby-mad as she was.

"Hi, Jack. Chilly tonight, isn't it?" Jai, a student who'd joined the club last season, rubbed her bare arms as she approached with a couple of the other young players.

"Oh, you'll soon warm up with the fitness drills we've got planned." She smiled at their horrified expressions but was distracted by a figure getting out of a car parked at the gate. The girl walked towards the players confidently, but Rowan could see hesitation in her expression. She looked strangely familiar, with thick, reddish-brown hair tied back from her very youthful face, which was covered in a sprinkle of freckles.

Oh no, don't let her be seventeen. I can't face the paperwork. She smiled as welcomingly as she could manage as the girl got closer. "Hi there, I'm Rowan Russell, club captain and assistant coach, although everyone here calls me Jack. I'm sorry, Kelly didn't give me your name." She held out her hand and the girl grasped it, looking relieved to see a friendly face.

"Elsie. Elsie Kennedy. I'm looking forward to getting on the pitch."

Rowan froze. *Fuuuuuuuck. Tess Kennedy's kid? No way.* She fought hard to keep the smile in place. "Elsie? I thought you looked familiar. I think I met you when you were young. Did your mum play here? You joined the minis for a while, right?"

Elsie grinned widely. "Yeah, I didn't think you'd remember. I thought you were so cool when we used to come to the club. I wanted my hair cut like yours, but my mum wouldn't let me. I was seven, so she was probably right."

Her grin was infectious, and Rowan found herself relaxing. "Well, it's great to have you back, Elsie. Why don't you go and change? We'll do some warmups and general stuff and then you can decide if you want to join the backs or the forwards."

"Thanks, Rowan." Elsie's smile widened. "This is my first senior team. I've just turned eighteen, by the way, so no need for any extra forms."

Rowan nodded. "That's a relief." She looked around. "Hey, Tank." The team's youngest prop was locking their car, and they turned and jogged across. "This is Elsie, she's new. Can you take her to the changing room and remind everyone they need to be out on the pitch in..." she checked her watch, "five minutes."

Elsie and Tank walked away chatting, and Rowan trotted over to where the head coach, Steve, was unloading kit from his car. "Steve, we've got a new player tonight. You'll never guess who she is?" She hauled a large net bag of balls from the boot and slung them over her shoulder.

Steve piled her arms with as many tackle pads as she

could manage and then a few more. "You're right, I'll never guess. Are you going to tell me?"

As they made their way to the training pitch, Rowan hefted the bag that threatened to fall from her shoulder. "Tess Kennedy's daughter, Elsie."

Steve looked blank for a moment and then his eyes widened. "Tess the ex-international? Played at fullback for a season till she got injured?"

"Got injured and never played again. Yes, that Tess. Don't you think it's strange her daughter would want to play here?"

Steve's brow furrowed. "I thought they moved away, and that's why Tess disappeared."

"Well, clearly, they're back." She was relieved to get her awkward load to the training pitch without dropping anything. "Or at least Elsie is. Maybe she's a student."

"Why don't you ask her?" Steve unloaded the kit from her arms and turned his back to lay out some cones.

"I will. I just thought you might find it strange that she'd want to go to a club where her mother had such a bad injury."

He glanced back at her as he moved away. "Things happen, Jack. And people get over them and move on."

She shoved her hands in her coat pockets and stomped back to the clubhouse. The season Tess had been at the club seemed so long ago, but she remembered it more clearly than many of the less memorable intervening years. The first time she met Elsie, she hadn't behaved very well...

October, twelve years ago.

Tess was the last to arrive. Rowan had been at the club all morning and was checking the pitch for divots when she saw Tess pull up, spilling out of her car with two small children in tow. Rowan checked her irritation. What was it about Tess that annoyed her so much? Other players often brought their kids to the games if they didn't have childcare.

Tess looked around, trying to find someone she could leave them with, Rowan assumed. She studied the grass beneath her feet with great interest, and when she looked up a few minutes later, the kids were with her dad, helping him put the flags out.

It felt like a betrayal. She didn't like thinking that way, but she couldn't seem to help it. She knew she should be more charitable towards Tess; the poor woman was clearly struggling to juggle her family life and continuing to play rugby. But all Rowan could see was someone who had marched in and taken her position on the pitch.

The older child, a girl she guessed—the dark red hair of both looked like it had been styled by cutting around a bowl on their heads—threw a small rugby ball onto the pitch and ran after it, giggling and trying to kick it while shouting, "Grubber kick!"

Rowan saw her dad look up and smile fondly, but she felt a flash of anger at her beloved pitch being treated like a play park. She strode over to the little girl, who was struggling to pick up the ball in her small hands. "You're not allowed to play on the pitch," Rowan said loudly as she loomed over the child. The little girl looked up, her delight replaced in a split second by fear. Her big blue eyes filled with tears immediately. Rowan stopped dead. *I'm a fucking idiot, what's wrong with me?*

"Ro, she's not doing any harm, love," her dad called from the other side of the pitch.

She dropped to her knees. "Sorry, I didn't mean to shout."

The little girl backed off slowly, her eyes still huge.

"Is that your ball?" Rowan indicated the ball that was clutched closely to her chest.

The girl nodded and stopped her retreat.

"Can I see?"

The girl shook her head, frowning, and pulled the ball even closer.

Fair play, I did just scare the shit out of her. "Were you doing a grubber kick?"

The girl nodded again.

"What other kicks do you know?"

The girl considered her carefully, as if trying to weigh up the chances of being shouted at again against her love of playing with her ball.

"Can I show you one?"

The girl solemnly handed her junior sized ball over. It felt tiny in Rowan's hands. She stood and did a gentle drop kick, sending the ball off across the pitch.

The child giggled and shouted, "Drop kick!" as she ran to retrieve it.

Rowan turned to see her dad observing her with a smile on his face. She liked to make him happy, so she was glad she'd been nice to the kid. He took the hand of the smaller child and headed back across the pitch toward the clubhouse, where the players were emerging for their pre-match training.

A tug on her shorts brought her attention back to the little girl. "Can you do another one?"

"We need to go back to the clubhouse now."

The kid's smile disappeared. Rowan took the ball. "Do you know what a high ball is?"

The girl nodded.

"Okay." She tipped her head at the approaching

players. "They're the opposition. I'll kick it, and you need to get to it before they do. Can you do that?"

The little girl nodded, smiling again.

"What's your name?"

"Elsie."

"Right, Elsie, are you ready?"

Another nod.

She booted the ball high in the air in the direction of the club building. The girl screamed in delight and ran as fast as her little legs would take her.

"Heads!" Becca noticed the ball on its trajectory towards the group of women walking onto the pitch.

They all looked up. Rowan's girlfriend, Sophy, ran to get under the ball and jumped to receive it before landing neatly. She'd spent a lot of time with Rowan since she came to the club, and although she complained constantly about Rowan's "boring" training schedule, her handling skills had improved massively. Sophy looked extremely pleased with herself until a small projectile hit her legs with such unexpected force, she staggered back and only just managed to keep her feet under her.

"That's my ball!" Elsie was red in the face from her run.

Sophy scowled as the other players laughed.

"She nearly took you out there, Soph." Mollie laughed.

Rowan had been on the receiving end of Sophy's temper enough times to recognise the anger on her face. She tried her best to hide her own smile as Sophy caught her eye.

"Can I have it back, please. It's mine." Elsie tried to jump to retrieve the ball.

Sophy held it way out of her reach, still watching Rowan, who was approaching as quickly as she could.

When she did look down, her smile was unpleasant. "Is

it really? You should look after it better then." Sophy kicked it hard, not out onto the pitch, but towards the back of the clubhouse into a patch of brambles.

The little girl let out a howl and went running after it. Rowan jogged after her, hissing at Sophy as she passed, "She's a little kid. You can be such a fucking arse sometimes, Sophy." She knew she'd pay for that later. She looked around for Tess, but she hadn't emerged from the clubhouse yet.

Elsie was crying in frustration, peering into the thick undergrowth, where her ball was barely visible.

"Hang on, you'll get scratched. Take this stick and hold the branches back." Wishing she was wearing more than shorts, Rowan quickly retrieved the ball and returned it to its owner, who beamed up at her through a tear-streaked face.

"Thank you."

Rowan found a tissue in the pocket of her training top. "Here, wipe your face. I don't want your mum thinking you've been assaulted while she's been gone."

They walked back towards the building as Tess emerged, scrum cap and water bottle in hand. Rowan's dad was nearby with the little boy, putting out a few chairs for some of the older spectators. Tess swung around and beamed as she saw her daughter and Rowan approaching.

Her smile drooped as she noticed the scratches dripping blood on Rowan's legs. "Oh, Elsie, you've not been making a nuisance of yourself, have you?"

"It wasn't her fault," Rowan said. Most players were now out on the pitch and, not wanting to be late, she jogged off without another word. She shouldn't have taken her frustration with Tess out on her daughter. She reminded Rowan of herself at that age before she'd had anything more important to think about than rugby. Next time she saw the kid she'd make an effort, but not for Tess's sake, she assured herself.

Rowan hoped Elsie's memory of their first meeting was more favourable, and less embarrassing, than her own. She swung open the door of the changing room. "Oi, you lot, I'm not standing out there waiting for you all night. Get out on that pitch." The girls looked up guiltily from where they had been sitting chatting on the benches.

Zoë, who played at number eight, jumped up and the others followed her lead. "Sorry, Jack, we were just getting to know Elsie. Did you know her mum used to play here?"

"Mum played in the team with Jack," Elsie said.

The younger players looked at Rowan with a mixture of interest and disbelief that she could be old enough to have played with someone's mum.

"That's right. Now stop changing the subject and get your arses out there." She chivvied them all outside, and Elsie hung back to walk with her across the pitch. She might as well get the answers to her questions. "So how is your mum, Elsie? And what brings you back to these parts?" She glanced at her, so like her mother in her rugby kit.

"We've moved back to the old house. Mum and Dad rented it out back when we moved away so quickly. And when they divorced, Mum got that house in the settlement and not much else, so it made sense to move back. And I'm hoping to go to Haresby Uni next year, so she likes that she'll be close. She wants me to live at home, but I'm trying to encourage her to move into town. I'm not living out there in the middle of nowhere."

"I'm sorry to hear your parents have split. That must be

hard." She wasn't sorry. Tess's husband, Pete, had been vile the few times he had bothered to meet with the rugby crowd. And then there'd been the club dinner incident. She wondered how much Elsie knew about that, if anything.

"Not really. I can't remember a time when they got on. They only stayed together because they thought it was best for us. They both seem happier now. Dad, in particular, appears to be making up for lost time." She rolled her eyes. "But you can ask my mum how she's doing for yourself. She's picking me up after training, and she said she'd like a quick chat if you've got time? I texted her while I was changing, and she was really pleased you're still involved with the club."

"Ah, that's good. It'll be great to see her." She thought she managed to get that out casually enough. Inside she was feeling very differently. It had always been a regret that she never got to see Tess after the accident. It was her own fault she hadn't visited Tess at home like the other players had.

Jules had been her source of information for a while, but then they'd had a fight and that vague link with Tess had dried up. She'd gone over her apology a thousand times in her head over the years, what she'd have said if she'd ever had the chance to say goodbye. Now suddenly that opportunity was a reality, and she wasn't feeling prepared enough.

Rowan dragged her thoughts back to the present. They were approaching the training pitch, where Steve had been joined by Mollie, their long-standing scrum half, and their team captain and fly half, Hannah. She called them over to meet their newest member.

"So, Elsie, are you a back like your mum?"

Elsie laughed. "Oh, no, I don't have her pace. I've

mostly played hooker, but I've got experience at blindside flanker as well. I'm happy to play wherever I'm useful."

Rowan caught Steve's eye. Their hooker, Sue, couldn't carry on forever, but she was so consistent it was difficult to give anyone else enough playing time to develop them. If they had a player with experience, who was also happy to play in different positions, that could help them out no end.

Steve nodded. "Okay, let's get you warmed up, and we'll try a few things."

Rowan followed them onto the pitch and tried to empty her mind of anything except rugby. She was usually totally focused from the moment she tied the laces on her boots, but tonight she found her thoughts drifting to the memories of Tess that she'd tried to bury over the last decade. Tess had treated her like no one else ever had, and now she was going to see her again after all these years. The ball that hit her hard in the stomach, and the laughter from her teammates that accompanied it, pulled her back to reality. She put her thoughts aside until after the training session.

THREE

Rowan was pleased with how the session had gone. A good turnout like tonight meant they could play a practice game, and she'd been pleased with the performance of the first-choice team. They'd tried Elsie in a few different positions, and her ball handling and understanding of the game were impressive. She recalled her admiration of how well Tess could read the game. It must be genetic.

Some of the younger girls were getting showers in preparation to go out, but Rowan preferred the comfort of her own bathroom, so she pulled on her warm training top and swapped her boots for trainers to drive home.

Elsie was waiting at the door. "Mum's outside. Have you got five minutes?"

Damn. "Yeah, of course." She shouldered her boot bag, straightened her shoulders, and followed Elsie across the car park, hoping her smile didn't look like a grimace. Rowan followed her towards an old Volvo estate.

Elsie pulled the boot open and threw her kit bag in. "Hi, Mum, I'll be back in a minute." She jogged over to where the other players were chatting.

The driver's door opened, and a figure emerged. Rowan kept the car between them. She rested her elbows on the cold metal roof as the shorter figure turned towards her.

"Rowan Russell, it's so good to see you."

Tess's Yorkshire accent was as strong as ever, and Rowan was reminded how much better her name sounded when Tess said it. She must be in her forties now, but she appeared younger. She did look tired, which wasn't surprising if she'd just gone through a house move and a divorce, but she moved with that cheerful enthusiasm Rowan had always envied.

Tess scooted around the car, and Rowan couldn't stop her gaze moving down to Tess's leg. She must have made it obvious.

"It gets a bit stiff in the cold, but mostly it's fine." Tess moved close and wrapped her in a warm hug. "It's *so* good to see you after all these years."

She emphasised the "so" with an even tighter squeeze. Rowan forced herself to hug back and nodded wordlessly.

"I'm sorry I never came back to say goodbye, but Pete's job came up so quickly, and I still wasn't able to drive. I've always felt terrible about it. I loved this club." She stepped back and looked Rowan up and down. "You're looking great. How's life?"

Rowan felt as though she was in a surreal movie of a moment she'd imagined for years. "Uh, just the same really, you know?" Eleven years to think about it, and that was the best she could come up with.

Tess laughed lightly. "Chatty as ever, I see."

She opened her mouth to apologise, but Elsie had returned.

"Mum, the others are going for a quick drink at the pub

down the road. Can we go, please? Just for half an hour?" She smiled sweetly at Tess and turned to Rowan. "Are you going, Rowan?"

Rowan panicked. "Oh, I can't, sorry. I need to get back." To what? Did they know she lived alone? She decided not to expand and just stood there, wishing she could disappear.

Tess gave her a long look and turned to her daughter. "As it's your first night, one quick drink, but I'm not making a habit of it. We can't leave your brother alone all night, and we've got an early start tomorrow. Go with one of your new friends, and I'll see you there." She turned back to Rowan. "I just need a quick chat."

As Elsie ran off, Rowan felt conflicted. How could she both want to be in Tess's company but at the same time be desperate to flee? Tess had always observed her with an understanding that Rowan had found comforting, as though someone really saw her for who she was. But now she felt vulnerable, and she wasn't sure why.

Tess looked around to make sure her daughter had left. "I wanted to talk to you about Elsie."

Rowan nodded, glad of a conversation topic. "What about her?"

"I think she's a good player, and I want to encourage her to get as far in the game as she can. I was remembering when she was little, and you used to give her a different drill before every game and then test her skills afterwards. She was so determined then, she reminded me of you. So...I wondered if you would take her under your wing a bit?"

Rowan wasn't sure what Tess was asking. "Well, I help coach, so I'll be around. I could maybe give her a bit of advice about a training plan for the other days of the week if you think that's what she wants?"

"Could you ask her? I don't think she needs to know I've been poking my nose in." Tess rubbed at her face. "I think this club will be great for her, but she only turned eighteen a few weeks ago. I'd like to feel that someone was looking out for her. And you're the person here I trust the most."

Rowan tried not to show her surprise that Tess would still think that about her. She couldn't spoil it by asking if Elsie knew what had happened at that stupid club dinner. "You're right. She *is* good, and the setup we've got will really help to bring her on as a player. I'll keep an eye on her and give her some advice if she wants it. She'll be safe with us, I promise."

"Thanks. I really appreciate it, Rowan. We've got a busy year ahead of us. It's Elsie's A-level year, and Archie has his GCSEs so I'm still driving them to school back in the town where we used to live."

Rowan couldn't hide her look of disbelief.

Tess rolled her eyes. "Yes, I know it sounds ridiculous, but it's not much more than an hour's drive if the motorway's clear, and they can get the train home. It's only until revision leave starts." She smiled, but it didn't hide the weariness in her expression. "Right, I've kept you standing too long in the cold. I'll head off to drag Elsie away from her new friends, and let you get going." She walked towards her car and turned. "It really was good to see you, Rowan."

Rowan nodded. "Yeah, you too. Bye." She watched Tess drive away, her thoughts churning, then she turned back to the clubhouse. Steve had locked up, but she still checked the doors and the alarm before she left, wishing with all her heart she'd agreed to go and sit in the pub so she could listen to Tess Kennedy's warm voice for a while longer.

Rowan turned to see where Becca had got to. She was jogging as slowly as she could, but her best friend was way behind, her face a sweaty, purple grimace of pain. Rowan didn't want to put any extra pressure on her, but she felt sad Becca had got so out of shape. Becca had never been fast like Rowan but since pairing up in cross country races at school, they'd run together for years, as well as playing rugby, until Becca's other commitments had taken over and her running had declined. She knew Becca wished she had more time to exercise, but something always took precedence.

She sat down on the wall outside her flat and retrieved the two bottles of water she'd left out. Becca staggered up and collapsed onto the wall next to her. She opened the bottle and handed it over as Becca pulled off her glasses and wiped the sweat from her face with her T-shirt.

Becca had been more difficult to pin down than ever. Between caring for her brother Ben since her mother had given up on them, the ridiculous hours she put into her job as a journalist, and her girlfriend, recently become fiancé, she was rarely free. But she was always there for Rowan when she needed her.

Becca took a long swig of her water and turned to Rowan, still breathing heavily. "How are you feeling?"

Typical Becca, always talking about feelings. But she'd known Rowan long enough to understand that if she didn't ask direct questions, she wouldn't get answers. "I don't know. Confused, uncomfortable."

"Are you pleased she's back in town? Lord knows you were gutted enough when she left."

Becca had been the one who'd taken her home that

night after the club dinner. And she'd sat with her, talking into the early hours, reassuring her she had no choice but to get involved when she'd seen what was happening. And then the following week, when Rowan had been hysterical with worry for Tess and eaten up by guilt, she'd been there for her too. Becca was the only person who got to see that side of Rowan. Everyone else, including her dad, thought she was strong and stoic. "Yes. Of course I am." She didn't look away, even though she wanted to. "I'm glad to see she's safe and out from under the influence of that bastard."

"Does she seem happy about it?"

"She looks tired." She took a swig from her bottle. "But yes, content, I think." She looked back at Becca, who continued to watch her as her breath started to slow to a normal rate. "What?"

"Have you talked about any of what went on? You've been dwelling on it for so long, maybe it would be good to actually discuss it with her?"

"I met her in the car park, Becs, with no prior warning. You know I'll need weeks to even think about what to say."

"So, what *did* you say to her, when you met?"

Rowan bit her lip. "Not much. I felt a bit awkward, to be honest."

Becca chuckled. "Really? I'm shocked."

Becca's gentle teasing was always just the right tone to make her laugh. Rowan's laugh faded into a sigh. "You're right, though. Elsie's going to be playing regularly, so I'll keep bumping into her. I need to clear the air."

"The air may be fine, you know. You do have a tendency to dwell in the past. Tess's sights are probably focused on the future. And how's Elsie? She was such a keen little player as a kid, she must be a great asset to the team."

"Yeah, I think she's going to be amazing." Rowan drained her bottle. "Are you coming along on Sunday?"

"I can't make it this week. I'm going over to Gerri's for the weekend. I'm going to try to tie her down about wedding plans."

Becca could never keep the wide smile off her face when she mentioned Gerri's name. On the few occasions they'd met, Rowan hadn't seen that same enthusiasm in Gerri's expression when she looked at Becca. She hoped Becca wasn't getting in too deep, too soon. They'd only been together a few months, and it seemed quick to be getting engaged. But what did Rowan know? It could take her that long just to build up to speaking to someone. She was in no position to be questioning Becca's judgement. But she'd been hurt before, and Rowan hoped this relationship would last. She stood. "I need to get back. Work is ridiculous, and it's not going to improve while I'm sitting here chatting."

Becca swallowed her water and stood too. "You always did know how to end a conversation." She wrapped her arms around Rowan. "Good luck for the weekend. Text me the result, okay?"

"Only if we win." Rowan grinned. "Say hi to Ben and Digby, and happy wedding planning."

"I'll be there for the next home game, I promise. Put me down for the bar rota. Maybe Gerri will even come with me. She knows how important the club is to me."

Becca smiled widely but behind her glasses, her eyes were less certain.

"Come round one night next week with Ben and Digby for pizza and a film."

"Yeah, great." Becca handed over the empty water bottle. "I'll check out my work assignments and let you know what's good for me."

Becca jogged off slowly, leaving Rowan to have a quick shower before she walked back to the factory. As she headed back, she thought about Becca and her tendency to jump headfirst into relationships. She knew Becca had the same misgivings about her own overthinking everything until she missed her opportunity.

But Becs was right. For her own peace of mind, she would take Tess aside after the match to ask if things were okay between them. Tess had said she trusted her and that was a good sign.

She groaned as she saw the company van still waiting in the loading bay. Stefan and Charlie were good workers generally but often, if not chivvied along, they would lose track of how much needed to be done by the end of the day. She jumped up onto the dock and went in search of them, knowing exactly where to find them. They both looked up from their mugs of tea as she swung the door open. "Ah, guys. You were in here when I left. I thought you were taking the Mathiesons' delivery first, so we could reload the van for the morning?"

Stef stood first, and Charlie quickly joined him. "Sorry, Rowan, we didn't know if you wanted to check it over first."

She let out her breath slowly. What was the point in getting annoyed when she needed to get busy. "Right, Charlie, let's check it over together. Stef, be ready to leave in ten, okay?"

Stefan nodded, and she led Charlie to the van. "Where's the delivery note?"

He held it out.

"You check it off. I'll read out the labels."

They'd done the basic job in five minutes, so she didn't understand the need for delay. She watched as they drove away. Maybe she needed to be clearer with instructions.

They'd been doing the job for so long, she didn't get why they needed handholding but clearly, they did. When her dad was around more, he'd spent time working alongside them, but she just didn't have the time now. Her people skills weren't always the strongest...except when she was on the pitch. Then everything made sense.

FOUR

As the traffic slowed to a halt for what felt like the hundredth time that morning, Tess groaned and slumped in her seat. The morning drive to school wasn't too bad, and it gave her a chance to chat with the kids. Often, Archie would sit up front while Elsie lounged in the back with headphones on, listening to whatever subject she was being tested on that day. She relished the time with Archie, especially since he'd struggled so much with the divorce. Her strictly enforced no-phones-in-the-car rule meant they got to talk about school or his plans for staying with friends. She'd promised as soon as the house was fully furnished, he could have his friends over for the weekend. Anything to minimise the impact the move had on him.

But the solitary drive back home was a different matter. It dragged on endlessly, as if to remind her how much time she was wasting each day when she should be out looking for a job. It helped to dwell on something pleasant, and her thoughts drifted to Rowan. Had she been pleased to see Tess after all these years? It was so hard to tell. She'd anticipated the awkwardness. It had never failed to amaze her that Rowan was such a natural team player, confident and inspiring on the pitch, but sit her down and expect her to hold a conversation, and you had to be prepared for a lot of long silences. When Tess had been part of the team, Sue, the hooker, and that nasty piece of work, Sophy, used to tease Rowan for being slow on the uptake. But Tess had guessed, looking into Rowan's silvery grey eyes, it was more a case of so much going on inside her head that she took a while to get it out.

Rowan looked well. Jules had told Tess about Rowan's dad's illness. They were so close, Tess guessed that it would have taken a toll. But physically, she was in great shape as far as Tess had been able to tell under the muddy training kit. In fact, if Tess was being honest, she looked amazing. Tess laughed. Amazing wasn't a word she should be using about her daughter's coach. But she had always admired Rowan's athletic physique and her large, strong hands that could control a ball so skilfully. Tess shivered as she pictured them and chided herself. She shouldn't think of such distracting details as she drove, not that this snail's pace required much concentration. She had never denied, to herself at least, her attraction to Rowan, and her fantasies had been harmless inside her head and a way of coping with the day-to-day grind of her life back then.

But maybe her attraction had been more obvious than she'd thought because Jules had started teasing her about sexual tension. Rowan hadn't seemed to notice or care, and their friendship was always rocky, as any connection they started to build was often knocked back by the tension around rugby positions. And then Pete had chosen the night of the club dinner to address his own insecurities, and everything had changed for ever.

. . .

May, eleven years ago.

Tess couldn't believe she'd convinced Pete to come to the end of season meal, but he'd realised it could be in his interest to socialise with the more affluent club members. They could be potential clients for his wealth management services. He'd let Tess know he was doing her a massive favour and insisted she drove to save on taxi fares.

He stuffed his pocket with business cards then poured himself a very large whisky before they left. Tess raised her eyebrow.

"What, you want me to face your bunch of lesbians stone-cold sober? All they ever talk about is bloody rugby."

It's a rugby club. Tess knew better than to voice the observation and wondered if she'd made the right call to invite him. But she wanted to play a full part in the club, including the social side, and while it was acceptable for players not to bring partners to most events, Christmas and end of season dinners were the two formal events that most people brought their significant other to. She had bowed out of Christmas with an excuse about family commitments, so this time she'd decided to bite the bullet and go for it. As they got into the car, he looked her up and down. Knowing how draughty the clubhouse could be, even in summer, she'd opted for a smart shirt and dark green wool trousers.

"You have to dress like one of them too, do you?"

"Oh, for fuck's sake, Pete, grow up. I'm not wearing a stupid dress and heels just to look the part of your loving wife." She got in the car as he slammed his door harder than was necessary. She started the engine. "And lay off the comments about my teammates' sexuality, please. It's offensive."

"So, they're all straight then? They certainly weren't at

your old place." He laughed. "That's why you've always loved it so much."

God, I hate him. "No, they're not all straight, but the point is, it's none of your damn business, so keep your stupid comments to yourself. Equality is taken very seriously at the club so if you want to ingratiate yourself with the old boys, you'd best keep your bigotry to yourself."

They drove the rest of the way in frosty silence. Her hands were aching from their grip on the steering wheel, and she needed to calm down. She'd been to plenty of club dinners. It would start off civilised and quickly descend into a drunken party, and she wouldn't even get the chance to relax and join in. She hoped to escape when the eating was done before Pete got too drunk.

The clubhouse felt warm and welcoming after the frosty atmosphere in the car, and Tess soon started to relax a little. Jules had saved them a place at her table. Sue and her partner were already seated and waved a greeting, and Emily, the team captain, came and sat with her husband, who she introduced as Luke.

Pete pulled up the chair next to Luke and snagged a bottle of red wine from the centre of the table. "So what business are you in, Luke?"

Tess slumped down on the other side of him and looked around casually.

"She's on that table in the corner." Jules dropped into the chair next to her. "With her dad, and Becca, and some of the committee members."

Tess looked over her shoulder quickly to ensure Pete wasn't eavesdropping, but he was deep in a one-way conversation with poor Luke. "No idea what you're talking about, Jules. I was just looking around to see who I know. There are a few unfamiliar faces."

"Some of the older club members have very little to do with the club other than a couple of meals a year. But they pay good money for the prestige of being part of an old club. So, we humour them and only call them old farts when they're out of earshot."

Tess looked around and tried not to let her gaze rest too long on the table with Rowan, Becca, and a group of older men, including Derek, Rowan's father, around it. The men were all in club shirts and ties. Rowan was wearing a smart, open-necked white shirt with the club logo on the chest. "No Sophy?" She turned back to Jules.

"Ha ha, I knew it." Jules grinned knowingly. "She cried off, apparently. Said she wasn't going to spend her Saturday night in a draughty room filled with boring old men."

"How very club-spirited of her." Tess stood. "I need to get a soft drink before the food comes. Do you want anything?"

"No, I'll drink your share of the free wine, thank you."

Tess turned to the rest of the table. "Anyone need a drink?"

Pete looked up, already a little blurry-eyed. "I'll have a large whisky, darling."

She smiled through gritted teeth and made her way to the bar, stopped occasionally by people at the surrounding tables. Her route didn't take her near Rowan's table but as she stood waiting to be served, she recognised a familiar scent and turned to see Rowan squeeze through a gap to stand next to her. Recognising her perfume wasn't a good sign. "Hey, Rowan."

Rowan turned, and her face lit up. "You look nice. That green really suits you."

Rowan looked as shocked as Tess felt at the

compliment, and she quickly looked away to get the attention of the bar staff.

Tess felt the heat in her cheeks. "Thank you. That's the best feedback I've had so far tonight."

The server finally came their way and further conversation was halted while Tess put her order in, insisting on buying a drink for Rowan, her dad, and Becca. The drinks appeared on the bar, and they gathered them up.

"Well, have a good evening. I'll see you at the game next week. Final match of the season! I'm looking forward to having a lie-in on a Sunday, aren't you?"

Rowan shrugged. "Yeah, I guess. Thanks for the drinks." She gave a small smile before she turned away.

When the food was finished, and speeches and toasts had been made, Tess chatted with Jules. Pete hadn't embarrassed her too much so far, although he'd drunk a lot. He was currently sitting with a couple of the first team players, talking about golf, a half-empty bottle of whisky between them. She wasn't looking forward to the drive home. "I'm going to head off soon, Jules, if I can drag him away from his new mates."

Before trying to get Pete moving, she slipped to the bathroom, surprised to see no one else around in the silent corridors. As she headed back to the party, she jumped when a figure stepped out in front of her. "Shit, Pete, what are you playing at?" She stepped back instinctively as his face twisted into a sneer. The sound of a fire door opening further down the corridor made them both turn.

Pete grabbed her arm hard enough to hurt as he pulled her through an open door into the kit store. He didn't relax his vice-like grip, and she began to wonder how drunk he was. It was unusual for him to lay a finger on her; he preferred verbal and emotional attacks.

"Pete, you're hurting me." She tried to pull away, but he pushed her hard against a cold metal cupboard, pinning her with his bodyweight.

He wrapped his hand around her throat. "You evil bitch. You think it's funny to bring me here and then tart about with your little friend in front of my face?"

His whisky breath was sour as he hissed into her face. She looked up into his eyes, trying to get a clue about what had upset him as she attempted to push him off her. "What the fuck are you talking about? I've been at the table the whole night."

"Except when you went to the bar and that lezzer followed you. I saw the way she checked you out. And you fucking loved it, you greedy bitch."

Footsteps sounded in the corridor, and she stopped struggling. *Oh, please don't find me like this.* That she was more concerned about being seen than she was about being in the position in the first place was something she would think about later. For now, she just needed to get out of there. The door opened, and they both stayed still as the footsteps approached. Tess maintained eye contact with Pete but caught the glimpse of a white shirt out of the corner of her eye. It passed and she exhaled, but then the steps stopped.

"Tess?"

Fuck, Rowan. Please just walk on and let me deal with this.

Pete swung his head around without releasing the pressure on Tess. "Piss off. Can't a man have a bit of quiet time with his wife?"

"Tess, tell me you're okay, and I'll leave," Rowan said quietly.

"Rowan, just go." It was hard to speak normally with Pete's hand clamped around her throat.

Rowan stepped into the room. "Why don't you get your hands off her and let her speak?"

Pete's weight lifted off Tess as he changed his stance to deal with the new threat. He didn't remove his hand.

"Oh, look, Tess, it's your little dyke in shining armour. I knew something was going on." He turned back to her, snarling. "Has she fucked you yet?"

Tess raised her arms to push him off, but suddenly his hand was gone, and she watched in horror as Rowan dragged him across the room by the front of his shirt.

Tess pushed herself off the metal door and went after them. "Rowan, please leave it. I can handle this."

"You shouldn't have to." Rowan dragged Pete out into the corridor.

Someone must have heard the shouting, because people were spilling out of the bar to see what was happening. Pete straightened in Rowan's grip and swung for her face as hard as he could. She ducked easily and punched him sharply on the jaw. He dropped like a rag doll. Rowan stood over him, as if willing him to stand up.

Tess thought she might be sick as she looked around at her stunned teammates. She stepped forward, fighting herself to keep calm. "Rowan, everyone, please just go. I've got this."

People started to turn away and move back to the party, except for Rowan, still with fists clenched, watching Pete.

Tess moved to her side and whispered, "I asked you not to get involved. I do *not* need rescuing. Now leave me alone to clean this mess up." She forced herself to turn away from

Rowan, hauled a groggy Pete onto his feet, and led him toward the exit.

"You're gonna do time for this, you vicious little bastard," he slurred over his shoulder.

"Shut up, Pete, and keep walking." She couldn't look back. On the drive home, she struggled to see the road through the tears streaming down her face. It wasn't Pete's behaviour. She was accustomed to him destroying anything good in her life. But the look on Rowan's face when she'd told her to back off was hard to forget. Knowing she'd hurt Rowan and how much pain that caused her forced her to acknowledge that she needed to put some distance between them. But that should be easier now that she'd been so dismissive.

At the match the following week, fate had done a better job of giving her that distance than she could have imagined, and she'd never seen Rowan again. And that had filled her with a sense of loss that she'd never really addressed.

Tess looked around and realised she'd missed her road entirely as she'd been lost in her memories. She tried to refocus. Whether Rowan was pleased to see her or not, she had agreed to keep an eye on Elsie, so that was a relief. But maybe she should keep her distance and let Elsie build her own relationships within the club without her hanging around.

She finally got back to the house and pulled out her laptop. Every tab in her browser was open to a different recruitment site, and she sighed as she pulled up a chair. Job searching was tedious as well as soul-destroying, but she wasn't going to give up looking, even though it seemed like a hopeless task. She looked at her watch. Ten thirty already. How was she going to find a job when she couldn't show up before eleven? A few supermarket shifts, maybe. But she really needed to earn more than minimum wage to keep the house going and meet the kids' needs, especially if she could only fit in a few hours a day.

She got back to her search with another long sigh, wishing she had more to offer than an abandoned nursing career and a few years as a school classroom assistant. As she scrolled through the endless lists of jobs she wasn't qualified for, her thoughts kept going back to the way Rowan chewed her lip when she was thinking. It was surprising it was such a perfect pink and not covered in bite marks, such was the ferocity she attacked it with. Tess groaned. Obsessing about Rowan's lips was not only unhealthy, it was also unproductive. She reminded herself that if she didn't get a job soon, she'd have to ask Pete for money, and that was enough to focus her thoughts for the rest of the morning.

FIVE

Rowan stared blankly at her computer screen. She'd tried long ago to bury the memory of Tess's warm and compassionate nature, but now she was back, giving Rowan those inappropriate feelings all over again. She wasn't sure how to behave around her.

She'd always regretted how standoffish—and even rude —she'd often been with Tess when she was young. Back then, her position on the team had seemed more important than a new friendship, and her feelings for Tess had been confusing.

But Tess had been difficult to push away, and she'd found herself drawn into long conversations after matches. Tess had a way of asking the right questions, and before she knew it, they would be engrossed in a discussion about films or art, subjects no one else was ever interested in hearing Rowan's opinion about. They were usually interrupted by their teammates' banter about getting a room. Tess would just laugh it off, but Rowan would glare until people shut up. She'd missed Tess more than she could admit after she left so abruptly, so she'd tried to put her out of her thoughts.

When she *had* thought about her, Rowan imagined her struggling along miserably in her abusive marriage, her situation made worse by Rowan's stupid behaviour. But whatever Tess had been through since they last met, she appeared to have emerged with her positive attitude intact. All the shit she'd had to deal with, and she was still more upbeat than Rowan had ever been.

She shook herself and pulled her laptop closer. She really needed to focus on this week's big order. If they messed it up it could cost them a valuable customer. She jiggled her mouse to wake the screen and tried to make sense of the figures in front of her. She loved working alongside her dad, but the job had never thrilled her. She did her best to make it successful, and she enjoyed the new technologies she'd had to get to grips with, but she'd always felt like it was someone else's job.

She was rescued half an hour later by her dad carrying in two steaming mugs of tea. She swung around in her chair as he perched on the edge of his desk. He looked well today. Sometimes she was terrified by how frail he'd become. He watched her for a minute. Neither of them liked to rush what they had to say. They enjoyed a good silence and didn't feel the need to fill it with nonsense. That was one of the many reasons they got on so well. "Are you okay, duck? You seem a bit, I don't know, distracted."

She pushed her chair back and swung her feet onto the edge of the desk. "All good here. These figures had me confused for a while, but the customer made a mistake in one of the totals. It's fixed now. We'll get everything out on schedule." She tried to give her best carefree smile.

"I wasn't talking about work. I mean when you came in this morning. You looked like something was bothering you. Are you worried about the start of the season?"

"No." She tipped her chair back as far as she dared and put her hands behind her head to stretch. "I don't think about rugby *all* the time, Dad."

He looked at her closely. "There's something."

Damn it, he wasn't giving up. The problem with being so close to her dad was that she couldn't hide much from him. "Remember Tess who played for the club about ten years ago? The ex-international?"

"Of course I remember her. She was lovely, had a bit of a soft spot for you, I remember. You punched her husband." He laughed for a moment and then stopped suddenly as he remembered the full story. "Then she had that horrible accident."

"Punching someone isn't funny, Dad, and she definitely didn't appreciate my actions. I never got a chance to apologise." She'd never forgotten the way Tess spoke to her, and her expression as she walked away.

Her dad shook his head. "Are you still being dramatic about that, all these years later? It's water under the bridge, love."

"If I hadn't made such a big deal about being fullback, she wouldn't have offered to play at centre and that accident would never have happened."

Tess had been tackled badly and suffered a horrible injury to her leg. The sound of her screams as she lay on the ground was burned into Rowan's memory. It still made her feel nauseous.

"Anyway, her daughter has turned up at the club. She's a pretty good little forward and a potential replacement for Sue, if she ever retires."

"I remember little Elsie. She was the most determined player in the minis that season. The boys were all relieved when she left. She used to make them look bad with her skills." He chuckled. "If she's got half her mum's ability, she'll be a great asset." He picked up his mug. "But I thought they moved away?"

"Marriage breakup. They're back in the area."

"Well, if you see Tess, give her my love. She really was a lovely person. And tell her I'm glad she's rid of the knob in the flashy car."

Rowan smiled. Typical of her dad to be able to sum someone up in so few words. "I did see her, and she's well. I'll pass on your message." She downed the last of her tea. "I think I'll see if Jules is available for lunch."

How could Jules have not mentioned Tess's return? They didn't see much of each other anymore, but even a warning by text would have been something. When Rowan had returned to the club after university, Jules had taken her and Becca under her wing. They'd all been close for a few years, until Jules stopped getting picked for the team regularly. She hated being on the bench and moaned about wasting her entire Sunday for the chance to play fifteen minutes of rugby. Finally, she'd stopped turning up for training. Rowan understood how hard it was to be repeatedly overlooked in favour of younger players, but she didn't understand how Jules could just give up everything when the club had been such a big part of her life. They'd finally argued about it on a rare night out, and Rowan had accused Jules of lacking commitment. Jules snapped back that if Rowan had anything else going on in her life she wouldn't be so obsessed with the club. They didn't speak much for a long time, and now when they met up, they never talked about rugby.

Jules laughed as she picked up. "I was *so* expecting this call. Lunch is on you."

Half an hour later they were in a local café. Rowan

picked at her pasta salad and Jules tucked into a pepperoni pizza.

"Do you want a slice? You're putting me off my food with your miserable face."

Never one to mince her words, Jules could either lift Rowan's spirits or make her feel worse. "No, I don't. I don't know how you can stomach pizza for lunch." She needed to tone down the grumpiness. No wonder Jules was always busy. "Why didn't you tell me Tess was coming back to town?"

Jules paused, the slice of pizza drooping in front of her lips. "Honestly? Because I thought you'd work yourself up into a mess worrying about it." She bit into the slice before the toppings could drop back onto the plate.

"So you figured it was better for me just to bump into her at the club?"

Jules shook her head slowly as she finished chewing. "I didn't actually know that was going to happen. Tess didn't mention it until afterwards." She wiped her mouth. "What was it like seeing her after all these years?"

"Oh, how would I describe it? Surprising?"

"You know what I mean, Jack. Was the spark still there?"

Rowan drew in a long breath. "There was never a spark, Julia. That was just in your head." She set her knife and fork down on her plate, her appetite lost.

Jules sat back. "Oh, come on, you know you had a thing for her. All the other nonsense aside, you really liked her."

"I liked her. I *like* her. She's a good, caring person, and she's had a hard time."

Jules's lips twitched into a smile.

"But that's all it was, Jules. And I never really made her feel welcome at the club because I was so worried about losing my position. I didn't understand why she made such an effort to be nice to me. Pity, probably. But that was all it was, and now she wants me to keep an eye on her kid. I don't know why you always persisted with the idea of there being something between us."

Jules wasn't even trying to hide her smirk now. "Well, you punched her husband. Hard, if I remember correctly."

"Why does everyone have to keep bringing that up? He was an abusive prick, and I found him with his hand around her throat."

"Your life revolves around a rugby club. You've known a lot of pricks, but I don't remember you punching any others."

Rowan rubbed her face. "Please leave this, Jules. Can we just eat? I'm sorry I brought it up."

As she made her way back to work, Rowan thought about what Jules had said. It was true Tess had been kind to her at a time when she needed it. Her return home from university shortly before Tess moved into the area had been a hard time for her. All the pain and memories of her past had caught up with her as she struggled with her dad's illness and the reality that she'd be helping him with his business for the foreseeable future. Then Tess had turned up, with her genuine interest in Rowan and what was going on in her life. She'd talked to Tess about things she'd never fully shared with anyone, even Becca. And that had scared her. Their competition for a position on the pitch had made it easier to push Tess away, and much simpler than facing up to her emotions. But now Tess was back, and so were those feelings.

She looked up at the gates ahead and put thoughts of Tess out of her mind for now. Work was getting out of hand. She was trying to minimise her dad's workload, knowing how important it was for him to still play a part. They had plenty of customers, but her dad's business model had always been to keep things small and only to take on as much work as their small team could handle. But with business booming and Rowan doing everything she could to reduce the responsibility and stress for her dad, she needed another pair of hands. It was difficult enough to sustain her enthusiasm for the job on a good day, but when the workload became overwhelming, she had to fight the urge to run away from everything. *If we win on Sunday, he'll be in a good mood. I'll raise it with him then.*

———

Thursday's training session was all about preparation for the big game at the weekend. It was a home fixture, which gave them some advantage, but the opposition were currently sitting at the top of the league with a comfortable lead.

"All the more rewarding when we kick their asses," Rowan said when Jai pointed out that it would be a hard game. She looked around at their anxious faces. "Come on, you lot. We really do have a chance to win this. Think how good it'll feel afterwards."

While Steve focused on the technical side of the coaching, she made an effort to think about how the players would be feeling. She watched for insecurities and worked on them, encouraging individuals as they went. They had a good game of first team against reserves and by the end of the session, there were more smiles on faces. When Hannah asked what they were going to do on Sunday, Jai had shouted, "We're gonna win!" and everyone had cheered in agreement.

The players put away the equipment while the selection committee went indoors to decide on the match day team. Generally, if it was a straightforward decision they would announce it immediately, or if more deliberation was needed, they might call the players later with their decision. She hated those calls, when she had to give a team member the bad news that they hadn't been selected to play.

"Jack."

She turned as Elsie approached, a heavy tackle bag hoisted over her shoulders. She was out of breath and had clearly run to catch Rowan before she went into the clubhouse. Elsie was too new to be considered for the squad so she would be unlikely to hang around afterwards, especially with her mother in a perpetual rush.

"Just wanted to say I'll be there on Sunday to watch. If there's anything you need me to help with, I'm in."

Rowan smiled, admiring her commitment. "Bring your kit anyway. You can do the training session and warm up with the team."

Elsie nodded and promised to be there early. Poor Tess. Another long drive to factor into her weekend. Rowan did her best not to acknowledge the wave of pleasure that went through her when she realised she'd see Tess on Sunday. *Damn you, Jules.*

SIX

Tess turned to Elsie in horror. "What? It's my weekend too, Elsie, and I'm really pleased you're enjoying the club, but I'm so tired of driving." She banged her head on the steering wheel. "And you're not even getting a game yet."

Elsie smiled weakly. "It's okay, Mum, I can get the bus to town. I'm sure one of the girls can pick me up on the way past. I'll ask in the WhatsApp group."

"It's Sunday, Elsie. Buses don't run that early." Tess berated herself as she rubbed her head, wishing she hadn't been so dramatic. She wanted this club to be successful for Elsie. She had real talent, and she got as much out of being part of a team as Tess once had. "I'm sorry. I'm happy to take you, really. Let's see if we can drag Archie along, and we can go for a pub meal somewhere on the way home."

Elsie had shown an interest in rugby from a very early age, and Tess had done everything she could to encourage her. The first time she'd played had been at Haresby, and Tess could still remember her excitement.

· · ·

November, twelve years ago

After weeks of chipping away, Tess had finally convinced Pete to take Archie out for the day to the zoo while she drove Elsie to the club early on Sunday morning to try mini rugby. "She might not like it, Pete. Even minis can be pretty intimidating when you're most likely the only girl and all the dads take the mickey out of any boy you tackle. Let's see how it goes. If she wants to continue, we'll find a way."

And as her little girl jumped out of the car, smiling from ear to ear in a tiny pair of pristine white shorts and a new club jersey, she was glad she'd made the effort. They'd got to the club early, as Tess was determined her daughter wasn't going to suffer from Tess's usual tardiness. Elsie looked to her for permission then ran across the pitch to where a few men and small boys were gathered, seemingly totally at ease in her new surroundings.

As she followed Elsie across the grass, she heard her name being called. She turned to see Rowan piled high with tackle pads, trying to stop them from falling. She turned back to help, relieving her of as many as she could. "I swear you're the only person who does anything at this club. Couldn't this lot have brought these out?" She tipped her head towards the chatting men.

"They forgot, apparently, and shouted to me when I got out of the car."

"Piss-takers." Tess didn't lower her voice as they approached the men. She dropped the kit at their feet as they looked up.

"Cheers, ladies." A tanned man with a neat beard and twinkling blue eyes smiled at Tess. He held his hand out. "I'm Andy, the head coach for mini rugby. You must be Tess. We've heard all about you."

Tess kept her gaze cool as they shook hands. "And I've heard this is a good setup to bring my daughter to. I'll be trusting you to look after her."

He nodded and straightened his shoulders. "Of course." He nudged the younger man next to him. "Come on, Scott, let's get the kids moving."

She turned to see Rowan watching her with a small smile. "Want a cuppa while they get set up?"

Tess hid her surprise and followed Rowan back across the pitch.

Rowan looked back and smiled. "That put Andy in his place. I swear he thinks mums only bring their kids here so they can chat with him."

"Oh, I've met plenty worse than him. I do want Elsie to feel safe here, though. Rugby is still a really macho environment, and she's only seven." She followed Rowan into the clubhouse. She hadn't taken her turn on the cooking rota yet, but this wasn't what she'd expected. She'd never seen such a sparkling rugby club kitchen. In fact, it was cleaner than hers at home. She hoisted herself up onto the aluminium worktop while Rowan filled the kettle. "How much time do you spend here, Rowan Russell?" She liked the alliterative sound of Rowan's name and allowed herself the pleasure of saying it.

Rowan leaned back against the worktop while she waited for the kettle, her hands resting on the surface and long legs crossed at the ankle. "Well, for home fixtures, most of Saturday for the men's games, running the bar and sorting the food. Then I get the hotdogs on for the minis and juniors on a Sunday and clean up the changing rooms before the women arrive. Then kitchen or bar duty after the game. And training Tuesdays and Thursdays. And then there's the grounds maintenance stuff." She looked at Tess.

"Does that sound sad? I love it here. It's all I've ever known."

Did she have time for anything else in her life? "No, it's not sad. You and your dad are the main reason this is such a great setup. I'm hoping to spend a long time coming here." She nodded in the direction of the children on the pitch. "Hopefully long after my own playing career is finished."

"Thanks." Rowan turned away to make the drinks. "We've only got instant, I'm afraid."

Tess usually carried an insulated mug around with her, so she didn't have to risk this exact thing happening. But she'd forgotten it this morning in her haste to make sure Elsie was on time. "That'll be fine. Just black, please." It absolutely was not fine, but she didn't want Rowan to think of her as a coffee snob on top of everything else.

Rowan turned back, two mugs in hand. She placed one next to Tess on her perch and held the other, blowing onto the surface to cool it. With the height advantage, Tess was suddenly on a level with Rowan. She watched her silver-grey eyes flicker with hidden thoughts. Tess found herself wondering what it would be like to lean forward and nip that juicy bottom lip between her teeth. She forced herself to look away and pick up her coffee. She took a large swig that made her gag and nearly coughed it into Rowan's face. The moment was gone, and Rowan looked confused for a moment, before she laughed.

"I knew that coffee wouldn't meet the standard. I've been trying to convince the committee to invest in a machine. We'd make the money back in a couple of years, but they don't get it." She sipped her own drink. "I stick to tea here, to be honest."

Tess laughed. "Remind me to do the same in future."

She jumped down. "Now, let's go and watch some tag rugby."

Tess brought herself back to the present. It was disconcerting that so many of her memories revolved around Rowan. She'd spent Elsie's training session sitting in a pub drinking coffee as she continued her job search on her laptop. For the umpteenth time she wished the house was closer to town. Being stuck out in a village added another complication to finding a job. Pete had chosen the location because he could park for free at the train station in town and get a quick connection to central London, where he'd been working at the time. It hadn't been convenient in any other way. When he moved jobs, they'd moved once again.

She'd hated relocating when the children were small. They'd struggled with the change, and she'd found it difficult to get to know people. When she was younger, she'd always had a large friendship group. As an only child of older parents, when she'd lost them while still in her teens, she felt a deep sense of being alone in the world. The friends she'd made, first at university and then through rugby, had filled that void. Starting her own family had made her feel less alone, but she'd sometimes wondered if Pete liked to keep them on the move to limit her circle of friends.

When she'd finally managed to take up rugby again, she'd relished the social life, even if she'd been forced to juggle it with the needs of her family and her work commitments. It may have been a short-lived return, but she had good memories of her season at Haresby.

And now here she was again, in the middle of nowhere with no real friends except Jules. But she had a plan. Elsie's first choice university was Haresby, so it made sense to put the village house on the market and try to find a house in town, big enough to give the three of them some space. Somewhere near the railway station, so Archie still had the freedom to go and visit his dad without relying on lifts. *And I don't have to be subjected to Pete's stupid smug face.* Elsie was less enthusiastic about keeping contact with Pete, and she did it out of a sense of duty, if nothing else. She hadn't been a fan of how Pete had treated Tess during the breakup or before. With the benefit of hindsight, Tess was having doubts that staying with Pete for so long had been the best thing for her children after all.

"What are you thinking about, Mum? Your face has gone a bit sad," Elsie said.

"Nothing really, love. I was just thinking about all the moving we've done over the years and how hard it's been for you two."

"It wasn't that terrible. We've stayed in the same place all through secondary school, until now. I remember when Dad wanted to move again when I was in Year 10, and you put your foot down." Her smile shone in the darkness of the car. "You've done a good job, Mum. It's not your fault Archie can't cope with change."

"Oh, don't say that, Elsie. I'm worried enough about him starting at a new school. He resents me for it, but this travelling every day doesn't make sense."

"He doesn't resent you. If Dad had done the decent thing and let us stay in the house instead of digging his heels in and threatening a messy divorce, we wouldn't be in this situation. And Archie knows that. I think he's really disappointed in Dad, but he finds it hard to talk about things."

Tess let out a long sigh. She was proud of Elsie for

having such insight, but it seemed a big burden for a teenager to be carrying around. Her intention had been to stick it out another few years until both the kids were away from home, but Pete's behaviour had gradually become more upsetting and emotionally abusive, and she couldn't have survived much longer.

Elsie reached across and squeezed her knee. "It'll get better, Mum. Archie will get through this year, and maybe a new Sixth Form is a chance for him to meet more people. Once exams are over and we move to town we can get settled, it'll be so much easier for you."

Tess was horrified to feel the sting of tears. She didn't need Elsie to know how much she was struggling. She hoped the darkness would hide her.

"Oh, Mum. I worry about you. I want you to be happy."

She sniffed and got herself under control. "I am happy, Elsie. I have two smart, talented, and lovely children. And we've got a comfortable home and enough money." The last part wasn't anywhere near true, but Elsie didn't need to know. "I have to remind myself of that sometimes."

When they got home, Archie was nowhere to be seen. She shouted up the stairs and got no answer, so she headed to his bedroom. She heard nothing, so she hammered on the door. Still nothing. Figuring she'd given him enough warning, she swung the door open to find him in his gaming chair, eyes glued to the computer screen. She lifted his headset, and he jumped and looked up at her, guilt clear in his eyes.

"Come on, Archie. I told you when I left, you needed to log off by eight. It's half nine. You're not going to get any quality sleep if you're shooting aliens until nearly bedtime. You really need your rest for studying."

Archie rolled his eyes as he snatched his headset back.

"They're not aliens. And I didn't realise it was so late. It's not my fault."

Tess felt another pang of guilt. She'd moved him away from all his friends to this village in the back of beyond and then left him in the house on his own for whole evenings at a time. The rugby club was a thirty-minute drive, so trying to get home in the hour and a half of Elsie's training session was pointless. She hoped Elsie passed her driving test soon because she couldn't keep spinning plates like this.

She hauled Archie out of his chair for a hug and pulled his head down for a kiss on the cheek. He wasn't tall for his age, so he'd been thrilled when he finally got to be taller than her, but he'd always be her baby, and a part of her wanted to be able to cuddle him forever. "I'm sorry this is difficult, sweetheart. It will get better, I promise." She held him at arm's length, so he had to look her in the eye. "Did you get the physics homework finished?"

He nodded. "Yeah, it wasn't hard. Do you want to check it?"

"No, I trust you. And I wouldn't really know if you'd made it all up anyway." She laughed and ruffled his hair. "How about you get in your PJs, and I'll make us all hot chocolate before bed?" She left him to get changed and tramped wearily downstairs. She was definitely having a shot of something in hers.

She worried about Archie. He was an introverted boy, and Elsie was right, he didn't cope well with change. The break-up had affected him much more than his outgoing sister, who was already surrounding herself with friends in her new town. He wasn't interested in sport or anything other than his computer games. He excelled at the sciences and maths, and she didn't have any concerns about him getting good GCSE results. But his small circle of similarly geeky friends had taken him a long time to build, and she was concerned he would become even more insular now that he'd moved away. Whatever job she managed to find, it couldn't take her away from her time with the kids. There were so many things she needed to prioritise, and sometimes she couldn't help but feel overwhelmed by it all.

She set the kettle to boil, leaned on the worktop, and took a few deep, slow breaths until the tightness in her chest eased. It was a lot, but she would get through it. She had to.

SEVEN

Tess smiled fondly as Elsie jumped out of the car almost before they'd stopped, hauling her bag from the back as she went. "Will you be okay, Mum? I need to go and find the team." She leaned into the car as rain started to soak the front seat.

"Just get inside, Elsie. I'll be fine. Good luck!"

Tess watched the rain drumming against the windscreen, wondering what she could do to occupy herself until the game started. Kick-off wasn't for another two hours, but for once she hadn't brought her laptop. She needed a day off from her fruitless job search, and she'd been planning on a long walk to get her head in a better place. She peered up at the thick rainclouds, but there was no sign of a break in them.

It wasn't often she had time to herself. Archie was with his dad. He'd been horrified at the thought of being forced to stand in a field all day, away from his beloved games console, so he'd gone behind her back to phone his dad and beg for a rescue. Tess had lost her temper with him and sent him to his room for the evening, after removing the power cable to his console. So, it had been a bit of a relief when Pete had arrived this morning to pick him up. Tess had opened the front door to see a smiling young woman in the passenger seat of Pete's car. She'd forced herself to smile sweetly and thank him.

"I didn't have much choice did I, if the poor kid was going to be forced to watch women pretending to play rugby all day?"

She'd kept the smile plastered in place. Pete had also played rugby at university; that was how they'd met. But as soon as he realised his limited skills weren't going to bring him the glory he'd envisaged, he'd given up. He'd resented Tess's successes and didn't bother to hide his pleasure when starting a family had meant she had to quit playing. When she finally started again, he gave her no support at all, which was why her children had spent a season sitting in the clubhouse on Sunday afternoons. She'd known it wasn't sustainable, and her injury had taken the decision out of her hands.

On the positive side, Pete had reluctantly agreed Archie could stay overnight, and Elsie had a study day tomorrow, which meant she didn't have to get up at five in the morning. Talk about being thankful for small mercies.

A sharp rap at her car window startled her from her thoughts. She recognised Rowan's dad, Derek, and while she was aware everyone had got older in the years she'd been away—herself included—the change in Derek was shocking. He had his hood up, but she could see white, wispy hair under it, and his skin had a greyish hue. His illness must have taken a heavy toll. She smiled warmly and wound down the window.

"Tess Kennedy! I heard you were back in town. What

are you doing out here? We can't have Haresby's most capped player sitting out in the rain."

She laughed. "Those caps were a lifetime ago, Derek. My time for basking in glory is long gone." She got out of the car and slipped on her raincoat. He wrapped her in a warm hug. He was always more of a hugger than his daughter. They were alike in temperament as well as looks though. Tess knew his pleasure in seeing her was genuine, as he wasn't the type to put on an act.

"It's good to see you again," she said.

"You too, duck. Let's get you inside with a nice hot chocolate. That's my job around here now, getting the kettle on."

She locked the car, and they strolled towards the clubhouse. Or Tess strolled. Derek's progress was more of a shuffle. She remembered the quiet but vibrant man she had known over a decade before. In his mid-fifties then, he hadn't long been retired from first-team rugby and was heavily involved in coaching, both the men's team and the girls', which he'd established when his daughter had reached the age she was no longer allowed to play with the boys' team.

She followed his slow progress to the bar and sat on a stool while he fiddled with the coffee machine. "Have you got a mocha by any chance, Derek?" A hot chocolate sounded comforting, but she really needed a caffeine fix.

He glanced at her. "I've no idea what that is, but there's a button that says mocha, so your luck's in. Coming right up."

The machine started to gurgle into action.

"So how have you been?"

Derek turned back and rested on the other side of the bar. "Not too good, to be honest with you, Tess. I had a cancer scare years ago. I had surgery and got the all-clear, but it came back about six months ago." He pointed to his chest. "My lung. Seems a bit unfair—I've never smoked a day in my life. But these things don't always make sense, do they?"

Tess squeezed his hand. "I'm so sorry to hear that, Derek."

"I've had all the treatment they can throw at me. The doctors say it's looking positive. It's taken a lot out of me though, duck. I try to keep going. Rowan is amazing with the business, and it's doing better than it ever did under my control. She wants me to retire and let her get on with it, but I worry she does too much. There's never any downtime with that one. I don't think she knows how to relax."

"I remember that well. She never stopped training." Tess smiled as she recalled Rowan's intensity on the pitch.

"She's calmed down a bit on the playing side. She's so busy, pretty much running this place by herself. The men's side are rubbish at pulling their weight. But between this and the business, she hasn't got much time for herself."

"Hasn't she got someone to remind her to go home?" *Oh, very subtle.*

Derek's smile faded as he turned back to the coffee machine. "Oh, you know Rowan. She never did find it easy to talk to people. She always tends to end up with the ones who pick her. Usually for the wrong reasons. She eventually realises they're wrong for her, and she's on her own again."

"When I left, she was with that terrible Sophy."

"That lasted a couple of years until Rowan realised she was being messed around. I think Sophy still managed to convince her she was the one doing the leaving."

"That's a shame. She's got such a generous heart, she

deserves to be with someone who appreciates her." She hoped Derek didn't think that was too much.

"She certainly does. I just wish she would realise it." Derek's smile returned as he placed two mugs on the bar between them. "Now, Tess, tell me all about what you've been up to since you left."

The rain cleared before the match began, but the wind had an icy bite to it, so Tess went to her car to swap her waterproof for a jacket. She'd enjoyed her catch up with Derek, and she was looking forward to them watching the game together. As she went to join him on the touchline, where he'd set himself out a folding chair, she was delighted to see a short figure in a long coat making her way towards them. "Jules!" She hadn't seen her old friend since she'd moved back, and she flung herself into a warmly returned embrace.

"Hey there, how are you doing?" Jules held her at arm's length and looked closely at her. "You look knackered. How's that ridiculous school run working out for you?"

Jules had been very clear she thought it was a bad idea trying to move back here and keep the kids at their old schools.

She turned to Derek. "Afternoon, Derek. What's your prediction for the final score then?"

Jules kept the conversation going in her usual no-nonsense way, teasing Derek about his loyalty to the club and making them all laugh. Tess watched the team run out onto the pitch, led by the captain, Hannah, with Rowan close behind. She indulged her desire to watch Rowan, tall and strong in her rugby kit, for as long as she could before the game started. She felt the same pull she always had when she was near Rowan. But back then it had been impossible to let her imagination roam as to what that attraction could mean. Now they were both here, and single. But it wasn't that simple, was it?

With ten minutes of game time left, Derek's optimistic hope for the result was close to coming true, as Haresby were five points ahead. They had scored three tries, and Tess's favourite by far had been the one scored by Rowan. A pass from the back of a perfectly executed lineout had gone to Rowan. She'd taken the ball into the opponents' twenty-two before looking for someone to pass to. Finding no one close, she'd sidestepped two defenders to run the ball between the posts. She wasn't flashy like when Jai, the winger, had scored, jumping around and chest bumping her teammates. Rowan had simply grounded the ball and gone back to her position.

Now they were defending in their own half and a powerful looking winger was running the ball, almost unchallenged, towards the try line on the far side of the pitch. Rowan sprinted across the pitch to tackle her, but Tess groaned as she got her head on the wrong side of the opponent's body, leaving herself wide open for a knee to her face. Rowan's head rocked back with the impact.

Jules winced. "Ooh, that'll have done some damage."

Rowan still somehow managed to keep her arms wrapped around the woman and brought her to the ground. She spilled the ball, which was kicked into touch to much applause from the home crowd. Tess watched Rowan closely. She hadn't got up yet. As other players leaned over her, she slowly rose to her knees. "Shit, I hope she's okay."

"Oh, don't worry about Rowan. She's got a hard head, that one." Derek was out of his chair, the worry on his face belying his jovial tone.

Hannah leaned over Rowan and consulted with the referee for a moment then shouted over to the coach to bring the medical bag. Elsie ran on with the water bottles, and Tess itched to go and help, but spectators didn't just run onto the pitch.

Steve took one look at Rowan's face and called for a replacement. Rowan shook her head while holding a dressing against her nose. Steve waved his watch in her face and said something short, and she got up, picked up the medical bag, and stomped towards Tess and Derek.

The other players clapped her off. "Well played, Jack." Hannah patted her on the shoulder.

As Rowan approached, Tess could see the dressing was stained with blood. Steve had gone back to the other side of the pitch, and it didn't look as though anyone else was coming to look at her injury. She stepped onto the pitch, took the bag from Rowan, and led her to the chair Derek had vacated.

"I'm fine." Rowan pulled away, clearly angry at having to leave the pitch before the end of the game.

"Just let me take a look. I'm a professional, remember." Tess laughed as she pushed Rowan onto the seat, attempting to lighten the mood as she recalled how much Rowan hated fuss.

Elsie ran up to join them. "You okay, Jack?"

Tess was surprised to hear her daughter use Rowan's nickname. She knelt next to Rowan and moved the dressing away from her nose. "Ooh." She winced. "Were you particularly attached to how it looked before?" She was close enough to feel the rumble of laughter from Rowan.

"Not particularly, lucky for me. Is it bad?"

Tess wiped the blood away carefully. "The bleeding's about stopped." She touched the swelling that was already appearing on either side of Rowan's now less symmetrical nose. "It's broken though, I think. It'll take a couple of weeks to heal." She sat back on her heels. "And you're going to have a great pair of black eyes. Your right one is swelling up nicely. No high-powered business meetings this week, I hope?"

Rowan chuckled. "Nope, I think this week's pretty clear in that respect."

Tess continued to clean the blood away, trying to ignore the feeling of Rowan's warm skin beneath her fingers. "I don't suppose there's any chance of you going to A&E to have it checked out?"

Rowan started to shake her head and stopped to let out a hiss of pain. "I've broken my nose before. If it's affecting my breathing when the swelling's gone down, I'll get it checked out."

Tess sighed and stood, just as the final whistle blew. Elsie jumped up and down, clapping at their victory.

Derek cheered and patted his daughter on the back proudly. "Well done, Rowan. That was well earned."

"You probably want to get some ice on it sooner rather than later." Tess started to help Rowan up, but she stood quickly, presumably to show she didn't need assistance.

"Thank you. Well, luckily, I'm on kitchen and bar duty today, so—oh shit, I forgot to turn the potatoes up."

Derek pulled her into a careful hug. "Don't you worry, love. Me and Tess made sure everything was cooking nicely at half time. We even turned the chilli on low. You go and get your shower, and we'll have it ready." He turned. "Won't we, Tess?"

"Of course. You take your time and try not to make sudden movements with your head."

Rowan smiled at her. "Thanks for giving him a hand." She walked slowly back out to celebrate with her jubilant team on the pitch.

Tess did her best to ignore the way Rowan's smile warmed her whole body. The overwhelming desire to make Rowan happy wasn't something Tess was accustomed to. Yes, she had a natural desire to help people, but this was something much more intense. She needed to keep it under control.

EIGHT

The visiting team had long gone, the younger girls had left to continue the celebrations, and the few stragglers were making their way out. Rowan had used her injury as an excuse not to join the extended partying, but it really was aching enough to make her feel sick. In the past, even that wouldn't have been enough to keep her from joining post-match celebrations. She had once gone straight to the pub from A&E after having a gash in her leg stitched.

Maybe I'm starting to feel my age. She slumped on a bar stool with a half-melted pack of ice held to her face. Tess had insisted on taking over her bar duties and every now and then, she would replace the ice pack with a fresh one.

She did the same just now, coming around the bar to stand very close, almost between Rowan's knees. Rowan's whole body tensed.

"Let me take a look."

Tess's cool hand tipped her chin back and removed the ice. She couldn't open that eye now, and the other one was watering with the pain.

"It may not feel like it now, but the bruising will definitely be better if you keep icing it all evening."

She nodded slightly, which made her wince.

"Rowan, have you taken the painkillers I gave you? That must be hurting like hell."

Tess was so close she could feel her breath on her face. She started to imagine another situation with Tess between her legs. *What the fuck? What is wrong with me?* If she was honest, Tess in close proximity had always had this effect on her. It was one of the reasons she'd tried to avoid her when they were playing together, even though Tess made that difficult. She'd only really got together with Sophy to take her mind off Tess.

Rowan opened her eye. "No, I told you, I'm fine." She immediately regretted the irritation in her voice. Tess would think it was a reaction to her attentiveness when it was at her own ridiculous thoughts. She had never liked fuss but unexpectedly, she enjoyed Tess's attention. She put it down to her having a good bedside manner. Tess shrugged and moved back behind the bar.

Serves me right for being such an arse. Her vision was really blurred, so her dad had said he'd take her home. But that was good, it would give her a chance to have that new employee conversation with him.

"Right," Tess said.

She was back, not as easily put off as Rowan had thought. Tess swung the stool around so Rowan could see her from her left eye. She lifted Rowan's hand from the bar and placed two tablets in it then waited while Rowan picked up her half-finished pint and swallowed them down.

Tess nodded towards the beer. "You won't drink any more, will you? It's not a good idea with a head injury."

Rowan shook her head gingerly. "No. Don't need any

more reasons to feel like shit tomorrow. Dad's going to take me home." Soon, she hoped, as she was feeling like death.

"Well, the bar's mostly cleaned up. Kitchen too. Just leave the rest. Someone will pick it up during the week, won't they?"

"That'll be me. But yes, as soon as the girls leave, I'll lock up." She lifted her head with an effort to look at Tess. "I really appreciate what you've done today, helping Dad out." She hesitated. *Why do I find it so hard to accept help?* "And for looking after me." She felt warm fingers stroke the side of her face.

"You look like you need looking after." Tess cleared her throat, and the touch was gone. "You have to get a proper rota going for food and bar duties. These girls are too accustomed to you doing everything."

Rowan knew she was right; they did take her for granted. But it was her own fault for always taking things on. "Yeah, I know. I'll mention it at the next committee meeting." She held the ice to her face and leaned heavily on the bar as she stood.

"Here's your dad now. I'm going to get moving if that's okay?"

Her dad slumped down on the stool Rowan had just vacated, his face grey. She peered at him from her one good eye. *Fuck, I've let him overdo it.* "You okay, Dad? You don't look great."

"I'll be right as rain with a good night's sleep, duck. Let's get you home."

Tess stepped up. "I don't think either one of you is in a safe state to drive. Why don't you leave your cars, and I'll take you home?"

Rowan and her dad talked over each other in their rush

to protest. "We're fine. It's a really short drive, and you need to get back."

Her dad nodded. "You've got your early start in the morning."

"Actually, I haven't. Archie's at his dad's, and Elsie has a study day, so I've got a lie-in planned." Tess checked her watch. "And I've let Elsie go into town for an hour before I pick her up, so I'll only be hanging around. It would be rude not to let me take you."

Rowan didn't have the energy to argue, and she was relieved her dad wouldn't have to drive. She nodded. "If you don't mind, then that'd be good, thank you."

Tess laughed softly. "You must be feeling rough. That was too easy."

Tess insisted Rowan stay in the car as she took Rowan's dad into his house and got him settled. Rowan was secretly relieved, as any movement of her head now was agony. The painkillers didn't appear to have taken much of an edge off. She was vaguely aware of Tess getting into the driver's seat and the car moving again.

Tess had to ask for directions a couple of times before they arrived, and she parked in Rowan's space outside the flat. Rowan refused any help getting out of the car, so Tess stood nearby after hefting Rowan's kit bag onto her shoulder. She followed her closely to the front door.

"I can take it from here." Rowan reached out to take her bag, planning to collapse onto the bottom step as soon as the door was closed.

"I don't think so. It would be unprofessional of me in my new role as team medic not to make sure you're safely settled."

Tess's tone was gently teasing, but Rowan got the impression arguing would take more effort than she was currently capable of. She swung the door open and trudged up the stairs, knowing Tess was close behind.

"Right, you go and get your PJs on and get into bed, and I'll bring you a nice cup of tea."

Rowan looked at her in horror. *I don't want you anywhere near my bedroom.* That wasn't entirely true.

"Just do it, Rowan. I have a lot of experience with difficult patients."

Ten minutes later, she was tucked up in bed, covers pulled up around her neck protectively. A gentle tap at the door announced Tess, as she appeared with two mugs in hand. *Oh God, she's going to sit on my bed and drink tea.*

"Elsie texted to ask for another half hour, so I thought I'd join you. That lanky winger was in the background, encouraging her. I think she might be part of Elsie's new passion for Haresby Rugby Club." She rolled her eyes as she sat on the bed.

"Jai? She's a decent kid. In her first year at the uni, so if Elsie goes there next year, at least she'll know someone."

"She needs A-levels first, and she'll stand more chance of getting them if she's not out drinking the night before a study day." Tess scratched her head. "It's my fault. I should have more discipline...with both of them."

Rowan sipped her tea, amazed that Tess could give herself a hard time. "You're a great parent, working in difficult circumstances. From what I've seen, you give up everything to make sure they get what they need."

Tess's face lit up in a smile that wiped all the worry and weariness away in a second. "Thank you for saying that. It means a lot."

Rowan rested her head back against the pillow. Was this a good time to ask about the past? Despite the pain in her head, the intimacy of the moment made it feel right. "Did what I did to you ruin your life?"

Tess tilted her head. "What do you mean?"

"I don't know, all of it." She forced herself to make eye contact. "Punching your husband must've made things worse for you at home. And pretty much forcing you to change team position. You wouldn't have got injured like that if you'd been playing at fifteen. And then you moved away, and I never knew if you were okay." She finished her tea and placed the mug by the bed.

"Jules said she gave you updates. I always asked her to say hi."

"Yeah, I knew you were alive, but that's not the same as okay, is it?" Rowan placed her hand on top of Tess's. "I never forgot seeing that bastard's hand around your throat, Tess. And I never knew if he was doing it again."

"He didn't. It wasn't his thing." Tess sighed, staring into her own mug. She looked at Rowan. "While I was immobile, it made things hard. I was struggling to get the kids to school and just function from day-to-day. A couple of the other mothers from school were a great help. But then he pulled the rug out from under me and insisted we had to move. That was really hard. I knew no one in our new town, and I couldn't drive anywhere. I think he saw his opportunity to take total control, and he made the most of it."

Rowan squeezed the fist of her free hand so tight her fingernails dug into her palm as she tried not to let what she thought of Pete show in her expression.

"Oh, Rowan, I really don't want to discuss this if it's going to upset you. Can we talk about it when you're feeling better?"

So much for hiding her feelings. She gave a small nod.

"How's your sister doing? Did she come home after university? I forgot to ask your dad earlier."

Tess's choice of a safer conversation topic was typical of her attention to detail about other people's lives. She'd never met Willow; she'd been away studying when Tess had been at Haresby. But Rowan had talked about her often. She'd told Tess about all of it, her mum's accident, and Willow's injuries, and how she'd always blamed herself.

"No. She met Cara at university in London, and after they graduated, they moved to Brighton." Rowan tried to shuffle herself into a more comfortable position without jarring her face, which had finally stopped pounding with pain.

"Oh, nice. I've always wanted to live near the sea, but I've never even come close." Tess leaned over her and supported her shoulder while she plumped her pillows up. Rowan tensed, and Tess pulled back with an embarrassed smile. "Sorry, old habits die hard."

She stood and drained her mug, and Rowan realised the sinking feeling in her stomach was because she didn't want Tess to leave. How had she gone from desperate to escape to this, in a matter of minutes?

Tess took Rowan's empty mug from the table. "Try to sleep as upright as you can. It'll make the swelling less painful in the morning." She smiled. "I'll wash these and let myself out. Sleep tight, Rowan Russell."

The front door clicked quietly closed a few minutes later, but she didn't drop off to sleep for a while, her thoughts full of Tess's gentle, capable hands on her face.

NINE

The coffee shop was busy, and Tess resigned herself to a wait as a harassed-looking barista took her order. As she leaned against the counter, she thought back to her conversation with Rowan at the weekend. Asking about her sister had made her remember the terrible events in Rowan's childhood. No wonder she was so stuck in the past. She wondered if she'd ever looked for help with processing any of it. It had nearly broken her heart when Rowan had opened up to her all those years ago.

February, eleven years ago

Tess breathed a sigh of relief when she saw the gate to the clubhouse were open. The Russells' van was parked in the otherwise empty car park so Derek or Rowan must be working. She'd been relying on that. At the previous day's match, she'd left her earrings on a shelf in the changing room and hadn't remembered them until she got home. They were diamond studs that Pete's parents had bought her for Christmas a couple of years ago, and she knew how guilty he'd make her feel if she'd lost them.

She stuck her head inside the door. "Hello! Rowan? Derek?" There was no reply, but she thought she heard a door close further inside the building. She slipped in and made her way to the changing room, where she quickly located her earrings and put them in. She looked around at the dirty changing room. The teams had a rota for cleaning after their games and this week, the front row should have brushed up the mud and tape from the floor and left the room clean for the next match. But Sue, Tara, and Megan had been at the front of the food queue after the game, so they'd clearly left it for someone else to do. There was a broom leaning against the bench and if she wasn't on her way to visit a patient, she'd have spent ten minutes cleaning up so Rowan didn't have to. She noticed a pad of paper lying on the bench, and she picked it up. On the open page, there was a beautiful sketch of a fine-featured woman who bore more than a passing resemblance to Rowan. She was staring out of the drawing with a defiant half-smile.

Tess jumped as the door opened behind her. She turned to see Rowan in the doorway, her eyes puffy and red.

She held out the pad. "Is this your mum? I didn't know you were such a good artist."

Rowan took the pad and looked down. "It's the anniversary of her accident today. Sixteen years."

Tess waited, wondering if any more details would be forthcoming. Rowan had never mentioned her mum's death before. Tess recalled Jules telling her when she first came to the club that Rowan had lost her mum in a car accident when she had been very young, and Derek had commented once that Rowan had become withdrawn after her mother's death, but there had never been a good time to ask more.

Tess couldn't imagine what that would be like. Losing her own mum when she was eighteen had been hard enough.

"Would it help with what you're feeling if you talked to me about it?" Tess lifted Rowan's chin gently, aware of the intimacy of the gesture, but the pain she could see in Rowan's eyes was tearing her up inside.

Tears gathered in Rowan's eyes. "I don't know if I can, but I want to."

Tess took her arm, pulled her to the bench, and sat beside her. "Why don't you try and see how you do? If you want to stop, you can. I won't push you."

Rowan stared at the sketch. "I drew her from a photo. I can't remember her clearly enough now to do it from memory." She sounded so downcast, as though she'd failed.

"Oh, Rowan, she's so like you. And of course you can't remember well, it was most of your lifetime ago." She waved the pad at Rowan. "This is lovely. You are *so* talented."

"She was the real artist. Before she had me, she used to do exhibitions and everything. It was income from her paintings that kept our heads above water when Dad was first setting up the business."

"Well, you've inherited her talent." Tess handed the pad back, giving Rowan time to think about what she wanted to say.

"It was my fault, the accident."

Her voice was so quiet Tess thought for a moment she had misheard. "What was your fault?"

"Mum asked me to go shopping with her and help with my little sister, Willow. Dad was going to the club for a match, and I wanted to go with him. I loved watching him play. I kicked up such a fuss that my mum said she didn't need the hassle when she was already trying to do the shopping with a toddler. She told me I needed to grow up a bit and left the house. That was the last time I saw her. And Willow never walked again. I let them down."

Her face was a picture of misery as she stared down at the drawing. Had she really been carrying this around since she was a child? "It wasn't your fault, Rowan. You were a kid faced with a shopping trip or going to the rugby club."

"The police weren't sure how it happened, but she drove head-on into an oncoming truck on a straight stretch of road. They thought Willow may have distracted her and she turned to see to her."

"Ah, Rowan, you don't know what happened. You can't take responsibility for that. You were a child."

"Do you think no one ever told me that? It's all I heard after she died. But I've never been able to shift the belief that if I'd been there, things might have been different."

Tears streamed down Rowan's face and pooled onto the paper, making it bubble and distort the sketch.

Tess put her hand out to take it but stopped short. "Your beautiful drawing is getting ruined."

"It doesn't matter. I've got dozens." Rowan dropped the pad onto the bench. "That's why I need to be there for Dad. And Willow, when she needs me."

The tears had slowed, and Tess rummaged around in her uniform pocket for a tissue. She located one, checked it for freshness and handed it over. Rowan blew her nose noisily.

"Thank you for sharing that with me, Rowan. I can't imagine how hard it's been over the years. Have you ever thought about counselling? It might really help you with some of this."

Rowan shook her head. "I'm okay most of the time. But this day's always hard."

"Is there something you do to recognise the anniversary?"

"Yeah, we go to visit her grave. My sister's coming back from university. And then we go for dinner together and share our memories of Mum. We don't talk much about it otherwise." Rowan straightened her shoulders. "Are you working?" She nodded at Tess's uniform. "Am I keeping you back from something?"

Tess checked her watch. "I've got a visit I really need to do in the next half hour. She stood. "Will you be okay here on your own?"

Rowan nodded and stood. "Yeah, I'll clean up here and get back to work."

Tess smiled and squeezed her arm. "Take care of yourself, Rowan Russell." She turned towards the door.

"Tess."

She looked back. Rowan shoved her hands in her pockets, and she looked younger than her years.

"Thank you for listening. You're right, I probably do need to get some help. But talking to you has been a start."

"I'm glad I could help. Take care." She escaped the room and the powerful urge to wrap her arms around Rowan and try to make the sadness go away.

"Tess."

The barista calling her name brought Tess back to reality, and she picked up the coffee gratefully. She looked around the busy seating area until she spotted Jules, who had somehow managed to bag a sofa. She made her way across the room, deposited the coffee onto the table, and sank into the soft, deep cushions with a sigh. "You would not believe what a treat it felt to stay in bed until seven. That morning drive is killing me."

"That's what you get for being a breeder." Jules shrugged. "How much longer do you have to do it?"

"Another five weeks of this term, then study leave starts. It'll take the pressure off a bit, but they may have very different timetables so it could even make it harder. I'm totally relying on Elsie passing her driving test in January. I'm not sure it's doable without that." She frowned. "And I'm going to have to cope with them staying at Pete's more during the exams." She sat forward to take a sip of her coffee.

"It all sounds very eventful."

"So, what excitement have you got on the horizon? You know I need to live my life vicariously through you."

"Don't get your hopes up. Things are off with Tonia again, and she's decided to go to Paris alone."

"Oh, Jules, that's rubbish." She knew Jules had been looking forward to a romantic break for months. "Is it fixable?" Since Tess had known her, Jules had been in a casual relationship with a doctor called Antonia. She lived in Sheffield, and they spent occasional weekends together, but Tess had always assumed they were both happy with the arrangement, as it had lasted so long.

"I don't think so. She says she wants someone to settle down with, and I'm not that someone."

Jules said it lightly, but Tess could hear the hurt in her voice. "Do you want to be? You've always said the best thing about your relationship is that neither of you wants any more from it."

"I don't know, Tess. I always thought I liked things just as they were, but maybe if I'd tried harder..." She threw her head back and sighed. "She's probably right. If we never got any further than dirty weekends in fourteen years, we probably aren't right for each other."

"Fourteen years is a long time to be with someone. Is it worth trying to make a go of it? Perhaps if Tonia knows you're serious about the relationship, she might want to give it another try?"

"I don't think so. She's already eyeing up some young registrar at work. I should've seen it coming." She rubbed her face and finished her last mouthful of coffee. "Right, I know how to cheer us up. Let's go to my spa." She held her hand up before Tess had a chance to object. "My treat. We can have lunch and a couple of treatments, and you'll be home in plenty of time for the rug rats. It's a great idea, and you owe it to your best friend in her hour of need."

"I can think of a million reasons why it's not a great idea. I've got a house to clean, and I urgently need to find a job." But she was sick of always running around, and the thought some pampering was too hard to resist. "As long as I'm home by three. Come on, I'll drive."

As they made their way to the countryside spa, Jules asked about her job search.

"I've not found anything yet, but I might have a lead."

Derek had mentioned a possible position at the printing works when they chatted on Sunday, but she didn't know how serious he was. He was so kind, she suspected he'd offered because she'd told him how much she needed a job. He'd promised to talk it over with Rowan so she wasn't sure how it would turn out. "What does Rowan think of me?"

"Ha ha. You know I don't give confidences away between either of you. But I think it's fair to say you confuse the hell out of her."

"Well, I'm glad to know it's mutual."

"You know how I'm always encouraging you to get laid? You could start there."

Tess took her eyes off the road for a moment to see Jules grin. "Because that would make things *less* confusing?"

"It would do you both the world of good. Let off some steam."

"No offence, Jules, but I'm not sure I want to be taking relationship advice from you."

Jules nodded. "Point taken. Do you want to hear about the new contract I've just signed to design something ridiculously extravagant in the Lake District?"

Tess was glad of the change of subject, but as Jules regaled her with details of the luxury house she would be designing, she considered the thrill that had run through her at the notion of sleeping with Rowan. She needed to keep those kinds of thoughts at bay, especially if there was a chance of solving her money crisis with a job where Rowan would be her boss.

TEN

Rowan walked to work with thoughts of Tess spinning around in her head. She wasn't used to someone being kind to her with no obvious benefit to themself. Her last girlfriend, Kay, had seemed caring to start with, but when she realised Rowan wasn't going to drop the rest of her life to do everything she wanted, her selfish nature had come to the fore. It had still taken Rowan months to end it, and she'd since steered clear of relationships. She really needed to move on and to someone a lot less complicated than Tess Kennedy, who had just come out of a long and unpleasant relationship and who was, as far as she knew, straight.

She promised herself she would sign up to a dating site after work. She laughed to herself as she looked at her reflection in a shop window. She'd need to use an old photo for her profile. Her nose was misshapen, and her eyes were badly bruised, even if the swelling had gone down a little. It still hurt when she moved her head too quickly or leaned over, so she'd have to take it easy at work for a couple of days. That wasn't ideal with the number of jobs that were piling up.

Her dad wasn't in when she arrived, so she got on with the orders that needed to go out. He turned up around eleven, looking tired but less wiped-out than the evening before.

"I'm sorry, Dad, I need to be more organised about getting help at the club. You were run off your feet yesterday. Tess said the same thing."

"I'm just sorry I can't do more to help, love." He placed a kiss on her cheek and took a look at her before sliding into his chair next to her. "Nice pair of shiners."

"You didn't need to come in today. I've got it all under control."

"I know you do, Ro, but it's a lot for just you and the boys."

She saw her moment and seized it. "You know, I was going to talk to you about that. Profits are up, and we've got loads of orders to fill for the rest of the year. I think we could afford to employ a general assistant, even just part-time. And we could make it a six-month contract, so they weren't coming in with any long-term expectations. We just need someone with computer skills and a driving license. They could learn on the job." She stopped abruptly. That was a lot of talking for her, but she had been practising it in her head for days. She wondered what he would use as an excuse to disagree, but to her surprise he was smiling.

"Great minds, eh, love? I was about to say exactly the same thing."

"You *were*?"

"Yes. I know I've been unwilling to expand our team in the past. I think it's a big responsibility to give someone a job. But things have changed. I can't do the work I used to, and it's not fair on you."

Strike while the iron's hot! "Excellent. I'll get a job

description put together then. I was thinking we could advertise on local Facebook groups and put a couple of notices in supermarkets. I don't think we'll need to do any paid advertising."

Her dad's smile got even bigger. "I don't think we'll need to advertise at all. I've got someone in mind."

"Really?" Where had he found a candidate? He only got out of the house these days to come to work or potter around at the club.

"Tess Kennedy is looking for a job. She told me yesterday. Needs to fit around her school journey but we can be flexible."

No, no, no. That was the opposite of trying to stay away from Tess. She forced a laugh. "I'm not sure this is what she'll be looking for, Dad. You know, with her being a trained nurse and all?"

"Her registration lapsed years ago, she told me. She can't get a nursing job without retraining, and she doesn't have the time or money for that." His face relaxed into a satisfied smile, as though he'd solved a big problem all on his own.

"Even so, I don't think we can offer her the kind of money she'd be looking for. And it won't be very challenging."

Her dad looked into his mug.

"What? You've not already offered her a job? Seriously, Dad, this is something we need to talk about together." She rested her head in her hands, careful to avoid her bruised face. As well as the thought of having to cope with Tess at close quarters, she was disappointed with her dad. They had discussed the decision-making process when she had stepped up her management role in the business, and he had promised to always consult her.

"No, no, not offered, love. I just mentioned we might have something that would suit her. She sounded interested. I asked her not to mention it until I'd discussed it with you. I said you'd call her about it."

She swung around on her chair. "Why do *I* have to call her? You made the job offer." She immediately regretted her tone. Her dad looked upset, and she tried her best to keep him upbeat these days. "Sorry, Dad, it was just a bit of a surprise. I can talk to her if you want."

"She's lovely, Rowan. And she's all on her own with those kids. I just thought if we could help her, and she could help you, everyone would be happy."

Of course he felt for her as a single parent—he'd been one for so long. She cursed her insensitivity. If it made her dad feel good to know he was helping Tess, she could handle her stupid straight woman crush, or whatever it was. *She might not even want the job. Maybe she just didn't want to say anything to hurt Dad's feelings.* "Okay, I'll call her later and ask if she can come in for an interview."

Her dad frowned. "Do we need to interview her?"

"A chat then? Later in the week. We can talk to her together."

Her dad's face brightened. "Thanks, Rowan. You're a good girl, you know?"

"I know. I'm your little angel." She smiled and decided seeing him in good spirits made the potential awkwardness worth it. They did need help urgently, and if Tess was really interested in the job, maybe they could make it work. She just needed to keep her emotions to herself and act professionally.

Tess stood in the cold wind outside the factory. She wrapped her coat tighter around her one and only smart suit and pressed the buzzer. She was having serious second thoughts now. When he'd suggested the job opportunity at the clubhouse, Derek had outlined the perfect solution to her financial woes, but Rowan's tone on the phone the day before hadn't given her much reason for optimism. She'd made it sound like a formal interview and asked Tess to bring any relevant qualifications with her. Tess couldn't think of any qualifications she held that would be relevant to the general dogsbody job Derek had talked about. She was clutching an envelope with the few IT certificates she'd accrued over the years. It didn't feel like much to show for over twenty years of working, but she did have a clean driving licence.

She shuffled her feet to keep warm, and as her thoughts drifted to Rowan, she reflected on how seeing her get hurt had upset her so much. She'd had to force herself to remove her hand when Rowan had thanked her for taking care of her. She was a natural carer, so the general concept of wanting to look after people when they were hurt wasn't new to her but the intensity of it was surprising. Yes, Rowan was gorgeous, but Tess had no intention of ever again entwining her life with someone else's. She wanted to be the master of her own ship, to control her own destiny. She needed to focus on her current situation, yes, but she had high hopes for when the kids were settled into higher education, and she could really think about what she wanted to do with her life.

She jumped as the door opened to reveal Rowan, dressed in cargo pants and a pale blue DR Printing polo shirt. Tess felt a little overdressed as she stepped in.

Rowan held the door as she entered, and a smile lit her

bruised face. "You did a good job on my nose. It's not half as bad as I thought it would be. Thank you for the constant supply of ice. And for making me use it."

That was a pleasant start. Tess looked closely at the bruising as she passed. Four days later, it still looked pretty bad, but she remembered some of the cuts and bruises she'd turned up to work with back in her playing days. "Barely noticeable." She smiled back, hoping she looked more confident than she felt.

"Make your way into the meeting room down at the end and get comfortable. My dad and I will join you in a few minutes." Rowan waved towards a nearby door. "Would you like coffee? It's not too bad. We've got a filter machine, and I'll make a fresh pot."

Tess could have kissed her, but that would be a bad start to their professional relationship. "Thanks so much. My day has so far consisted of a hundred and twenty miles of motorway driving." *And a mad dash to find suitable interview clothes and get my ass here just in time.* She followed the corridor to the room Rowan had indicated.

A gas heater in the corner gave out a familiar but slightly unpleasant smell. It was warm enough to take off her coat though, so she was grateful. She dropped it over the back of a chair and stood as near to the heater as she dared, rubbing her hands.

From the direction of the corridor, she heard the welcome bubbling of the coffee machine as well as a distant conversation. Rowan's voice, along with a quieter male one she assumed was Derek's, carried down the hall. The voices stopped as a door closed firmly. Finally warm, she sat down, pulled out her sad envelope of certificates and waited, trying to think positive thoughts.

Rowan appeared five minutes later, two mugs with the

company logo in one hand and a pad of paper in the other. "Sorry, Tess, looks like it's just going to be me." She kicked the door shut. "Dad says he'd happily give you the job, so if I want an interview, I can do it myself." She smiled and shrugged as she sat. "I'm sorry if this feels overly formal, but we haven't employed anyone for years. Keith, Charlie, and Stefan have been here forever. I just think it's worth doing things properly, so we all know where we stand."

I don't think there's any chance of knowing where I stand with you. "Sounds good, Rowan. Where do we start?" She smiled in what she hoped was her most enthusiastic way.

An hour of discussion later and Rowan appeared convinced that Tess was capable of driving errands, answering emails and phone calls, keeping on top of the invoicing, and even helping with the printing in an all-hands-on-deck situation.

"As long as you're fine with me not being able to start until late morning, I'm happy to do whatever you ask of me, Rowan. I enjoy variety and I do love a challenge, so feel free to throw anything at me. If there are tasks I don't know how to do, I'll ask or work it out." She hoped Rowan was satisfied. It was hard to tell.

Rowan stood and smiled. "Let's go and tell my dad we'll give you a month's trial and see how things go."

Tess felt a weight off her shoulders. Even if it only turned out to be a month of work, it would solve a very immediate problem and avoid her having to ask Pete for anything. Derek was overjoyed when they told him the news, and Rowan took her to the staff uniform store.

She laughed as Rowan piled the items into her arms. "Ooh, I do love a bit of merch."

Rowan gave her a half smile. "Dad likes us all to look professional. Are you sure you can start on Monday?"

"Yes, definitely. I can't wait to get stuck in."

As she drove home, Tess enjoyed the feeling of elation. Okay, it was only a few hours a week, and it wasn't that much more than minimum wage, but it was more than most companies would pay for an inexperienced assistant. It was a start on her way to getting back on her feet, and she was grateful. She just needed to behave like an adult around Rowan, not the lovesick teenager she felt like inside.

ELEVEN

Rowan looked up as the door opened, and Tess rushed in, hands full of coffee and what looked like a box of doughnuts.

"Sorry, the motorway was awful again. I'll stay a bit longer tonight." She dropped the box on Rowan's desk and deposited a cup in front of her.

Coffee breaks had become a lot more attractive since Tess had started work the previous week. Fresh coffee and pastries made a welcome change from the battered filter machine and box of stale biscuits in the rest room.

"Thank you." Rowan took the lid off her cup. "And you don't have to work late, Tess. You do the hours you can. That's what we agreed."

Tess flicked the power button on her laptop and went to hang up her coat. She tipped her head towards the doughnuts. "Take what you want, and I'll leave the others in the rest room for the boys."

Rowan slipped a couple of her favourites onto a blank piece of paper, and Tess scooped the box up.

"I'll check on today's deliveries while I'm there."

Rowan watched her as she bustled around. "Tess, come and sit down for five minutes. You've been driving for how long?"

Tess checked her watch. "Close to four hours." She dropped into her chair and sighed. "Thanks, Rowan. I don't want you to think I'm taking this for granted."

"Hardly. You do more in the few hours you're here than those two do in a week." She tipped her head in the direction of the warehouse.

Tess smiled and slipped a doughnut out of the box. "Maybe I could have a small one with my coffee."

"Tess, you know you don't need to bring treats in every day. It must cost you a few quid." She had an inkling of how tight money must be for Tess from her willingness to take on any available hours. She'd already offered to come in on Saturday morning for a special job that needed to go out. It was lucky she had, as neither Stef nor Charlie was available. Rowan hoped she wasn't taking too much on.

"I like to treat myself to a coffee on my way in, so it's no trouble to pick them up." She bit into her doughnut.

"Well, take it out of petty cash. There's a budget for refreshments."

Tess shook her head as she licked jam from the corner of her mouth. Rowan was aware of how closely she watched that movement.

"It's fine, honest," she mumbled from behind a mouthful of dough.

Rowan knew she wasn't trying to ingratiate herself with her new colleagues. Tess genuinely enjoyed treating people and got pleasure from their happiness. Rowan watched her as she washed her snack down with a long swig of coffee.

"That's better." She smiled widely at Rowan as she stood. "I'm as good as new."

She lifted her uniform hoodie from the back of her chair and pulled it over her head. Rowan had the urge to stand up and pull Tess's hair free from where it was caught in the neck of her jumper but banned herself from such an intimate move. Instead, she sat back in her chair and watched Tess gather up the doughnut box and her clipboard.

"See you in a bit."

She disappeared through the door and Rowan felt her loss from the room.

As if overhearing her thoughts, Tess reappeared. "Oh, I nearly forgot. You might want to call your friend, Becca. I saw her out walking her dog this morning, and she seemed really odd. I haven't seen her since I got back, but I'm sure she'd remember me."

Oh yes, she'd remember you, with all the whining I did when you left. "Yes, of course she knows you. She's looking forward to seeing you at a game soon."

"Well, I pulled up next to her and said hello, but she completely ignored me and took off into a field with her dog." Tess scrunched her nose. "Becca was always such a lovely, friendly girl, it seemed strange."

"Okay, thanks, I'll drop her a text."

Tess was right. Becca would have been thrilled to see her and on the phone to Rowan immediately. She pulled out her phone and sent a quick message before getting on with the day's work.

By early afternoon, she still hadn't had a reply from Becca, and she was starting to worry. Even if she was caught up in something at work, she would usually send back something quick. Greg, the receptionist at the paper where Becca worked, had been in the Haresby colts team a few years ago, and Rowan still had his number.

Hi Greg, is Becca at work today?

His reply came back a minute later. *Hey, Jack. No, she rang in sick. Stomach upset, she said. If you speak to her, tell her I hope she's feeling better.*

She thanked him and sent another text to Becca. *Are you okay? If you don't reply, I'm coming round now.*

The reply came back almost instantaneously. *I'm fine. Leave me alone.*

Is something wrong with Ben?

What part of leave me alone don't you get? Ben's all right. Gerri broke up with me if you must know.

Rowan's heart sank. She'd gone into this relationship as she always did, wholeheartedly, and she'd be gutted it was over. Becca was a lot to take on, with her commitment to her brother and her relentless work schedule. Gerri had never seemed as involved as Rowan thought she should be.

I'll be over after work, whether you like it or not. I'll bring food.

Whatever.

She tried to put worry about Becca aside as she got on with her work, but when Tess reappeared in the office she said, "Thanks for the heads up about Becca. Her fiancé's dumped her."

"Oh, I'm sorry to hear that. Of all our old teammates, I'd have thought Becca would be settled in a relationship by now. She's such a sweetheart."

"Yeah." Rowan didn't know what else to say. If being a decent person was a guarantee of a happy relationship, they'd all be in a different place right now.

By the time Rowan arrived at Becca's, Ben was home from his day centre. She'd chosen Chinese for their takeaway as Ben loved it, and if he was enthused about eating, that was one less thing for Becca to worry about.

Ben answered the door with a wide smile. "Hello, Rowan. What's for tea?"

"Why don't you guess, Ben?"

"Chinese?"

"Good guess! Here you go." She swung the paper bag in his direction, and he was off into the kitchen at a sprint. She wandered into the living room and found Becca lying on the sofa, staring at the TV, which was showing a superhero film with the sound blaring at full volume.

Her eyes flicked to Rowan and back to the screen. "You're persistent."

Rowan picked up the TV remote and muted the volume. "I am when I'm worried about you. How are you feeling?"

Ben bounded back into the room, balancing a plate full of food. "Chicken noodles!" He grinned at Rowan as he took the TV remote from her and turned the volume back up.

"Let's go into the kitchen and leave Ben to his TV."

Becca didn't react, so she hauled her to her feet. "Come on, Becs. Let's go and eat." She did most of the work propelling Becca into the kitchen and onto a seat at the table. Rowan scooped out some of Becca's favourite dishes and set the bowl before her. She scooped food into her own bowl and sat opposite. "Eat up, Becca. I know you won't have eaten all day."

"I'm not hungry."

Becca's voice was dull in a way that made Rowan's heart ache. Her best friend was normally so enthusiastic, seeing her like this was heartbreaking. "You can talk about it or not, it's up to you." She pushed the bowl towards her friend. "But you're going to eat, or I'm staying all night."

Becca rolled her eyes half-heartedly and picked up some chopsticks from the table. "Fine."

"And *do* you want to talk about it?"

Becca looked up. "There's not much to say." She manoeuvred some food to her mouth and chewed. "Gerri said it was too much of a commitment too soon, and she needed some space." She returned her attention to her bowl.

"I'm so sorry, buddy." Rowan wasn't sure what else she could say.

"You knew it, didn't you? That she wasn't that into me, and I was making an idiot of myself?"

Becca's eyes weren't accusing, they were just sad. Rowan thought for a moment. "I knew how much you liked her. I didn't have any insight into what she thought, Bec. I only know you should be happy. If Gerri's not the person to make that happen for you, she doesn't deserve you."

Becca pushed her bowl aside and groaned as she lowered her head to her arms. "I really don't want to talk, Ro. Thanks for bringing food, but I can't do this now."

Rowan felt for her. "How about we go and watch the film with Ben, and I'll stay the night? I can take Digby for his walk in the morning?"

"Yeah, if you want." Becca pushed herself up from the table and trudged back toward the living room.

Rowan sighed, tidied up the remaining food into boxes and cleaned the kitchen before returning to the lounge. She had to manoeuvre a horizontal Becca until she was sitting behind her on the sofa. Becca dropped back against her chest. They stayed in that comfortable position for the rest of the evening, and when it was time to go to bed, she pushed Becca up the stairs ahead of her.

As she lay on the hastily made sofa bed in the spare room, she stared at the ceiling, wide awake. Being in love was wonderful, until it ended. If she made a move with Tess, would she one day end up crying on her sofa with a broken heart? She couldn't imagine Tess inflicting pain on anyone, but that was how love worked, wasn't it? You put yourself on the line and just hoped the other person felt as strongly. And when they didn't, it left you broken.

TWELVE

Rowan packed the last of the boxes into the back of the van. For the first time in a while, they were on top of their orders. A few weeks of Tess's involvement had made more of a difference than she could have possibly imagined. Rowan had extended her contract for a full year and Tess had been so grateful, it almost made Rowan uncomfortable. But she was a grafter, she picked tasks up quickly, and most importantly, she wasn't afraid to comment when she thought things could be done differently or more efficiently. Some small tweaks to their processes had greatly improved output. This wasn't a surprise to Rowan. She'd always thought she and her dad were a bit too involved in the day-to-day side of the business to see the opportunities for change, but there'd never been anyone else to come up with ideas. And her dad was even more set in his ways than she was. She found it difficult, though, to let go of total control when she'd taken responsibility for so long. Not that Tess wanted control, just small changes. But Rowan wasn't great with change.

Tess appeared at the door to the loading bay, looking

cute as anything in her navy uniform hoodie. She shoved her hands in the pocket and stood watching as Rowan closed up the back and locked the doors.

"Another job finished. It's such a satisfying feeling when it's all done ahead of time."

"It sure is. Thanks for helping to get things sorted around here, Tess. It's made a lot of difference." She couldn't have imagined her saying something like that a few weeks ago, but Tess was easy to talk to.

"Are you sure you don't want any help with the delivery?"

She couldn't think of anything she would enjoy more than running this job with Tess sitting alongside her in the van. But she knew how hectic her life was, with her school run in the morning and then having to be home to make dinner, and wash uniforms, and help with revision. She couldn't ask Tess to stay late just for her own entertainment. She jumped down from the loading dock and opened the van door. "No, of course not. You get off home now, and I'll see you in the morning." She jumped up and slammed the door, waving to Tess as she pulled out of the yard. Tess waved back and disappeared inside.

She seemed happy in the job and turned up smiling each day. Not that she wasn't always smiling, but she seemed more relaxed these days. Rowan hoped the arrangement would last, as it really seemed to suit everyone. Her dad was coming into the office much less regularly now he knew Rowan had some help. And Rowan couldn't deny how much she looked forward to seeing Tess every day. She hoped it wasn't obvious that sometimes she created situations for them to work closely together, just to spend more time in her presence.

The rugby season, such an important part of Rowan's

life, was looking positive too. Their last few fixtures had been easy wins, including the recent home game against the team who'd sat at the bottom of the league all season. Zoë, the number eight, had been unable to play because of a family emergency, so Emily had moved to her old position and Elsie started at flanker. She'd played brilliantly considering how little time she'd been with the team, and Hannah, Rowan, and Steve, confident of a win, had decided to give her the last twenty minutes at hooker. While she needed a lot more experience in the scrum, she held her own and even set up a try at the end of the game. Tess had been overjoyed to see her playing so well and that had made Rowan happy.

Now they had a final away game this week, followed by one more home game, then a three-week break for Christmas. Rowan had talked with her dad, and they'd agreed to give Tess a full two weeks paid holiday over Christmas. They wouldn't be able to take that much time themselves, but her dad was worried Tess must be exhausted after a full term of her long motorway commute and now a busy job as well.

Rowan knew Tess wouldn't be easily convinced to take a paid break, but if her dad raised it, she'd be much more likely to agree. She was painfully aware that no rugby or work meant they would have little reason to spend time together. Should she be concerned about how much she was enjoying Tess's company? Tess was a joy to work alongside, and Rowan felt herself becoming chattier and opening up more due to her time with Tess.

She'd also got into the habit of picking up Elsie for away games. It was a little out of her way, but she loved the idea of Tess having some time to herself. The first time, she'd left Tess a bottle of wine and a scented bath bomb when she'd arrived to collect Elsie. She'd had to go back to the car to get them after chickening out but Tess had been so pleased, it had felt right. Today, on her lunch break, she'd found a relaxation candle in her favourite gift shop in town, with a scent she thought Tess would love. She planned to give it to her when she picked Elsie up on Sunday. She knew it wasn't normal behaviour. She'd never paid her girlfriends this much attention. But it felt so good to make Tess smile, she couldn't help herself.

At lunchtime, Rowan was sitting with Tess in the break room when Tess's phone rang. She looked at the number and pursed her lips.

"Oh no, what now?"

She picked up and mouthed "Archie" at Rowan in explanation. Rowan could hear an excited voice at the other end.

"No, Archie, I'm not coming to get you. You need to work on this project at school. I can't help you, but Mr Poynter knows what he's talking about. If you're being too ambitious with your project, maybe you should scale it down a bit." She held the phone away from her ear for a moment. "No, I'm not saying *dumb* it down, Arch, but you've got a busy few months ahead of you, so you need to keep it in perspective." She put her hand over the phone to let out a groan of exasperation, and she rolled her eyes at Rowan. "He's got this project work to get finished." She turned back to her conversation. "Okay, we'll talk about it tonight. You can try to explain to me what's going wrong, and we'll decide what to do about it, all right?" She paused to listen. "Okay, just stick with it for now. Safe journey home. I love you, bye." She hung up and dropped the phone on the table.

"Problem?" asked Rowan and then cursed herself for the stupid question. Tess was distressed, and she wanted to help.

"He's got this project for computer science, and I think he's overstretched himself. He's losing his shit over it, and I can't help him. I've no idea what he's talking about."

Rowan didn't want to intrude, but she hated seeing Tess feel so useless. "I'm not exactly an expert, but I did do computing at GCSE. Can I try and help?" She braced herself for Tess telling her to mind her own business.

Tess's face brightened immediately. "Oh, Rowan, that'd be amazing. Will you come and have dinner with us tonight, and you can ask Archie about his project?"

"Tonight? Yeah, I guess." She saw the look of doubt on Tess's face, as if she'd asked too much. "Of course I can. I might not understand it either though, so don't get your hopes up."

As Tess left to go home at her usual time, Rowan promised to be at the house by six thirty.

"Thanks again. I really appreciate you giving up your evening. I'll make it up to you with a good home-cooked dinner. Do you like chilli?"

"Yeah, anything will do me, thanks. It'll just be a novelty to not cook for myself." And she really didn't have anything better to do. Maybe a bit of sketching and a run. She could do that anytime, and she couldn't turn down the chance of an evening in Tess's company.

She rushed through her last few tasks as quickly as possible and locked up on time so she could run home for a quick shower and change of clothes. As she dried her hair, she wondered if Tess was looking forward to the evening as much as she was. Of course she wasn't; it was just a run of the mill evening with her kids, trying to juggle schoolwork, and housework, and all the other things Tess's life revolved around. The only bonus in entertaining Rowan was that she might be able to help take the pressure off one aspect. Well, at least that was something.

She pulled on her favourite short-sleeved shirt and buttoned it up, before checking her reflection in the mirror. She liked to look smart in those rare moments she wasn't in work clothes or rugby kit, but tonight she felt herself making a special effort. *This is a family meal on a school night, get a grip.* Even so, she took a final look in the mirror before she left.

———

"Hey, thanks again for coming over." Tess pulled her in for a hug and dropped a quick kiss on her cheek.

The spot burned with heat and Rowan hoped it wasn't visible. Tess pulled her by the hand into the kitchen. Rowan's visits so far hadn't extended beyond the hallway. Not that Tess hadn't invited her in but she'd always found an excuse, not wanting to intrude on Tess's precious time with her family.

The kitchen was long, with a dining table at the far end, large enough to seat four comfortably. The table was old, stripped and stained in a shabby chic way.

"Are you admiring my handiwork? I didn't want to buy new, so I searched the charity shops and gave them a new lease of life. Someone's probably turning in their grave at what I've done to their prized G-plan." She pointed at a sideboard, grinning.

"It looks great." Rowan meant it. Tess clearly had an eye

for colour and had made the worn furniture a combination of homely and fun.

Tess indicated a chair. "Sit and keep me entertained while I finish up."

Rowan sat slowly and placed the bottle she'd brought on the table. What was she meant to talk about? Why didn't she find this stuff easy like other people?

Tess turned the bottle to read the label and nodded approvingly. "Good choice."

She leaned over Rowan to stretch up to the top shelf of the unit, and Rowan got a glimpse of milky white skin as her T-shirt rose. She looked away quickly as Tess placed two glasses in front of her and slid a corkscrew across the table.

"Make yourself useful and pour us a glass. Maybe if you get me tipsy, I'll stop trying to make you talk."

"Sorry." She concentrated on opening the bottle to hide her disappointment in herself.

"I'm teasing you, Ro. I don't expect chatter from you. Luckily your conversation is of a high enough quality to make up for its scarcity."

Rowan looked up, but Tess had her back to her now, as she removed pots from the hob and started to dish up. As if sensing her gaze, Tess threw a smile over her shoulder that made Rowan feel dizzy inside. How did Tess have this effect on her? She needed to rein it in big time if they were going to be friends as well as colleagues.

"Elsie, Arch, I said six forty five. I meant six forty five."

Tess's yell broke her out of her reverie, and she focused on pouring the wine with a steady hand. Elsie and Archie strolled in. Archie was looking at his phone, but he glanced up to see Tess's glare and quickly slipped it into his pocket as he went to help serve. Elsie lowered herself into the seat next to Rowan, elbowing her in a playful way as she passed.

Rowan returned the poke and smiled. Rugby banter she could deal with.

Tess placed a steaming bowl of chilli in the middle of the table, and Archie followed with rice and sour cream.

"Thank you, Archie." Rowan smiled at him, hoping they'd get on okay. It would make the homework thing easier.

"You're welcome. Mum says you know about computer science. Can you help me with my project?"

Well, that was a lot more straightforward than she'd imagined. She liked a conversation that cut to the chase. "Maybe...I hope so. Let's enjoy our dinner, and we'll go and look at it after, okay?"

Archie nodded as he started to serve himself, but Rowan was only aware of the look Tess was giving her. Was it affection or something more? This wasn't her strong suit, so she wasn't sure, but whatever it was, it wasn't helping the odd feeling in the pit of her stomach. Feeling bold, she looked up and caught Tess's eye. Tess glanced away quickly, but then looked back, a half-smile on her face, and something in her eyes that made Rowan wish she hadn't made eye contact.

"So, Jack, what's your prediction for Sunday's game?"

Elsie's question jolted her back to reality and she reminded herself she was at a table with Tess's children. "We should be okay. A win will put us in a good place for the second half of the season, and it'll definitely make the Christmas party more of a celebration. You planning to come along?" She tipped her head at Tess. "Families are welcome."

"Ah, yeah, please come, Mum. That'll be so much fun."

Tess lowered her fork and looked at Elsie. "Do you think that'll add to your fun? Having your mum there?"

"It's not that kind of party. It's the whole club getting together. It's a good fundraiser." Rowan wondered if she was trying too hard.

"But more importantly, it's fancy dress. Mum loves to dress up." Elsie laughed. "And I mean as an Ewok or a Smurf. No costume is too much work for her."

Tess cleared her throat. "Hey, I can do glamorous too!" She rolled her eyes. "But I usually opt for comedy. And comfort."

"So, I'll book you a ticket?" Rowan tried to look casual.

"Let me think about it."

"Mum, you have literally nothing else to do. Two tickets for us please, Jack. Unless Archie wants to join us too?"

Archie mimed a vomiting action. "I'd rather sit at home in the dark."

Rowan smiled for the rest of the meal. When the time came to look at Archie's project, she was pleased to find she did understand what he was trying to achieve. She ran through the parts he'd overlooked and helped him plan the rest of the project, watching as he wrote thorough notes of what he needed to do. She looked around the room at the gaming chair, the posters, and the console that took prime position in the room and wondered if she could help Ben too.

"Archie."

He looked up from his notes.

"I've got a friend who doesn't live too far away, and he loves gaming. He's a bit older than you, but he's got some additional needs. He doesn't make friends very easily, and he mostly plays games on his own."

Archie nodded, as though he'd been in the same situation. "D'you want me to show him how to get online? He could join some of my games if he likes the same stuff?"

"That would be very kind." She indicated the posters on the walls. "These are the games he likes to play." She felt a rush of happiness that she'd thought of a way to help Ben and Becca.

"Let my mum know, and I'll go over to show him how to set things up."

She nodded and stood. "Thanks, I really appreciate it. Are you sorted with your project now?"

"Yeah, it makes more sense, thanks."

"Just give me a call if you run into any other problems, okay?"

He nodded and returned to his notes as she left the room.

Tess squeezed her arm tightly as she got ready to leave. "I really owe you one, Rowan. Let me know how I can repay you."

All she could manage was a nod as she pictured the many ways she would like Tess to return the favour. A warning bell went off in her head but being with Tess made everything feel so right.

On the drive home, she forced herself to evaluate her feelings. Tess seemed to enjoy her company, and that made her feel like she might be a little interesting. But Tess had just come out of a bad long-term marriage, and Rowan had no reason to think that even if she did want a new relationship, that it might be with her. The last thing Rowan wanted was to be someone's rebound experiment.

Maybe Tess's kindness affected her so much because she'd never been with the right person. She seemed to attract all the wrong people. Her dad always said she needed to take the bull by the horns and just talk to someone if she liked them. But that was easier said than done, wasn't it? Her dad thought she was perfect and great company. Most of the women she'd dated would disagree.

Maybe she should revisit the idea of online dating. She could take her own time making contact if she found a profile she liked. And in the unlikely event they replied, they wouldn't expect an immediate response. That she could do. She drove home with a determination to get herself out and meet someone new and take her mind off Tess once and for all.

THIRTEEN

As Tess pulled up outside Becca's modest terraced house in the middle of the town, a stocky young man she assumed was Ben swung the door open. His hair was fairer than Becca's, but the family resemblance was clear. He wore a wide, open smile and waved enthusiastically. Archie waved back. He had been keen to come over and help as soon as Rowan had told him about Ben's situation. Tess guessed he knew what it felt like to not have many friends, and she was pleased Archie was showing kindness towards someone else.

While Rowan had arranged the meet up, she hadn't made it clear whether she would be there herself tonight. Tess wasn't concerned about spending an evening with Becca, even after their recent one-sided encounter now that she knew the reason for Becca's behaviour. But she couldn't deny she'd be thrilled if Rowan was around too. Archie jumped out with his rucksack containing his gaming gear and left her to juggle the food she'd prepared and lock up the car. Becca had promised pizza, so Tess had made some fresh sour cream dip and her favourite guacamole for them to dip the crusts into. She'd also baked some white chocolate cookies, allegedly for the boys, but she knew Rowan loved them too.

Archie followed Ben inside, and Becca appeared at the door. She looked tired, but her smile was genuine.

"Sorry, Tess, do you need a hand?"

"I think I've got everything, thanks." She followed Becca inside, where she was quickly relieved of the tray of cookies.

"I'll hide these until after Ben's eaten, if that's okay?" She inhaled. "Oh, wow, they smell amazing. Maybe it's me they need to be hidden from."

She led the way into the kitchen, and Tess followed, immediately filled with happiness to see Rowan chopping salad at the worktop. *This is getting ridiculous. I saw her a couple of hours ago.* Rowan looked up with a smile that seemed to echo Tess's pleasure. Or was she imagining it?

"Rowan, Tess has baked cookies. I'm supposed to be getting fit, so you need to intervene." Becca waved the box of cookies under Rowan's nose.

"They do smell good." Rowan grinned at Tess. "White chocolate?"

"And strawberry—which is a fruit, so they're healthy." Tess felt herself beaming back at Rowan, who took the box from Becca and placed them out of the way.

"Pizza's nearly done." She tipped her chopped salad into a large bowl and added it to the food already spread on the small kitchen table.

"I'll get the boys to eat before they get too engrossed, then we can leave them to it and chat." Becca turned to Tess. "We've got a lot of catching up to do."

Tess realised the small kitchen wasn't going to fit three of them. "Do you want me to do anything?"

"Sorry, it's a bit cramped." Becca pulled a bottle of wine out of the fridge and indicated with her elbow to a cupboard as she handed it over. "Glasses are there. Corkscrew in the drawer below."

Tess pulled out two wine glasses and a tall glass for herself. She saw an opening at the sink and filled the glass with water. She took it and the wine into the lounge and sat down on an old, battered sofa. She liked the friendly informality of Becca's home, she thought, as she poured the wine.

"Ben!" Becca's voice roared up the stairs. "Pizza's ready."

Two sets of thundering footsteps and the pad of canine paws followed. Ben was even heavier-footed than Archie. She stayed out of the way while the boys piled their plates and made their way more slowly back upstairs.

"This is a special treat, remember, Ben. If those plates don't find their way back down to the kitchen, it'll be the last time. And don't give Digby any pizza." Becca poked her head into the lounge. "Help yourself, Tess. They've left us a few slices."

Tess found Rowan at the small table, holding out a plate for her.

"Hi." Rowan held the dip bowl while she scooped some out and added a few slices of pizza, then she followed Rowan back into the room. Rowan pointed to her glass of water. "Sorry about you having to do all the driving."

She sat down on the sofa next to Rowan. "The downside of living in the sticks. But hopefully, that'll soon change."

Becca followed them in and dropped into her chair. "Yeah, much appreciated, Tess. Maybe we could do a return visit sometime?"

"Of course. I could cook for you." Tess smiled at the thought. She'd missed having a group of friends like this.

"I'd need to give you Ben's list of acceptable foods. It's not very long, so it might cramp your style a bit."

"Tess's food is delicious." Rowan lifted a dip-laden crust into her mouth and nodded in appreciation.

It pleased Tess that Rowan enjoyed her cooking.

"Oh, yeah, I hear you've been spoiling her with home-cooked food." Becca grinned at Rowan as though she was sharing a secret and poured herself another glass of wine. She took a healthy swig before she put the bottle down.

"I'd feed her more often if she'd let me. It's the least I can do when Rowan saves me from having to drive Elsie all around the county and beyond."

Rowan finished chewing. "You don't have to feed me. I'm driving there anyway. It's not a problem."

The conversation moved on to rugby, and Rowan updated Tess on how Elsie's game was developing.

Becca grabbed the bottle from the table and frowned to see it was empty. "I'll just get another." She hauled herself out of the chair and left the room.

Rowan scratched her head. "She's drinking more than I've ever known her to."

Tess sensed Rowan's feeling of helplessness and put her hand on her leg. "She's going through a rough patch. Just be there for her, Ro."

Becca returned, an open bottle in one hand and the plate of cookies in the other. She filled her glass to the top and reached towards Rowan's empty glass.

Rowan moved it aside. "Not for me, Becs. I've got to drive in the morning."

Becca pouted. "Drinking on my own is what I do every night. I was hoping for some company tonight."

"It's a weekday evening, Becca," Rowan said. She leaned forward and picked up a cookie, biting it in half. "Ooh, these are so good," she mumbled around the crumbs.

Tess thought about how long it was since she'd enjoyed a glass of wine with friends. "Why don't you all come one weekend and stay over? There's enough room if you don't mind sofa beds."

"Rowan can bring her new girlfriend," Becca said and grinned.

Rowan pinned her with an icy stare as she chewed her cookie.

Tess swallowed down the bitter taste of jealousy and forced a smile. "Who's the lucky woman?"

As Rowan looked from Becca to Tess, her expression softened, and she looked awkward. "I don't really know her yet. It's just a first date," she mumbled.

Becca chuckled. "Rowan's been looking for love online."

Tess raised her eyebrow.

"Shut up, will you, Becs? I'm not looking for love, I'm just going for a meal."

Rowan was saved by the sound of canine feet padding down the stairs, followed by the door swinging open. Becca's dog appeared even larger in the confines of the living room.

"Hey, Digby, are the boys too engrossed to pay you any attention?" Becca scratched behind his ears.

He swung his big head around and spotted Tess. His tail banged against the side of the chair, but Becca held on to his collar.

"Woah, not everybody's a fan, Digby. Tess may not want to fight off your big, sloppy chops."

"Let him come and say hi," Tess said with more confidence than she was feeling. As he padded closer, his head was almost on a level with hers. "Hi, Digby." He leaned in to sniff her, then sat, his tail beating against the floor. A giant paw landed lightly on her knee. She shook it very formally. "Pleased to meet you."

"Wow, he's really on his best behaviour with you." Rowan laughed, which drew the dog's attention, and he jumped up to run to her. She fussed him, and he somehow managed to crawl up into her lap, looking like a giant puppy, as he squirmed for her to scratch his belly.

Becca rolled her eyes at Tess. "Ro's always spoiled him. He knows who the soft touch is around here."

Rowan laughed and petted him, her face looking younger as she forgot about the earlier line of questioning. Tess wondered why she was making the effort to go on a date when the idea clearly made her anxious. She looked at her watch and jumped up. "Oh, wow, I didn't realise the time." She turned to Becca. "I'm so sorry, we have to be up at silly o'clock in the morning, so we have a strict bedtime curfew on school nights." She started to gather their plates, but Becca stood and took them from her.

"I'll take these. You may want to go and extract your son from whatever mission the two of them are enrolled in."

Tess climbed the stairs, identifying Ben's room by the noise coming from it, as well as the hazard tape decorating it, along with a sign that said, "Do not disturb—gaming in progress." She knocked loudly. "Archie, we need to go, love."

Archie's head emerged, his headset in hand. "Do we have to? We're in the middle of something."

Tess waved her watch under his nose. "Yes, we do. And I thought the point of tonight was getting Ben online, so you could play together all the time?"

Archie gave an exaggerated snort. "All riiight." He disappeared back into the room.

Tess headed back downstairs, where Becca was tidying up in the kitchen. "Thank you so much for feeding us. And it was nice to get out and chat."

"You don't know how much I appreciate Archie doing this for Ben. He loves gaming so much, but none of his friends at the centre are into it, so it's such a relief for him to find a friend."

Tess could only guess at how much of her personal energy Becca spent watching out for her brother. She squeezed Becca's arm and pulled her into a hug. "Come over to us soon."

Becca pulled back and smiled. "Thanks, Tess, I will."

Archie ran down the stairs, his rucksack over his shoulder. "Thanks for having me. Ben's a good gamer."

"He's well practiced." Becca laughed.

Tess pulled on her coat and threw Archie's to him. She stuck her head inside the room, where Rowan was now lying full length on the sofa, with Digby on top. "We're off now."

Rowan heaved the dog from her and stood. "It was good to see you, Tess." Her smile was gentle. "Outside of work, I mean."

Tess hugged her and enjoyed the fleeting moment of their bodies pressed together. "See you in the morning, Rowan."

"I like Ben, he's fun. And Digby's great. Can we have a dog?"

"Absolutely not. But I'm glad you enjoyed yourself." It was unusual to see Archie so animated, and she'd had a pleasurable evening in good company, not just Rowan's, who was increasingly her favourite person to spend time with, but Becca was a lovely woman too. When she'd known her over a decade ago, she'd been a mature young person with a wealth of knowledge on current affairs. Now, it seemed the weight of her responsibilities had taken its toll, but Tess could still see the passionate nature that had always driven her.

She wondered if making new friendships would be enough to keep her in this town when her kids had moved on. She wanted her freedom, but the thought of moving on again was losing its shine. And could she keep her relationship with Rowan platonic? She was going to have to if Rowan's foray into dating went to plan. Jealousy flared again. She'd started to think Rowan was having similar feelings about the two of them, but her tiny flame of hope had been snuffed out. And it wasn't like she'd given Rowan any clue that she was interested, so she couldn't blame her for not seeing her that way at all. She needed to get over herself and get on with her own life. She'd promised herself she wouldn't get involved again, and this was a good reminder why. Archie's voice, chattering about his game with Ben, brought her back to reality. She put aside her self-centred thoughts and focused on her son.

FOURTEEN

The drive to the restaurant took longer than Rowan had factored in. It really was in the middle of nowhere, and she'd missed the turn on the winding country road she felt she'd been navigating for hours. When she finally arrived outside the traditional country pub turned high-end restaurant, she was already feeling anxious.

Anna, the woman she'd been chatting to online had thought it was a good place to meet, and she said the food was out of this world. Rowan was sure she'd be too nervous to eat, but this place looked upmarket enough that the portions were unlikely to be large. Just her luck, she'd have to try and negotiate fancy menu items while thinking up witty conversation. She laughed at herself as she got out of the car. Any conversation would do. More likely she'd just freeze up and mutter one syllable answers. Anna would soon get bored.

She pulled on her coat as she walked up the path to the door. No point shooting herself in the foot before she even entered. She'd agreed to come, she needed to make an effort.

The inside of the restaurant was equally impressive,

modern while still retaining the beams and older features of the pub.

A short man in a white shirt met her at the door. "Welcome. Do you have a booking?"

Rowan tried to smile confidently. "I'm here to meet Anna Lane. The booking is in her name."

He consulted the iPad in his hand. "Ah, yes. She's already here, I believe."

Of course she was, because Rowan was—she checked her watch—seven minutes late. Not as bad as it could have been but still a poor start to the evening. She recognised Anna immediately as they moved into the main room of the restaurant. She was sitting at a table against the wall, sipping water and reading the menu in her other hand. She looked very like her online photos, a couple of years older than Rowan, with shoulder-length reddish hair. Rowan's brain stuttered. Had she subconsciously sought out a redhead? She needed to put Tess out of her mind as she approached, putting on the friendliest expression she could muster as Anna looked up with a smile of recognition and possibly relief. "I'm so sorry." She slipped into the seat opposite. "I got lost and kept missing my turn."

"That's okay. I come here a lot. I forget how difficult it can be to find." Anna held out her hand, and her smile was warm and genuine. "It's nice to meet you, Rowan."

Rowan shook her hand firmly then loosened it a little as she reminded herself she wasn't greeting a customer. "You too."

Anna picked up the menu. "I'm starving, so let's order and then we can get to know each other."

Rowan picked up her own menu hastily and looked at the choices, prepared to navigate her way through the foams and reductions, to find something she might enjoy. She coughed to disguise her laugh as she saw squirrel was on the menu. Tess would love that. She called them tree rats and was in a constant battle with them digging up her lawn. She'd probably appreciate a squirrel pie as revenge.

"Is everything okay?" Anna was watching from over the top of her menu.

"Uh, yes, sorry." She poured herself a glass of water. "Bit of a dry throat."

She went back to her menu and opted for a mushroom starter and the salmon. They couldn't mess salmon up too much, surely. Relieved she'd made a choice, she dropped her menu and sat back.

Anna slid the wine menu across the table. "You choose. I'm still deliberating."

Rowan froze. She enjoyed a glass of wine, sure, but usually it was someone else's choice. Left to her own devices, she'd opt for a beer. She guessed it wasn't an option tonight. "Shall I wait to see what you're eating?" She had a vague idea about red with meat and white with fish, but that didn't seem much to go on.

Anna waved a hand over her menu. "No, go ahead. I'll drink anything. It's entirely up to you.

Fantastic. She took a deep breath and consulted the wine list. White had less potential for disastrous spillage. New World or European? She finally decided on a random choice just as the waiter appeared.

"Are we ready to order?"

Anna put down her menu and smiled. "I am. Rowan?"

"Yes, all good." When they'd ordered their food, Rowan requested the French wine she'd selected, and Anna nodded her approval.

"Good choice."

Definitely more luck than judgement if that was true,

but Rowan breathed a mental sigh of relief. She hadn't blown it yet. With the menus gone, she now had no choice other than to look at Anna. Her hair did have a reddish tint, but that was where the similarity with Tess ended. Anna's hair was straight, and smooth, and her nails were perfectly manicured.

Anna looked at Rowan with a half-smile on her shiny lips. "So, Rowan, tell me about yourself."

Rowan made an effort not to bite her lip, but her fists were firmly clenched under the table. She managed to open her mouth. "I play rugby."

"I know that from your profile. Tell me the stuff that's not on there. What do you like to do to unwind?" Anna took a slow sip of her water. "I'm getting the impression good restaurants aren't on that list."

Shit, she was coming over as rude. She wished she had a beer. "I'm sorry, no, I like eating. Out, that is. Eating out."

Anna chuckled. "That's good to hear. What else? Theatre?"

Her gentle coaxing helped Rowan relax, and they were soon talking about live music and the best venues in the region. By the time their starters arrived, Rowan was beginning to believe she could get through this without making a complete idiot of herself. The food was delicious, and the small glass of wine she allowed herself also helped her to unwind. The rest of the evening was surprisingly enjoyable, and after the food was finished and they sat chatting, the conversation moved on to sport.

"So, you play rugby? You must be tough. Hockey's enough for me. I prefer to stay on my feet."

"It's not all rolling about in the mud. Especially as a back. It's more running and passing."

"And tackling." Anna poured more wine.

Rowan shook her head to another glass. She was enjoying herself now and wished she could, but she was driving.

"I've watched enough rugby. There's no way I want someone hitting me at that kind of pace."

Rowan smiled. "You'd just need to run faster then." They continued their casual chat until Rowan realised the time. "I'd better get back. Work in the morning." She waved to get the server's attention. "I've enjoyed this a lot. Thank you."

"So have I." Anna reached across the table and put her hand on Rowan's.

Rowan tensed.

"Can we do it again soon?" The silence went on for too long, and Anna quickly withdrew her hand. "Or not. Why don't you call me if you want to?"

Rowan gathered her composure and smiled. "Yes, of course I will. I've had a wonderful evening, Anna, thank you."

Rowan kept her eyes on the winding country lanes as she drove home in the dark, but her thoughts were everywhere else. Apart from the slightly uncomfortable ending, she had enjoyed the meal, and she was definitely attracted to Anna. She was kind, funny, good company, close to Rowan's own age, and she played sport. They had plenty in common, and they'd had an enjoyable evening. So why had the thought of another date made her panic? She needed to try harder with this. She rang Becca's number. It was late, but Becca was her emergency contact. She wouldn't sleep until she knew Rowan was alive. Not that she was sleeping much lately anyway.

"No SOS texts, so I'm assuming it went well?" Becca asked.

"It did. Better than expected. She was lovely."

"So you're going to meet up again?" Becca didn't wait long into the pause. "Oh, for fuck's sake, Ro. Tell me you arranged to meet up again."

She tapped her hand on the steering wheel. "I don't know, Bec. I said I'd call her. I need to think first."

"Think about what, you muppet? You like her. Did she like you?"

"Yeah, she said she wanted to do it again soon, so I guess I didn't bore her too much."

"Will you shut up about being boring. That's all in your head, courtesy of a couple of nasty exes who used it as an excuse to mess around on you. You're a great catch, Rowan. You're fun, gorgeous, financially stable, and you've got no complications in your life to scare people off."

Rowan felt guilty at that. Compared to Becca, her life was pretty straightforward. "I'm going to call her, okay. She just caught me off guard."

Becca's splutter burst through the speaker. "Because she asked to meet again at the end of a fun date? You're one of a kind, Rowan. But I love you dearly."

"What have you been up to?"

"Let me see. I fixed Ben's gaming headset because he'd pulled a wire loose, then I groomed a ridiculous dog and have enough fur to knit a jumper. And now I'm sitting down to a two-thousand-word article that needs to be submitted in three days. And I've not started the research yet. Just a regular Wednesday night for me."

Becca was never full-on self-pitying, but Rowan could hear the weariness in her voice. "I'm sorry you don't get much of a break." She checked the time. "It's late, Becs. Can't you pick that up tomorrow?"

"I'll get an hour or two in before bed. You know me, I don't need much sleep."

"I know nothing of the kind. You choose to work instead of sleeping. It's not good for you."

"Okay, okay, Aunty Rowan, I'll call it a night."

Rowan heard the sound of a laptop being closed. "I don't believe you. But don't stay up all night, okay? People care about you, Becs."

"Yeah, people like my gorgeous, unavailable best friend."

"Ah, Becca." She knew her friend was feeling at rock bottom if she was going down this route.

"I'm sorry. I'm sorry, okay? I didn't mean to say that. I'm just fed up, Rowan."

"Do you want me to come over?"

"No, of course not. You're right, I'm tired and it's late. Great journalism is not going to get done tonight. I'm going to bed. When I wake up, my life will be amazing again."

"Becs..." She didn't know what to say to make Becca feel better.

"It's okay, really." She paused. "Do you fancy a run tomorrow night? I could do with some fresh air."

Rowan smiled. Exercise made everything better. That was something she could be relied on to help with. They made arrangements, and she rung off after making Becca promise to put her laptop away for real.

She rubbed her eyes. She'd told Tess once that there had never been anything between Becca and her, but that wasn't entirely true. The summer after their A-levels, things had got a little strained between them. They'd spent months in each other's company revising for their exams, and then the sense of release after it was all over had made them a little giddy. After they'd almost kissed one night in Rowan's car, they'd had a serious talk about it and agreed they didn't want to risk their close bond. They had agreed, it was true, but Rowan had always known she'd been more enthusiastic about the agreement than Becca. They'd continued their friendship, but Becca struggled to hide what was on her mind, and sometimes she blurted out things that made Rowan wonder if their feelings were quite different. She loved Becca dearly as her best friend, nothing more.

She compared that to how she felt about Tess, who she was desperately trying to think of as a friend. But when she was near Tess, her whole body felt alive, and she just wanted to be closer still. It was a very different feeling indeed. She hoped her new venture into dating would help her clear her head of Tess, and maybe they could be comfortable being friends too.

FIFTEEN

Tess scrolled through their ordering system, one hand on the mouse and the fingers of the other drumming a rhythm on the desk. Being at such close quarters with Rowan was driving her crazy. It was self-inflicted. Not only had she accepted the job, but she couldn't help orchestrating situations to see even more of Rowan. The job had been a lifesaver, well, an asking-the-ex-for-money-saver, anyway. And it was about so much more than money. She was enjoying it immensely. She loved having a task and seeing it through until the end. She was amazed at how much of a sense of satisfaction she felt when surrounded by a warehouse full of completed orders.

And Rowan was helping Archie. He'd talked about his project all the way to school today, and even though Tess wasn't entirely sure what he was talking about, she could see Rowan had given him the confidence to see it through. She had told him she was on hand to help him further if he needed it, but she'd encouraged him to have a go on his own first. Tess couldn't begin to describe how much that meant to her, and it just intensified her feelings for Rowan. Feelings she had no idea what to do with.

The object of her thoughts suddenly burst through the door.

"Shit, shit, shit." Rowan dropped a pile of brochures onto the desk in front of Tess.

Tess resisted the urge to ask what was wrong and picked up one of the brochures instead, a regular job for a local estate agent. Opening it, she could see the problem immediately. The images were all distorted. "Oh. That's not good. It must've come in like that."

Rowan stood with her arms folded. "Probably, but we should've noticed and fixed it. Dad took the job, and it's the first thing he's taken on for weeks so I can't say anything. Fox's are such an important customer, and they need them by tomorrow morning for an open-house event. Bollocks." She dropped into her chair and rubbed her face. "If Keith had been here, he'd have noticed, but Charlie should've picked it up. He can stay and redo it with me. We'll be here all bloody night."

Tess stood. "We'll sort it, Rowan, and your dad doesn't need to know. You fix the file, and I'll go and talk to the boys." She slipped out, leaving Rowan to her muttered curses.

Stefan and Charlie stood staring at the mountain of brochures in horror. "Right, lads, what do we need to do to get this sorted?"

Stefan turned to her. "Sorry, Tess. I should've done a final proof before I set the job going."

"It's water under the bridge, Stef. We need to sort this, though. Can you both work late? Rowan's going to fix the images, and we can get it running again."

Stefan's face dropped. "I need to do the school run, but I could come back when Kasia gets home from work."

"Don't worry, Stef, we'll manage. Charlie?" She looked at the older man hopefully.

"I can't, Tess. In fact, I need to leave a bit early. We've got tickets to the match tonight, and I'm driving my dad there. I can't let him down." He shrugged.

Charlie had three brothers, all local, so she suspected it was just a convenient excuse, but she couldn't force him to work late. Not even Rowan could do that. "Fine, when Rowan sends the new file over, both of you do what you can until you need to leave. I'll get the rest done." She marched out, frustrated. Why were they so lacking in commitment? She'd only been here a couple of months, but she appreciated what a good business this was to work for. Stef and Charlie had worked for Rowan and her dad for years. Surely, they deserved some loyalty.

She texted Elsie before she returned to the office and got a quick reply. *We'll manage, Mum. If there's a major emergency in the world of printing, the least we can do is step up to the challenge.*

Don't be a smartarse, Elsie. All I'm asking you to do is heat up a bowl of stew.

Will do. Over and out.

When she got back to the office, Rowan was focused on the job, so she sat down and checked the delivery details. As long as they got them dropped off tonight, everything should be fine. Packing and delivery would take as much time as the actual printing, but she was sure they could get finished by ten. She might even be in bed by midnight.

Rowan turned her chair. "All sorted and sent to print. Are Charlie and Stef on board?"

"Well, not exactly. They'll get the print run started, but

they both need to leave. I've got the kids sorted, so I'll stay and pack them, get them in the van, and deliver tonight. Don't worry."

Rowan's expression darkened. "Whoa. No way, Tess. You need to be up at five tomorrow. I'm not going to be responsible for you crashing on the motorway."

It was nice that Rowan was concerned for her welfare, even if it was in a health and safety kind of way. "I'm used to not getting enough sleep, Ro. And I should get a few hours. I'll be fine, honest."

Rowan stood. "I'll go and get those two sorted. Why don't you order us some food, and we'll crack on until it's done? It's not a massive job, and we'll get you home as soon as possible." She stopped on her way out. "Thanks, Tess. It's good to have someone I can rely on." Her face reddened as she spoke, and she ducked out quickly.

Tess smiled to herself. She wanted to be the person Rowan relied on, but what did that mean for their future?

Tess rubbed her eyes as she drove through the dark country lanes. She and Rowan made a good team. They'd finished the job and got it delivered faster than she could have thought possible. She'd stayed away from coffee for the last couple of hours in the hope she might get a few hours of quality sleep, but she was flagging now. She opened the car window, hoping a blast of cold air would invigorate her, but it just made her shiver. *Great, now I'm sleepy and cold.* She shook herself. She'd be home in five minutes and in bed in another twenty. She'd be asleep before her head hit the pillow.

She jumped as her phone rang out loudly. The car was

a million years too old for handsfree, so she reluctantly pulled over, hoping the kids were okay and Rowan hadn't had another emergency. She retrieved the phone from the passenger seat, where she'd tossed it earlier, to see Jules's name flash up. She glanced at the time as she picked up. Ten thirty was late for Jules to be calling. "Hey there. Everything okay, Jules?"

A long sigh sounded down the line. "I'm sorry, I know it's late."

"It's fine, it's Friday tomorrow, and I've got a quiet weekend ahead. What's up?" Tess made an effort to hide her own weariness.

"I don't know really. I've been working alone on a job all week, and I've barely spoken to another person. I wondered if you were free for a cuppa?"

Tess leaned back against the headrest. This felt like the longest day of her life. "Of course. Now? I'm nearly back home, but I can turn round."

"I can come to you. Get the kettle on."

Tess breathed a quiet sigh of relief. "Lovely. I'll see you in a few minutes."

It didn't take her long to get out of her work clothes and check in on the kids, who were both occupied in their rooms, and she'd already made a pot of tea before Jules arrived.

"That's not some camomile nonsense, is it?" Jules sniffed as Tess poured two mugs.

"Hardly. Proper Yorkshire tea." She slid the mug across. "Is everything all right?" She had seen less of Jules since she started her job. Jules was a freelance architect and enjoyed a lifestyle where she could take a long lunch or a visit to the spa to break up a busy day. Tess had shared those opportunities with her while she could, but there was just no time now. The least she could do was find time for a chat if Jules wanted one.

"I guess so. Just feeling a little isolated, and I've been missing my partner in crime for lunchtime adventures."

Tess led the way into the living room, and they settled on the sofa. Tess balanced her mug on the arm. "I'm sorry. There doesn't seem to be much time for fun lately."

"And how are things working out with being at close quarters with the irresistible Rowan?" Jules grinned before taking a sip of her tea.

Tess let out a groan. It was all so complicated.

"Going well then? Why don't you just ask her out, Tess? What are you afraid of?"

Tess's deepest fear was getting into something she couldn't escape, but before she even addressed that, there were so many other barriers. "For a start, she's seeing someone. Well, she's been on a date, anyway. I couldn't quite bring myself to ask how it went." She lifted her mug and blew on the tea. "But even if she was available, what do I want from her, Jules?"

"Why are you asking me? You fancy the pants off her, you enjoy her company in every situation, and you trust her. Rowan won't hurt you, Tess. It's not in her nature."

"I know. But I like my life as it is. It may be chaotic and too busy, but I make all the decisions, and I've only got myself to blame if things go wrong." She couldn't suppress an enormous yawn.

"Sorry, I'm keeping you up." Jules finished her tea and stood. "I forget not everyone has the privilege of rolling out of bed at eight thirty." She placed her mug on the table. "Freedom is a novelty for you at the moment, and you should enjoy it. But don't write Rowan off as a bad idea. The two of you have a connection that's palpable. I don't think that comes along too often. It certainly never has for me. Don't miss out on the chance of something amazing just because you're too scared of it going wrong."

Tess pushed herself out of the chair and followed Jules into the hallway. "I'm sorry. You came for a chat, and you've ended up giving me a counselling session. Are you really okay?"

Jules shrugged her coat on. "I'll live. Just promise me next time the kids are away at their dad's, you'll come to the spa."

"That's such a hardship to put myself through, but for you, I'll cope." She kissed Jules on the cheek and opened the door. "And you promise me, if the weather's not too bleak, you'll come and watch a home game again soon."

Jules laughed. "Almost as much fun as the spa. No promises, but I'll think about it."

Tess watched as the rear lights of Jules's car disappeared down the lane. Jules was the most independent person she'd ever know. She didn't rely on anyone for anything. But was she happy? Tess was never quite sure.

She went upstairs quietly and got ready for bed as quickly as she could. She'd be up again in five hours. But it was nearly the weekend. Rowan would be picking Elsie up for rugby and maybe she'd stop for dinner. Tess should be looking forward to a weekend of rest and not running around after people, and yet here she was hoping she got to cook for Rowan.

She sighed as she finally dropped onto her bed. It had never felt like such a luxury. And yet, could she sleep now? Of course not. Rowan roamed through her thoughts. She couldn't stop wondering how the date had gone a couple of weeks ago. She could never ask, but maybe Becca would mention it again. If she and Rowan were going to be friends, she needed to be able to talk about that aspect of Rowan's life without feeling the pangs of jealousy. She didn't want a relationship. Rowan had every right to date who she wanted, and she deserved to be happy. Tess couldn't avoid the inevitable image of the faceless date woman making Rowan happy. She groaned and pulled the pillow over her head as if it could act as a shield against her unhelpful thoughts.

SIXTEEN

A pang of disappointment hit Rowan as she pulled onto the driveway on Sunday morning and saw Elsie waiting on the doorstep. She'd set off early, hoping for a few minutes chatting to Tess while she waited. To her joy, Tess appeared at the door with a bad case of bedhead and dressed in red flannel pyjamas that made Rowan simultaneously want to hug her and rip them off to see what was underneath. Thoughts like that were getting more frequent.

Her second date with Anna hadn't gone so well. After they'd covered so many subjects in their first encounter, she'd struggled to think of anything else to talk about. When she caught herself thinking that never happened when she talked with Tess, she'd realised she wasn't properly committed to trying to meet someone, and that wasn't fair to Anna. She'd apologised to Anna for wasting her time and explained that she was interested in somebody else. Anna had taken it surprisingly well and wished her luck. She'd gone home and suspended her account. She might have no chance with Tess, but she didn't have any interest in meeting anyone else either. And now she was sitting here feeling foolish about the emotions she couldn't deny when Tess was nearby. Tess leaned against the doorframe, sipping her ever-present mug of coffee and watched Elsie put her kit bag in the back of the car. She caught Rowan's eye and smiled. That smile drove away Rowan's hesitation, and she jumped out of the car, grabbing the paper bag from the passenger seat. She couldn't stop the matching grin that spread across her face. The closer she was to Tess, the happier she felt, that was the truth. She held out the bag. "I got you a candle. I thought it might help you chill out after the week you've had. It's supposed to aid relaxation." The moment seemed to drag on. Was it too much? Then Tess reached out to take the bag, her laughter sounding like music.

"Thank you, Rowan. The wellbeing programme in this company is better than you'd get at a multinational. I promise I will return to work tomorrow fully re-energised."

Rowan knew she was being teased, but the employer/employee relationship made her uncomfortable. "It's not...it's nothing to do with work. You deserve to have some time to yourself."

Tess's eyes twinkled. "I know you imagine me lying in a roll top bath, surrounded by bubbles, while you two are off getting muddy."

Rowan willed her face not to turn bright red.

"But I've got a week's worth of school uniforms to iron, a house to clean, and a grumpy teenager to help with algebra revision. Algebra!" She shrugged. "I'm not even sure what that is. Is it the one with the letters or the triangles?"

Rowan jumped at the chance to think about maths instead of baths. "Letters. I might be able to help if he's really stuck, but it's been a while."

"Thanks, Ro, but I'm sure we'll manage. And I really do appreciate this." She motioned to Elsie, sitting patiently waiting in the car.

And I appreciate the five minutes it gives me in your company. She was so screwed. "We'd better get moving. I can't lecture the team on being on time and turn up late myself. We should be back by eight." She reluctantly turned to go and waved as she got to the car, drinking in one last look at Tess in her red tartan pyjamas.

She pulled on her seatbelt. "Right, Eek. Let's go and win some rugby."

Elsie beamed at her new nickname. It was a combination of her initials and the noise Jai swore she had made the first time she'd been tackled in a training session. As rugby nicknames went, it could have been much worse.

"You like my mum a lot, don't you?"

Oh God, this was going to be a long journey. "She's a wonderful human being, Elsie. I'm sure you're aware of that too."

"Yes, she's amazing. But I mean you *like* like her. It's so obvious. You bring her presents all the time, and you look at her with little puppy dog eyes."

Her laugh was as musical as her mum's. Rowan gave her most intimidating glare. "Shut up, Elsie." She turned the radio up loud, but that just made Elsie laugh even more. She sighed and turned the volume back down.

"Are you going to ask her out? On a date?"

"No. Of course not. You don't need to worry about that."

"I'm not worried. It would be perfect. She deserves to be happy. I think she's very lonely."

Rowan sighed again. The conversation wasn't going away, and they still had an hour of this journey to go. "If

141

there's one thing I've learned in nearly twenty years of relationships with women, it's don't go after the straight ones. It never ends well."

"Wow, are you really that old?" Elsie smirked. "But just for the record, Mum's not one of the straight ones. She dated women *and* men before Dad. I know because he used to have a go at her about it, calling her greedy."

That made Rowan want to go back all those years and punch Pete a few more times. "That doesn't mean anything, Elsie. Sometimes people say things they don't mean when they're insecure."

"Well, he found plenty to criticise. He didn't need to make things up. She doesn't talk to me about who she finds attractive, but I think it's pretty self-evident. She looks at you with the same saddo expression you give her."

The thought that it might be true made her heart race, but Elsie wasn't the person to be talking to about this. "Is that the same way you look at a certain winger?"

Elsie looked away and turned the radio back up. Rowan laughed and reached over to ruffle her thick hair, until she joined the laughter.

"I'm just saying you should give it some thought," said Elsie.

They spent the rest of the journey in silence as Rowan processed this new information. Did Tess really feel the same way she did? She talked a lot about her independence and going her own way once the kids had left home. Rowan was going nowhere. She doubted Tess would want to get mixed up with someone like her. But maybe Tess wasn't looking for a relationship, just some company. She could fall for Tess in a big way. How would she feel if Tess didn't feel the same? If Rowan was just a distraction or an experiment along the road of Tess's new life. She had a feeling that would hurt like hell.

———

Tess heard the car pull up shortly before eight. She and Archie had eaten earlier after an afternoon of maths revision that had challenged them both. She'd prepared two plates to reheat, in the hope Rowan might stay.

Elsie burst through the door, already chattering about having played her first full game and that they'd secured a narrow win, which put them in the top three of the league. Tess was pleased to see her so happy. She hugged her before sending her to unpack her dirty kit and prepare for dinner.

Rowan stood on the doorstep, hands in her pockets, smiling the sweet, shy smile Tess had seen a lot of lately.

"All hail the conquering heroes. Come on in. I've plated up a roast for you both. You must be starving."

"Oh, that's okay, we had a jacket potato after the game." Rowan scuffed her toe on the step. "I probably need to get home."

"To what? A reheated bowl of last night's pasta?" She knew she'd hit the mark by Rowan's expression. "Just eat, then I'll let you go, I promise. You must come in and smell this candle anyway. It's awesome."

Rowan's smile widened as she stepped inside.

From the way they both demolished their food, Tess could tell they'd burned up plenty of calories on the pitch. She sat with them, nursing a glass of wine. Rowan had refused any, saying she'd already had a pint after the game.

"Rowan got player of the match. Again." Elsie's voice was half-teasing, half-admiring.

Tess liked Rowan's involvement in Elsie's life. She was a good role model, proving that hard work paid off.

"Elsie played well at six. I'm not sure if Zoë will be back. She's caring full-time for her mum at the moment, and I think she may relocate back there so she's close to her. If Elsie keeps playing so well, she'll be getting a lot more starts in that position."

Elsie beamed as Rowan put her knife and fork together on the empty plate and sat back.

"And we'll keep working on her hooking. She'll get match time in the easier fixtures. Maybe by next season she'll be playing hooker more regularly." She turned to Elsie. "We need to take it slowly. There's no rush. Just keep learning."

Elsie nodded and scooped up the empty plates. "I'm off to do some homework. I'll leave you two to chat."

She gave Rowan a wink as she left. Tess wondered what that was about, but Rowan's expression was unreadable. Maybe Elsie had asked her to talk to Tess for her. She hoped Elsie knew they could discuss anything, without judgement. Whatever it was, Rowan didn't seem to be in a rush. After a couple of minutes of silence, Tess said, "I think it's so funny you can talk about rugby for hours and as soon as the conversation moves on, you're the quietest person in the room."

Rowan raised her eyebrow. "Are you calling me a rugby bore?"

She laughed. "Quite the opposite. You're so knowledgeable, it's always a pleasure to listen. But maybe you're more comfortable talking about things you feel confident with." She saw something flicker behind the inscrutable expression, but she wasn't sure what. "Anyway, I know I keep banging on about it, but this job has made such a difference to my life, Ro. I'd forgotten how much I enjoy having a purpose other than running around after those two."

"Tell me why you stopped nursing. You loved your career. I was shocked when Dad said you weren't a nurse anymore." Rowan chewed her lip.

Tess thought carefully. She knew Rowan was sensitive about how she got injured, but she didn't want to hide any part of her life from her. "It was a number of things, really. I couldn't drive for a while after we moved, so that didn't help." She saw Rowan's face drop. She stood and took her by the hand and sat them both down on the sofa. She kept Rowan's warm hand in hers, it felt so right there. "You've really got to get over that, Rowan. I have, and I don't want to skate around it anytime I talk about the past. Okay?" She squeezed her hand, and Rowan gave a small nod. "Even when I got back on my feet, there were no part-time job opportunities, and I wasn't prepared to leave my children to be looked after by someone else." She released Rowan and ran her hands through her hair. "You have to do so many hours of practice and training a year to stay registered, so it slipped pretty quickly and soon, nursing wasn't an option. It felt like a loss at first, but I got used to it eventually." She wasn't sure whether she should say it, but she added, "Like playing rugby."

Rowan's shoulders slumped.

"I found a teaching assistant job at the kids' primary school. It was perfect. Archie was thrilled I could be there at the start and end of his day, and I really enjoyed the work. I stayed there for years, even after the kids moved onto secondary school." The upbeat ending to her tale hadn't done anything for Rowan's downcast expression. How could Tess make her see she didn't need to fixate on things that had happened so far in the past? "Rowan, I've lived a bit longer than you, and one thing I've learned is that most things don't last forever. Look at my kids. I've spent the last eighteen years prioritising them over everything else, and in the next three or four they'll be gone, living their own lives. If you can't adapt to change, you're stuffed. You've got to make the most of what you get and not spend too much time looking back."

Rowan straightened her shoulders and looked at Tess with determination in her eyes. Tess wondered what she was thinking of. As she opened her mouth to speak, they were interrupted by a thundering of heavy steps on the stairs before Archie burst into the room.

"Mum, Dad's on the phone. Oh, hi, Rowan, I thought you'd gone home. Sorry, he wants to talk about next weekend."

"Archie, tell him I'll call him tomorrow evening, okay? It's nearly a week away, how urgent can it be?"

"I don't know. He told me to get you." He looked at Rowan. "He's on my laptop."

He shrugged as if that explained why it was so immediate.

"I'll call him tomorrow." Tess kept her voice firm but calm. Now she would never know what Rowan had been about to say. Did even she want to know?

Archie rolled his eyes and ran out without another word, crashing back up the stairs.

"Sorry."

"Reminds me of Willow and my cousins when they were young. I forgot how loud teenagers can be." Rowan smiled and stood. "I really do need to go now. Early delivery in the morning."

Damn. Tess didn't want her to leave, and she was

dying to know what she'd been about to say. *I'll see her tomorrow morning. Get a grip.* "I'm sorry I can't help more at the beginning of the day. As soon as the kids are on study leave, I promise I'll do some early starts." She loved working alongside Rowan, but it really was all work. These little moments of intimacy were what she craved. But to what end? Rowan seemed to like to hang out with Tess. Was that a sign she'd like something more, or was she just a thoughtful friend who could see Tess was lonely?

"It's fine, really. I've been managing on my own for so long, just having you there in the afternoons is such a help."

She stretched her back, and her muscles popped. Tess wished she could offer a post-match massage. For a moment, she imagined straddling Rowan's bare back and running her hands over her tight muscles. She dragged herself back to the current situation and stood quickly. From the look on Rowan's face, she had definitely missed something. "Sorry?"

"I said thanks for dinner, and I'm glad you like your candle."

"Mum! He says it needs to be now. He's got flights to book," Archie shouted from his room.

She rolled her eyes apologetically and followed Rowan to the door. "You're very welcome at our dinner table any time. See you tomorrow."

Rowan turned away, biting her lip.

"Mum!"

The moment passed, Rowan smiled her goodbye and was gone. Tess made her way up to Archie's room to see what the fuss was about, but her mind stayed with Rowan. The tension between them was increasing, but where was it going? Where did she want it to go when she was just getting her life back together? If Rowan was already seeing someone, why was she bringing Tess thoughtful presents and staring into her eyes with such intensity?

"Tess, are you listening to a word I'm saying?"

Pete's aggressive voice brought her back to reality. She sighed and leaned over Archie's shoulder to hear what Pete had to say.

SEVENTEEN

Becca made it to the last home game before Christmas, sadly pointing out she had nothing better to do. She turned up to help set up with Ben and the ever-boisterous Digby. Ben had been helping with post bags and flags since he was a teenager, and Rowan knew she could depend on him to get the job done. Digby, on the other hand, was a nightmare.

"Becs! Can you keep Digby indoors with you?" Rowan's yell brought Becca to the door of the clubhouse. She regarded her dog as he bounded around the pitch while Ben looked on, laughing.

"He'll do less damage out here. He's not gonna mess up your precious pitch."

"He'd better not," Rowan muttered as she put the last post in place. She knew Becca found the dog hard to manage. She'd adopted him when Ben had become obsessed with dogs, and he was still a handful.

She turned to see if Ben had finished. He'd put up the post protectors and was standing back to make sure they were perfectly aligned. She took the chance to sneak up behind him and tickle him. Ben giggled and squirmed in her grip, reversing their positions and wrestling her until they ended up on the grass. Digby bounded over and joined in, licking and nipping as he barked with joy.

"Will you lot stop messing around and help me clean these changing rooms?" Becca asked loudly. "They're a right mess."

Rowan groaned and pulled Ben to his feet. "Come on, Ben. You can show me your mopping skills."

When everything was done, Rowan threw herself onto one of the bench seats in the clubhouse and checked the time. She could hear Becca outside with her brother, laughing as they threw a ball for Digby. She hoped they were keeping clear of the match pitch. She would never understand how Becca managed to spread herself over so many different things.

Rowan could barely cope with her job and the club. She knew she gave too much of her life to rugby, but she needed it as much it the club needed her. While she had a few minutes to herself, she pulled out her sketchbook and flicked to a drawing she'd started this morning. It was a sketch of the team playing on the pitch outside. Predictable, but she enjoyed drawing what was going in her head, and today's game was so crucial, she could think of little else.

Even when she'd been small and they were a regular family, rugby had been a big part of her life. She could remember dragging tackle bags out onto the pitch when they were bigger than her. When her mum had died, the club had become the dependable thing in her life. So much about that time was just a blur of grief, but the desperate feeling that she needed to be there for her dad and Willow, to try to make amends for what had happened remained as clear as if she was feeling it now. Her sister, after she recovered from her injuries, had gone to live with their aunt and her family. But Rowan had been unshakable from her daddy's side.

She roused herself from her thoughts. It never did any good to reflect on that stuff. It could make her feel miserable for days if she started. She was optimistic about the game. At the selection meeting this week, they'd agreed it had been a long time since there were so many good players to select from. The seven players on the bench had all been starting choices last season. There would be even more competition for places when Elsie started as replacement hooker. She'd need to get game time, which meant she would probably be on the bench for every game, especially with the added bonus that she could also play in the back row.

Rowan didn't bother denying to herself how much she was looking forward to seeing Tess. She lit up any situation, and when that smile was turned on Rowan, she didn't care about anything else.

"Who's that?"

Rowan looked up to see Ben and Becca looking over her shoulder, looking at the sketch. Ben loved to see her drawings and Becca was her biggest fan, always trying to convince her she should try and make a living using her creativity and talent. She looked down at the pad with horror as she realised her thoughts about Tess had been reflected in the small sketch she'd added in the corner of the scene. A face looked back at her with gentle dark eyes and a warm smile. It was so obvious who it was. Becca wouldn't be fooled.

"Is it Archie's mum? Are you going to show her the picture? It's very good. I think she'll like it."

Rowan closed the pad in a panic and looked over her shoulder at Becca for help.

"Yes, it's Tess, Benji."

Rowan silently begged her to find a way to keep Ben quiet.

"But I think the picture is a surprise for later, so we mustn't spoil it, okay?"

Ben nodded. "Surprises are a secret. We won't tell, Rowan."

Rowan jumped up and stuffed the pad back in her kit bag. "Thanks, Ben. I'd better get my kit on for the game." She managed to make it out of the door without looking at Becca's face and the wide smirk she knew she'd see.

When the whistle blew to end the first half, Rowan ran with the other players to huddle together on the pitch while Hannah talked them through their tactics for the second half. She tried not to look at where she knew Tess was standing, chatting with Becca and Jules, while Ben played with Digby nearby. She'd looked over earlier and seen Ben talking to Tess and had nearly missed the ball that had been passed her way. When she looked back a few moments later, Tess was kneeling, petting Digby, so she hoped they'd been talking about dogs rather than sketches.

She wondered what Tess and her friends had found to talk about after all these years. She knew Jules and Tess had stayed close, but how did Becca just pick things up so easily with someone she hadn't seen for years? That's what normal people did, she reminded herself. They just chatted, without constantly worrying if they were saying the right thing. She focused back on the game, adding in her few comments about keeping the defence tight and the threat of the opposition's attacking lineout. When they went to return to their places for the whistle, she ran to grab a drink from her water bottle before it was carried off the pitch. As she put it back in the rack, she looked up at the spectators and saw Tess watching her. She smiled, and Tess mouthed, "Good luck," before Rowan turned away to jog back to her place. The half-time break had chilled her in her muddy, sweat-soaked kit, but she suddenly felt warm inside. She shook her head at her own silliness as the whistle blew.

Rowan slid the padlock in place and looked at her watch with satisfaction. For once, she'd managed to get the club cleaned and everyone out at a reasonable time. This was mostly due to the practical and vocal support of Jules, Becca, and Tess in getting people to help with the clearing up, and because the younger players were on their way out to party after their convincing win. In the past, Rowan would have joined them out of habit but tonight, she just wanted to go home. She'd been here since ten, and she'd had enough.

As she locked up the building, Tess and the others waited in the car park. She slung her bag over her shoulder and joined them. "Thanks for all your help. It was good to have a team off the pitch as well as on."

"Oh, you know my weekends are wasted if I don't spend a few hours in a cold, wet field." Jules laughed to soften her dig. "It was a pleasure, Rowan. I had good company." She smiled. "Now, I'm off to find a nice meal to wash down with a bottle of red, but I'm guessing you've all got people to get back to?"

Tess gave her a hug that lasted long enough to make Rowan wonder what was being left unsaid.

"Sorry, I'm heading back to dinner with a teenager. I've even splurged on a taxi for Elsie, as it's Christmas. So, after dinner, I'm going to put my feet up for a bit and then get an early night."

Jules said her goodbyes as Rowan imagined herself sitting with Tess in front of the roaring log burner Tess always talked of owning. In reality, it would be an unpleasant living flame gas fire, but even that would be a good place to be, if she was there with Tess. She wondered if Tess enjoyed a foot rub. A nudge from Becca roused her from her fantasy.

"Well? I'm not standing here all night waiting for you."

She had no idea what she'd been asked and looked around for a clue. Tess's eyes were on her, as they often were lately. Her lips curled into a smile as she took pity on Rowan.

"Becca's just invited you round for dinner. Sounds like fish fingers are on the menu."

She turned to Becca. "Sorry, I was thinking about something else. Yes, please."

"Whatever was on your mind, it looked more enticing than my offer."

She shrugged. "It was a work thing, sorry. I can't think of better company than you and Ben."

Becca raised her eyebrow.

"And Digby, obviously." She needed to stop fantasising about Tess all the time. It was too distracting. "I'll drop my car home, and I'll be round in half an hour."

Becca waved her goodbyes, leaving her standing in the car park with Tess, who didn't seem in a rush to leave.

"Thanks for being there today. I know you have to, for Elsie, but I'm so glad you were." She ground to a halt and looked at the ground.

Tess chuckled. "I'm glad I was too. I love watching you play, Rowan. You're so much better than you think you are."

She looked up, wondering if Tess was teasing her, but her expression was full of admiration and something else Rowan didn't know what to do with.

Tess cleared her throat. "I'd better let you get to your meal, and I need to get back to Archie. Maybe he got bored of his game and made dinner, so all I'll need to do is sit down and eat."

Rowan joined her laughter and followed her to her car. Tess hugged her, and she relished the feel of their closeness.

Tess kissed her on the cheek. "Bye, Rowan, see you tomorrow."

Her breath tickled Rowan's ear, and she suppressed a shiver of pleasure. "Night, Tess. Have a good evening."

As she swung the car park gates closed and locked the chain, Rowan did her best to put the confusing thoughts of Tess aside and focus, but the way Tess looked at her kept coming back. Should she do something about how she felt? Tess was sending some pretty clear messages, wasn't she? Rowan groaned as she dropped into her seat. Maybe it was better to keep her distance for now. Not that it was easy with the amount of time she spent in Tess's company lately. She turned her thoughts to fish fingers and sloppy dog kisses and hoped Becca would leave her be. She didn't have the answers to the many questions about Tess.

EIGHTEEN

Rowan didn't look up as Tess wheeled her chair up close.

"Sorry, I know you're in the middle of invoicing, but I had to share my news."

Rowan let out a sigh as she sat back from her laptop and gave Tess her full attention.

"That call from Pete last week? I thought he was going to let poor Archie down again for the weekend, but he actually wants to take them to the Christmas markets in Frankfurt. Elsie feels she should go if he's making an effort. I didn't want to get anyone's hopes up too soon, but he sent the tickets over this morning. They're actually going!" She couldn't resist wheeling her chair around the office as though it was a dance partner. It was the best she was going to get as Rowan sat there, a neutral look firmly in place. Determined to get a reaction, she left the chair and came to rest with both hands on Rowan's desk, her face a few inches from Rowan's. In all honesty, she hadn't meant to get this close, and now that she was, she felt flustered. But she willed her enthusiasm to spread to Rowan. "So I get the whole weekend to myself! The bath bomb is actually going to get used!"

Rowan's face transformed into a sort of smile, but Tess suspected it was forced. She wished once again she could see inside that gorgeous head and understand what Rowan was thinking. And more importantly, what she was feeling. Being this close made Tess just want to lean over and kiss Rowan's sexy mouth, but she had no idea what reaction that would get. And they were at work, so it would be very inappropriate. She moved away quickly and turned towards her own desk. "And then the week after is school holidays so I can work longer hours if you need me." Talking about work felt a lot safer.

Rowan turned back to her invoice with a longer sigh. Did Tess annoy her? Or was she struggling with this too?

"That would be good. I'll have a look at what work we've got on and get back to you."

Tess got back to her tasks. Rowan's lack of enthusiasm was like a bucket of cold water over her excitement for her free weekend. She'd really been hoping they could spend some proper grown-up time together, even if they were destined only to be friends. But Rowan was acting strange and withdrawn, as if she had nothing to say to Tess anymore. Tess felt it like a physical pain. She told herself to focus on work, and she could worry about the weekend when it eventually arrived.

The rest of the week flew by as they got out the orders in record time. Tess often saw Rowan watching her, but she looked away quickly whenever Tess smiled or raised an eyebrow. She couldn't fathom what was going on.

She finished early on Thursday evening to drive the kids down the motorway with their weekend bags. They were both in high spirits about the trip, and Pete greeted them at the door with a big smile, as if to indicate to Tess what an amazing weekend they were going to have without her. Behind him, in the hallway, she could see the young, blond woman he hadn't yet bothered to introduce. Elsie had reported her name was Karen and that she didn't say much but seemed nice enough. Tess hoped she knew what she was getting into and inwardly wished her luck.

On Friday morning, child-free, Tess got to the office bright and early. Rowan was at her desk, a frown on her face as she stared at her screen. Tess got the impression she wasn't thinking about work. "No kids, no homework, no rugby. I bet you think I won't know what to do with myself."

Rowan looked up.

"How about this? Lie in. Check." She did an air tick for emphasis. "Breakfast in bed. I'll have to make it and go back to bed, admittedly, but still. Check. Romantic movie of a type not favoured by teenagers. Check, check, check."

Rowan was still staring at her silently.

"What about you? You must have plans for rugby-free weekends?"

Rowan's mouth moved soundlessly a couple of times. "Uh, Christmas shopping? Maybe." She looked away quickly.

Tess tried to ignore the sinking feeling inside. Why was Rowan so distant at times? She'd still harboured a hope that they might do something together this weekend, but Rowan's behaviour was making that unlikely. Her eyes burned, and she turned away to her desk. She wasn't going to show her distress.

Stefan came into the office. "Sorry, I'm stuck on the

newspaper run. Could either of you do the St Mary's school delivery, please?"

Rowan was halfway to the door before she could react. "I'll do it. I'm just finishing up here anyway."

Tess stood. "Are you sure? Let me help you load the van."

Rowan stared at her and then shrugged. "Yeah, sure. Thanks." She marched out.

Tess found her a few minutes later, backing the van into the loading bay. As they started to load the boxes, Rowan was piling them in a much more haphazard way than her usual process. Tess decided she'd be most useful inside the van, restacking the boxes neatly. She moved a couple aside and stacked a full pile to the roof of the van. As she turned back, Rowan staggered through the doors, piled high with boxes in front of her face. She somehow made the gap between the loading bay and the van without breaking her neck, but as she lurched into the back of the van, one of the boxes Tess had moved was directly in front of her feet. Seeing her trip, Tess dashed over and caught her by the elbow just as she started to fall into the stack of boxes. She pulled Rowan back against the side of the van and took the top box from the load she had managed to hold onto so she could see her face.

"Thanks." Rowan was flushed. "I didn't factor in being able to see where I was going."

She bent to put the boxes down, and Tess started to ask her why she was in such a rush. But when Rowan stood, her lips were so close, Tess was transfixed. Rowan froze, but her eyes darted around wildly as if searching for an escape. Tess didn't budge, and Rowan's eyes eventually settled on her own. They were full of so much emotion, it took Tess's breath away. "I can't stand this any longer, Rowan. You're driving me crazy. Tell me what I did wrong—"

Rowan let out a long groan, and Tess felt her hand in her hair, pulling her towards her mouth. She complied willingly and when their lips touched, it felt like electricity was flowing through her. Rowan kissed her hard, and she couldn't hold back her reaction as her tongue explored her mouth hungrily. Rowan had both hands in her hair now, and Tess kept her body pushed up against her, trapping her against the wall of the van. Rowan finally pulled back slightly and rested her forehead against Tess's. Both were breathing heavily, trying to regain control.

"I've been fantasising about this moment for weeks." Tess breathed into Rowan's neck. "But of all the scenarios I imagined, none of them involved the company van."

She chuckled, and Rowan raised her head, looking into her eyes as she joined in with the laughter. She pulled Tess in close and buried her face in her hair. She pulled back and looked at Tess as if she was seeing her for the first time.

Tess tipped her head. "If there's any more of those kisses on offer, I don't think I've had enough yet."

Rowan leaned in again and captured Tess's lips with her warm mouth. The first time hadn't been a fluke. Tess felt the kiss throughout her body and in some places more than others. She couldn't remember feeling anything like this before.

Rowan pulled away again and held her at arm's length. "This delivery can wait till later. How about we find somewhere to talk?"

"Who are you? And what have you done with Rowan?" Tess opened her mouth in mock horror and then smiled. "Yeah, I think we've both got a few things to say." As they got down from the van, she slapped Rowan's arse. "You can go first."

Rowan joined Tess's laughter.

———

Tess looked around the pub for a quiet table. Rowan had suggested they talk away from the office, so lunch at the local pub seemed like a good choice. It was busy with the lunchtime crowd, and she was lucky to find the small table tucked away in the corner. She hoped Rowan would be able to see her when she'd been served. Her head was buzzing, and she was glad of a few minutes to get her thoughts in order before they talked about what had happened.

Kissing Rowan had been even better than her fantasies. She had the softest, sweetest lips. Tess reminded herself that she hadn't kissed anyone she was truly attracted to for a couple of decades, so maybe her idea of a passionate kiss was slightly inflated. But Rowan had seemed to be enjoying it too, if her heavy breathing was anything to go by, when they'd eventually pulled apart. She remembered the feel of Rowan's hands in her hair, demanding but somehow tender at the same time.

"It's okay, I found you," Rowan said quietly.

"Sorry, I was looking out for you, but I got distracted." She felt her face redden.

Rowan smirked as she sat down. "Thinking of anything good?"

"Oh, yeah, really good." She smiled and was surprised when Rowan leaned across and kissed her gently.

"You are so gorgeous," she whispered, her voice husky.

"If you want to talk, we need to stop the kissing. I can't focus on both."

Rowan nodded. "Me neither." She cleared her throat, took a sip of her beer, and looked into Tess's eyes. "I wondered if you would like to go out tomorrow. For dinner, I mean." She hesitated. "I thought if you planned to stay over, we could share a bottle of wine with dinner."

Tess smiled.

"I've got a spare room. I didn't mean—"

"I would love to. All of that. And let's decide on sleeping arrangements nearer the time, shall we?"

Rowan nodded again and looked relieved.

"Why did you find it so difficult to ask me?"

Rowan stared into her pint before looking up. "It's not exactly a strength of mine, is it? I mean, I was getting a vibe from you, and I thought you might like me, but then, I thought you were straight, and Elsie said you've never talked about who you might be attracted to, and I really wanted to ask you out, but the time was never right—"

"Hang on a minute. You talked to Elsie about this?"

"No. Well, not exactly. She raised it with me. She said she thought I should ask you out because I look at you like I want to."

"Did she indeed?" *Good old Elsie, always a surprise.* "Well, I think we should just skip over the fact that an eighteen-year-old has been the most mature person in this situation." She groaned. "Sorry, Rowan, I've been acting like I'm the teenager, but it's all so new to me, feeling like this." Feeling anything at all, but she didn't need to say that.

"I know, and I don't want to rush you into something or make you feel you have to do anything you're not sure about."

She wasn't sure about any of it, but she knew how Rowan made her feel, and that was something she wanted to explore. "Let's see how tomorrow night goes and take it from there."

Rowan nodded, and they chatted about more mundane things while they finished their drinks. As they strolled back to work, Tess wondered how she would focus on anything else for the next twenty-four hours, especially without the kids to distract her. She wondered if she could get Jules to take her to her swanky gym so she could burn off some energy before the date, while somehow evading Jules's inevitable questioning. She looked at Rowan, walking beside her, oblivious to how gorgeous she was, and Tess couldn't keep the grin off her face.

NINETEEN

Tess pulled up outside Rowan's flat with plenty of time to spare. The anticipation of their date had built over the day, and she couldn't wait to get her arms around Rowan. But at the same time, she'd never felt so nervous. An afternoon of pampering and waxing at Jules's spa had left her feeling slightly more presentable, but the fact remained, her body hadn't been seen by another human being in a long time. *Dear God, I don't want to think about last time I was naked with someone else.*

Rowan's body was young and fit. Every glimpse of it she'd managed, and she'd been paying *close* attention, showed tight, toned skin. She shook herself. Her own body had served her well through sport and parenthood, and she'd never had a problem with self-consciousness.

She jumped as her phone buzzed.

Why are you sitting out there? Have you changed your mind?

She twisted in her seat and turned around towards the large house Rowan's flat was located in. She saw a figure wave from a top floor window.

She texted back, *Are you spying on me?*

No, this is my kitchen window, and I was getting a drink of water. And then, *Are you hiding from me?*

Tess smiled to herself, exited the car, and hurried to the building with her overnight bag. Rowan opened the door and led her back upstairs.

"This is the spare room. You can leave your bag there."

Rowan opened the door to a room that clearly doubled as kit store, office, and guest room. A futon bed had been unfolded and made with fresh white linen. Tess threw her bag onto the bed and turned, rested against the door frame, and looked at Rowan. "So where are you taking me tonight?"

Rowan moved closer and leaned down to kiss her. It began gently but soon heated up until Rowan pulled away. "Maybe we should go and eat before we do that again. Otherwise, we're going to miss the reservation at my favourite French restaurant."

Tess regained her composure. "Ooh, French. Are you trying to impress me with your sophisticated ways?"

Rowan frowned. "I have actually made it as far as Paris, you know."

Tess cursed herself for forgetting about Rowan's insecurities. "Why bother when you can get French food at home, that's what I always say. Now show me the rest of your place."

Rowan ensured they arrived in plenty of time for their seven o'clock reservation, and they were seated at an intimate table by the window, overlooking the canal.

Tess looked out at the view with interest. "I hadn't realised it was so lovely down here. I really need to get the house sold and move closer to town."

"There are some beautiful Edwardian villas on Oak

Lane. When I was a kid, I had a school friend who lived in one, and I always dreamed I'd own one someday." Rowan picked at the bread that they'd ordered while they waited for their food.

Tess laughed. "I know that road. It's beautiful. But those houses are way out of my price bracket. I'm not going to be able to be choosy when I do move, even if I get a good price for my house."

Rowan frowned. "You want somewhere you'll be comfortable that meets Elsie's and Archie's needs, though."

"I've got a list of must-haves and then some desirables if I can get them. I'm going to start looking as soon as I've got some spare time." She laughed. "Whenever that might be."

Rowan took her hand, rubbing her thumb across her palm in the most distracting way. "If it's quiet in the office, you know you can search then, don't you? You work so hard, neither Dad nor I mind you taking some time if you need to get things sorted."

Tess tried to focus on something other than Rowan's thumb caressing her skin. How could a simple touch have such an effect on her? "I know, but it's never quiet, is it? And I do need to get more organised with this." She looked up from their clasped hands. "I don't suppose you're any good at decorating?"

Rowan smiled warmly. "I know it may be surprising to hear, but I've got an eye for detail. Let me know when you need me and I'll be there, overalls and stepladder in hand."

Tess tried not to think about how much she missed Rowan's touch while they ate. The way she reacted to Rowan unsettled her. She couldn't afford to get carried away with a relationship when she needed to get her life in order. But maybe she was getting ahead of herself. No one had mentioned a relationship. She and Rowan were attracted to each other, and they were adults who could act on the attraction and see where it took them. And tonight, it was taking her back to Rowan's bed.

The look in Rowan's eyes suggested her thoughts were along the same lines. Perhaps Jules had been right all along, and she just needed to get it out of her system.

The stroll home from the restaurant was slower than Rowan would have wanted while they walked off their meal, so she focused on the sensation of having her fingers intertwined with Tess's. She was eager to get home but also nervous about where the evening would go next. They hadn't discussed sleeping arrangements again, but maybe it would work out without her worrying. Tess was far from the first woman she'd taken home to her bed, but this felt different, more important. But for Tess maybe it was just an experiment, a chance to blow off some steam after her disastrous marriage.

She unlocked her front door and followed Tess through, only to find herself pushed up against the hallway wall.

Tess took her face in her hands and looked deep into her eyes. "I have been dying to do this all evening."

It started almost hesitantly, as though they were both checking it hadn't been a fluke the first few times they'd kissed. But the fire was soon stoked once more, and Rowan wrapped her arms around Tess, pulling her closer still. She couldn't get enough.

When they broke for breath, Rowan guided her into the lounge. "Nightcap?" It seemed a little presumptuous just to drag Tess up the stairs, although she could think of doing little else.

Tess grinned. "Yeah, why not?"

When they were seated on the sofa with a drink, Tess turned towards her and tucked her feet under her. "Are you nervous, Rowan Russell?"

Her eyes twinkled in the light from the floor lamp in the corner.

"Of course not. I just need you to be sure you want this." She squirmed a little under Tess's lustful gaze.

Tess downed her drink in one, rose quickly, and pulled Rowan to her feet. She kissed her hard, then whispered, "Take me to bed, Rowan."

Her voice was husky, whether from desire or the whisky, Rowan had no idea, but the words were enough to banish any doubts. She led the way upstairs, kicking open her bedroom door as she turned for another kiss. Tess pulled her head down so she could reach her lips, and they staggered into the room and towards the bed, pulling off each other's clothes as they went. As she pulled Tess's shirt over her head, Rowan stared at the creamy skin of her breasts revealed above her emerald-green bra. Rowan had to taste them. She leaned in and kissed Tess's skin. She tasted as good as she looked, and Rowan groaned and kissed her way up to where Tess's neck was bared, her head thrown back. Rowan grazed her teeth across the sensitive skin, and Tess gasped. She pulled away and took the chance to slow things down. Tess looked at her, her eyes dark with desire. Not breaking eye contact, Rowan reached behind Tess, undid her bra, and pulled it away to gaze on the treasures she'd uncovered. She kissed them lightly and continued to move down, pulling Tess's panties slowly down her legs until she stepped out of them. Rowan inhaled her scent deeply. She needed to remove herself from the temptation if she wanted to take things slowly, so she placed a couple of light kisses in strategic places and moved back up. Tess didn't appear to be able to support her own bodyweight, so Rowan moved her back toward the bed. Tess sat, but as Rowan pushed her back towards the pillow she resisted, looking up with a strange look in her eyes.

"I want...I don't want this to..." She pulled Rowan towards her, still sitting up.

Rowan thought she understood, lowered herself onto the bed, and manoeuvred so she was sitting with her back to the headboard. Tess crawled between her legs and kissed her hard, pushing her back against the pillows. Tess slid her knee up to put pressure on Rowan's most sensitive place. Rowan knew her boxers were already soaking, and Tess must have felt the wetness on her skin. She pulled back with a look of tenderness and desire that filled Rowan with a need to sate that hunger. She ran her hands down Tess's body and revelled in the feeling of Tess's soft skin and hard nipples.

The need in Tess's eyes grew as Rowan moved one hand lower and pulled her closer with the other. She touched liquid satin as she gently parted folds to discover Tess's centre. She slid one finger gently along her lips, watching for a reaction as she went. Tess gasped and her hand moved to cover Rowan's own, increasing the pace. Rowan slowed. No way was she rushing this. She was transfixed by Tess's expression. She wondered if she had never made anyone feel this way before or if she'd not paid enough attention. Tess's gasps were becoming rhythmic now, her eyes unfocused. Rowan couldn't keep her on the edge much longer. She increased the pressure and pace of her strokes, and Tess moved her hips in unison. Rowan watched as she started to climax, almost there herself. *Fuck, she's beautiful.*

Tess rolled her head back, and her nostrils flared as she rocked against Rowan's hand. Rowan kept her other arm around Tess's waist, keeping her from falling backwards. The wave went on for what seemed like minutes and just as Tess's moan had reached its loudest, Rowan moved her hand to Tess's waist and lifted her weight. As she slid herself further down the bed, she pulled Tess towards her mouth. Tess barely had time to react before she was in Rowan's mouth and another wave of ecstasy hit her. Rowan felt the headboard behind her move as Tess grabbed the metal bars for support. She tasted like heaven, and Rowan wished she could stay there forever, giving her the release she so clearly needed. Eventually she became aware of Tess's motion against her slowing, and her hand grasped Rowan's hair. She stilled the movement of her tongue and allowed Tess to slide down her body until they were face to face. Tess slid her tongue into Rowan's mouth, and she must have liked what she found because she proceeded to run her tongue around every millimetre of Rowan's mouth. Rowan tried to keep her hips still, knowing the slightest pressure was all she would need. This wasn't about her.

As if she became aware of the tension in Rowan's body, Tess pulled back, but not before running her tongue over her lips for one last taste. Rowan's hips bucked involuntarily, and Tess smiled. She slid slowly down the bed. Rowan grabbed her hand before she went far. "You don't need to do anything you're not ready for. I can wait." She definitely couldn't wait, but Tess didn't need to know that.

Tess looked into her eyes with a look that made her hips buck once more.

"Oh, I'm ready. Just try and stop me." Her head moved down.

Rowan closed her eyes as teeth nipped her nipple. The feeling of Tess's light kisses moving down her body was exquisite.

Tess's warm finger slid inside the waistband of Rowan's boxers. "These need to go."

Rowan raised her hips and shivered slightly at the cool air, as the damp material slid off her sensitive parts.

"Ooh, are you feeling chilly?"

She felt warm breath and gasped. The anticipation was going to kill her. Rowan spread her knees wide in case of any confusion about how much she needed Tess to touch her. Tess slid her hot tongue lightly, experimentally, along the whole length of her, and Rowan's hips rose to meet it. Firm hands pushed her back down and moved up to hold her open. She had never felt so exposed. Tess's tongue returned, more firmly, focussing on the place Rowan needed it most. She reached down and grasped Tess's hair, torn between urging her on and trying to stop things from going too fast. Tess raised her head slightly and looked up at her. She was smiling, her face flushed. Rowan groaned loudly as Tess entered her and began to move. She pushed back against the penetration, crying out at the pleasure of it, as Tess's finger was joined by another. Her hips rocked, and she was vaguely aware she was making a lot of noise before Tess's lips returned to her aching clit, and she lost awareness of anything outside of the sensations in her body.

Tess blinked in the light coming through the curtains. She was a full-on blackout blinds, eye mask kind of sleeper, so she was sensitive to the change in light. It occurred to her why the light was different, and she rolled over. Rowan was lying on her front, face turned towards her. Her hair fell over her forehead and into her eyes. She looked peaceful, not to mention adorable. Tess resisted the urge to wake her to continue what had started last night and lasted into the early hours. She'd never felt so alive or so desired. At one point, her tears had fallen onto Rowan's chest, and Rowan had pulled her close, kissed them away, and told her how beautiful and amazing she was.

Now in the literal cold light of day, she wondered what Rowan would think about all that emotion. She had lived for so long believing she didn't want sex, being told she was passionless. But last night had opened something up in her that she hadn't even realised was closed. When she was young, she'd had plenty of experience with men and women, and although she preferred the emotional depth of encounters with women, she'd got caught up in societal expectations and found herself with Pete. She'd believed them to be compatible enough to be happy together, but their relationship quickly became more controlling, and sex had turned into yet another thing he used to manipulate her.

But last night had been different from anything she'd ever experienced. She'd never felt so connected to another person. She'd always thought that when people talked about mind-blowing sex, they exaggerated.

She continued to look at Rowan, her face relaxed and younger looking in sleep. After years of trying to feel as little as possible, Rowan made her want to feel everything. With that thought, a wave of panic hit her. If Pete had managed to control her with his pettiness and passive aggression, what could Rowan do when she could make her feel like this? But Rowan wouldn't ever try to control her, would she? She was gentle and supportive.

And Rowan was so experienced, this must just be normal for her. Nothing life-changing, just sex. Tess couldn't take the risk of being derailed from putting her life back on track by getting into something that felt too big, too scary. But that shouldn't stop her making the most of this time with Rowan. Her hand slid under the cover, seeking out her target, until Rowan started to stir, and turned to her with a sleepy but playful squint.

"Good morning. Are you looking for something?"

Tess leaned in, claiming Rowan's lips, and focused on the present.

TWENTY

For once, Rowan wasn't looking forward to the rugby club's Christmas party. It was usually the highlight of the social calendar, but her heart wasn't in it tonight. Since their night together, Tess had been friendly but kind of distant, and she'd avoided any further physical intimacy. Rowan missed her so much it hurt. She struggled to believe Tess hadn't found their night together as special as she had. She'd certainly been keen enough to start all over again the next morning. But they had parted with an agreement to see each other the next day at work, and then things appeared to have gone back to normal. She wanted to ask Tess what was going on, but she wasn't sure how. Any regular, well-adjusted adult would simply have a grown-up conversation. Unfortunately, Rowan wasn't regular or well-adjusted.

So tonight was going to be awkward. This year's fancy dress theme was superheroes. She'd gone for Wonder Woman, having heard Tess talk about how much she'd enjoyed the film. But now, looking at the skimpy costume hanging on the back of the door, she suspected she would just be cold and embarrassed, and hair from the wig would inevitably end up in her beer.

She got to the clubhouse in plenty of time to get the heating ramped up and to open the bar. Hannah, Mollie, and Kelly soon arrived to help with the decorating, and the other team members and their partners and friends, as well as the men's team, arrived in dribs and drabs.

Hannah took first shift behind the bar and urged Rowan to go and get her costume on. She reluctantly emerged from the changing rooms to see the party in full swing. The room was lit mostly by the disco lights and she peered around, looking for her friends. Feeling self-conscious, she worked her way to the bar, contending with wolf whistles and the occasional fake grope from her teammates. The men knew better than to come anywhere near her.

She squeezed herself a space at the bar, alongside a very short Incredible Hulk, who turned around to see what the pushing was about. Behind a thick layer of bright green face paint was Tess. She stepped back to take in Rowan's full costume. Her green jaw dropped, and Rowan was in no doubt as to what was going through her mind.

"You look amazing. Wow."

For Tess, that was as close to speechless as Rowan had ever heard her. "Looking pretty incredible yourself." Rowan was pleased with that. She often overthought a comeback for too long until the moment had passed. It was difficult to tell, but she thought Tess looked embarrassed.

"I thought it would be warm, but I hadn't really factored in the bulkiness. Or the face paint."

"Believe me, warm was a good plan." Rowan rubbed the goosebumps on her arms.

"I know how we can warm you up. Would you like to dance?"

No, I would not like to dance. I feel conspicuous enough without adding dancing. I want to take you back to bed and show you how I feel about you. "Yeah, sounds good." She let Tess lead her to the dance floor.

Later in the evening, Rowan felt more relaxed about her costume choice. A few drinks had eased her self-consciousness and the room had heated up to an uncomfortable level, so she was one of the few people not suffering. She and Tess had alternated dancing and standing at the bar chatting all evening, and she was happy for the night to go on forever if it meant she could stay in Tess's company.

"I need some air." Tess looked flushed. Her green hair was stuck to her head, and she had unzipped the back of her costume in an attempt to cool down.

She headed for the fire door leading out to the roof. Rowan grabbed her coat, threw her wig behind the bar, and followed Tess out. She found her sitting at the top of the fire escape steps, looking down on the pitch below.

Rowan had no intention of sitting down on the cold metal of the steps in her current state of dress. She squeezed past and stood a few steps down, so she was on a level with Tess.

Tess looked up at her through dishevelled face paint. "This costume was a big mistake, Rowan Russell."

Rowan laughed. "We could try and wash some of it off in the bathroom if you want. Don't let it spoil your evening."

"It hasn't. I've had a great time." She paused, studying Rowan's face. "This is probably a bad time to talk, but I've missed you so much. I know we see each other every day, but it's not enough."

How do I tell her it feels like I've been picked up and then dumped without making it sound too dramatic? Rowan stared out at the dark pitch while she tried to formulate what she wanted to say, the alcohol slowing her thought process even more.

"I'm sorry I've been distant since our night together, particularly as it was one of the most wonderful nights of my life."

The drink appeared to be having the opposite effect on Tess. Rowan looked at her in shock.

"I got scared about how good it made me feel, and I don't want to lose control of my life, but I love being with you." Tess stood up and took a couple of steps down toward Rowan. "Please can we try again?"

Rowan mentally slapped herself on the side of the head. *Say something for fuck's sake.* She moved closer and took Tess's face in her hands, ignoring the greasiness of the paint. "I'm such an uncommunicative idiot. I tried to give you some space after that night in case it wasn't what you wanted. And you seemed to back off, so I thought maybe it wasn't."

Tess opened her mouth and closed it again, saying nothing.

"Our night together was special for me too. I realised how routine I'd allowed my life to become." She let out a long breath. "Watching you come was as close to a religious experience for me as I'll ever have. I would very much like to repeat it. And I'm so sorry I didn't speak up and ask you what was going on."

Tess's face erupted into her familiar warm smile. "It was all my fault. I should have talked to you about my concerns. We need to have a longer talk about where all this is going. But for now..." She pulled back. "I want to kiss you, but I think it would be too messy."

Rowan pulled her in and kissed her hungrily, their faces sliding together with the face paint.

When she pulled back for a breath, Tess burst out laughing. "I think it's going to be obvious what we've been up to." She looked at her watch. "My taxi will be here in half an hour. I need to start rounding up Elsie, and Archie if he's turned up from his trip to town."

"Archie's coming here?" Rowan was surprised. Archie hated the club and steered clear when he could.

"He's got a friend from school staying for the weekend. They wanted to go bowling, so it made sense to all get a taxi together." She shrugged. "A twenty-mile taxi fare is a big investment. Might as well get our money's worth." She took Rowan's hand. "Let's get you cleaned up."

She led Rowan back up the steps and into the hot, noisy room. Tess pulled her through laughing teammates until they reached the toilets. They looked in the mirror together in horror. While Tess's face paint was looking decidedly smudged, Rowan had a large green smear down one side of her face, and she looked as if she'd been eating green paint. "You just let me walk through looking like this?"

Tess laughed. "I don't think they were under any illusions. No one goes out on the fire escape to actually get fresh air." She rummaged inside her costume. "I thought this might get messy, so I came prepared." She pulled out a pack of makeup wipes with a flourish. "What I've learned from years of bad fancy dress choices."

"You've learned to bring wipes rather than make better costume choices?"

"What can I say? I'm still learning." Tess got to work on Rowan's face, so she was soon looking presentable.

"Your turn. I don't think the taxi will take you looking like that." She put her hands on Tess's hips and lifted her to sit on the ledge near the sinks, where the girly girls applied their makeup after a game. Tess giggled, but her face was now level with Rowan's own.

She had her work cut out, but she pulled out a handful of wipes and did her best. "Soon have you back to your usual gorgeous self."

Tess scoffed. "Hardly. This makeup hides a number of horrors. Maybe I should wear it all the time."

Rowan carried on working. She realised Tess wasn't fishing for compliments, she genuinely had no idea how attractive she was. *Because no one's told her for years.* Saying what she was thinking wasn't Rowan's superpower, but she would need to try harder. Once she had made Tess as presentable as she could, she stood back to admire her work. "Nope, definitely gorgeous." She pushed herself between Tess's knees and took her face in her hands. "Tess, you are absolutely fucking beautiful. I can't take my eyes off you, and it doesn't make any difference whether you're dressed up for a date or painted green."

Tess was speechless, so Rowan took the opportunity for another kiss. They stayed that way for a few minutes until Tess pulled back. She had tears in her eyes.

"Thank you. Whether it's true or not, I like hearing you say it."

The door banged open, and Dora the Explorer and Moana stumbled through sideways, snogging the faces off each other. Realising they weren't alone, they detached themselves and turned slowly to look at their audience. Elsie's gaze flicked from her mum to Rowan and back, and she gave them a wide smile.

"Hi, Mum. Are you having a good time?" she asked, her speech slightly slurred.

Tess jumped down from her ledge, clearly flustered.

"It's nearly taxi time, Dora. Don't get carried away in here. Has your brother turned up yet?"

"Not seen him."

Elsie and Jai stared at them, clearly waiting for them to leave.

Rowan laughed and slung her arm around Tess to lead her out. She was glad when Tess leaned into her instead of pulling away.

"Ten minutes and the taxi will be here. Don't make me come looking for you." Tess called over her shoulder as they left. "I need to call Archie. If he's not here by the time the cab arrives, we're buggered. He promised me."

Rowan steered them outside where it was quieter, and Tess pulled out her phone.

"Before you do that and our evening comes to an end, I just want a couple more minutes with you." She wrapped her arms around Tess and nuzzled in close to her ear. "I know we're both busy, but I really want to see you again soon. Alone. Can we try and make it happen?"

Tess turned her head and claimed her lips once more, and for a moment she forgot she was standing in a cold car park, dressed as Wonder Woman.

"Mum! What the actual fuck?"

The return to reality was brutal. Tess pulled away quickly and turned to face Archie standing a few feet away, a look of horror on his face. A taller, curly haired boy stood nearby, looking on uncertainly.

"Dad's right about you, you're selfish. No wonder he couldn't stand to be with you any longer." He turned on Rowan. "I thought you were helping me because you were my friend, not because you were trying to get into her pants."

"Don't you dare speak to Rowan like that, Archie Kennedy. Who do you think you are?"

Rowan had rarely seen Tess angry. If Archie's expression was anything to go by, it wasn't a common occurrence at home either. His face went from incensed to scared and back again.

"Wait till I tell Dad. He knew it all the time."

What the hell had Pete been talking to his teenage son about? Rowan folded her arms, wanting to speak up, but she knew Tess would want to handle this on her own. They were interrupted by the crunching of gravel as a minibus rolled into the car park.

"The taxi's here, Archie, get in. Tell him I'll be five minutes." She nodded at Archie's nervous-looking friend. "Sorry about this, Max."

"I'll go and find Elsie while you get the coats." Rowan held the door open for her. As they went back into the warm clubhouse, she made a beeline for the toilets. She stuck her head inside to find Elsie and Jai where they'd left them, still snogging.

"Elsie, the taxi's here and your mum's just had a blow-up with Archie, so I wouldn't keep her waiting."

Elsie tore herself away from Jai. "I'll see you in a couple of weeks."

Or more likely on video calls every day. Rowan wished her own love life was so simple and carefree.

They met Tess on their way out, looking hot and bothered in her costume, and evidently still furious at Archie's outburst. Rowan pulled her aside before they were within view of the taxi. "I wish I could be there with you. It's going to be a long journey home."

"My kids, my problem." Tess gave her a quick kiss. "I'm

coming to town tomorrow for some Christmas shopping. Fancy lunch?"

"I fancy that very much indeed." Rowan hugged her goodbye and headed back to the party. She was falling hard for Tess, and she still wasn't sure what it was Tess wanted from her. Archie's reaction to seeing them together didn't bode well. Coming between Tess and her kids wasn't a place Rowan wanted to be. It felt like things could get messy, but she was powerless to stop them.

TWENTY-ONE

"You don't have to go, Elsie. Do what makes you happy." Tess felt the impact of Archie's outburst weighing heavily on her as she sat at the kitchen table watching Elsie make pasta. Pete had called her, presumably after speaking to Archie, and smugly announced he thought it would be a stabler environment for the children at their old house for Christmas. She suspected the girlfriend was spending Christmas with her family, and Pete didn't want to be alone. This had given him the ammunition he needed to get what he wanted.

"I know. But I think I should be there with Archie. I can challenge some of Dad's most ridiculous statements."

Tess drew a long breath. She often questioned if she'd done the right thing agreeing to share custody with Pete after the divorce. It had felt wrong to fight for sole custody, and the kids were old enough to make up their own minds, but she constantly worried about the influence Pete was having on Archie. He'd never spent much time with him in the past, always giving the impression he was disappointed with his quiet, studious son. But he'd seen a chink in Tess's armour when Archie had struggled with the divorce, and now he seemed to revel in it.

"Plus, I'll get to hang out with my friends from school." Elsie's school friends were suddenly getting some time now that Jai had gone back home for the holidays. "But will you be all right on your own here?"

"Of course I will. A few days to put my feet up and rest. I can't think of anything better." She smiled more bravely than she was feeling.

"Do you think Rowan will invite you over for Christmas dinner?" Elsie sounded hopeful.

"I don't know, love. I think her sister and wife are coming up. I don't want to intrude on a family gathering."

"Well, I don't like the idea of you sitting here all alone on Christmas Day. It's not right."

"Please don't worry, Elsie. It's been a really long and busy few months. The quiet and rest will do me the world of good." She couldn't think of anything she'd enjoy better than a couple of days with her feet up, watching TV and eating chocolates.

As Tess drove the kids down to Pete's a few days before Christmas she wasn't feeling so positive, but she hid it well, playing Christmas songs all the way there and insisting Elsie and Archie join in. Archie had refused and sat sullenly in the back.

Derek had insisted she have a break over Christmas. "Honestly, duck, there's hardly any work going on. You've been working your arse off on the pre-Christmas rush. We can cope for a couple of weeks."

Rowan had been nodding her agreement in the

background, so she'd given up and decided to appreciate the break. The previous day, she and the kids had gone to town and spent the day shopping. A quick meal had been the closest she would get to having Christmas dinner with them. They'd agreed to save present unwrapping for when they were back together just before the new year. Well, she and Elsie had agreed. Archie was still sulking, and no matter how hard she tried not to let it bother her, his attitude sucked some of the joy out of the day.

You can get through this. It's just another day. Memories of every year around the tree, hours spent building whatever ship, or castle, or other scenario had been gifted came back to her as she drove down the motorway. Admittedly, reminding herself she'd also spent those days in Pete's company tempered her nostalgia, but she knew she would wake up on Christmas morning missing the kids desperately. She told herself to toughen up. They'd both be off living their own lives in a couple of years anyway. That was the reason she'd stuck it out so long with that bastard. But somehow that made it even harder to miss one more Christmas with them.

The five minutes standing in Pete's hallway were enough to make her want to get back on the road as soon as possible.

"So, it's finally out in the open. What I've been telling people all along. You just used me to breed."

"Shut the fuck up, Pete. The kids are in the next room," she hissed.

"You didn't care what the kids thought when you were having sex in a car park with that rugby slag. Was it really that little dyke who assaulted me all those years ago? Have you just been waiting to go back to her?"

The anger flared up inside her, and she took a deep

breath. Elsie and Archie didn't need to witness their father beaten up in his own house. "It was a kiss, and it would have been no big deal at all if you hadn't poisoned our son with your own resentment." She pushed him aside and raised her voice. "Have a good Christmas, you two. I'll see you next week." She left before her tears spilled over.

Not far into her long drive back, her phone rang. Rowan had bought her a phone holder that attached to her dashboard, and she looked at the caller name and smiled, rubbing her tears away. "Rowan Russell. To what do I owe this pleasure?"

Rowan's quiet chuckle was instantly comforting. "I dunno, I thought you might want some company on your way home. How did it go?"

"Oh, not too bad," she said. "The kids will be fine."

"Of course they will. They're big kids now, Tess."

"Can we change the subject? What are you wearing?"

"Oh no, we are not doing phone sex while you drive on the motorway in the dark. That is *not* what that phone holder is for."

Tess laughed, and they chatted for the remainder of her long journey. As Rowan told her about her sister's plans to visit, her mind wandered. She loved that Rowan was always there for her when she needed her. Was this what a real relationship felt like? But hold on, was it a relationship? They'd managed some time together during a couple of extended lunch breaks at Rowan's flat and had made some plans for Christmas but nothing further into the future. Tess didn't want to do anything to make the situation with Archie any worse. However she felt about his opinions, the important thing now was to keep him working towards his exams with minimal drama. That had to be her focus. And as well as her own concerns about getting too involved, she had no idea if Rowan was looking for anything longer-term. Tess came with a lot of baggage. Rowan worked and played hard. She wouldn't want to tie herself down with a family, would she?

"It's not about you being okay on your own. I want to be with you."

Rowan was clearly getting a little impatient with Tess's insistence that she would be fine spending Christmas Day alone. They'd been together at Rowan's flat every night since the children had left, and it had been wonderful. But she was worried she wouldn't be able to cope with a return to normal. Spending Christmas Day alone would be a good reality check. And she really didn't want to intrude on the Russell family Christmas. Rowan's sister, Willow, and her wife, Cara, were coming up from Brighton. Their baby was due in March, and Tess guessed that they would want to have their own Christmases once they had a family. This might be the last time Rowan spent the day with her dad and her sister at the family home.

"Christmas is a time for family, Rowan. Go and enjoy your time with yours."

"But Cara will be there."

"Because she's Willow's wife."

"Because she's part of her life. You're becoming part of my life. I want to introduce you to my family." Rowan reddened. "I just mean you're important to me. And to Dad. He wants you there as much as I do."

She finally gave in. She couldn't deny she would love to spend the day with Rowan, and it was reassuring to hear her say their relationship was important. She didn't know where this was going in the long-term, but that could wait until after the turkey was all gone. For now, she could enjoy the day. "It's lovely that you want me to share your day. And now that you've played the Derek card, you know I can't say no." She leaned across the dinner table and kissed Rowan. "I would be delighted to spend Christmas Day with you and your family."

"Fantastic. I was wondering if you could sort the potatoes. And the veg. I've got the turkey covered." Rowan cracked up at Tess's outraged expression. "Joking. I'm a monster in the kitchen. I don't even like people coming in to fetch cutlery."

Rowan had become more relaxed in the last few days. They'd had no distractions with work, or the kids, or even rugby. It had given Tess a view of what her life could be like if it was less hectic. When she'd imagined a future where she could do what she wished, it had involved no one else, but now she'd had a taste of being with someone in a caring relationship and she liked it. And Rowan seemed to be enjoying it too. Tess decided it was all too complicated to worry about for now. But sometime soon she was going to have to think about what she wanted for her future.

TWENTY-TWO

Tess was a little nervous about meeting Rowan's sister. She wanted all of Rowan's family to like her. She asked Rowan about her as they stood in the kitchen prepping veg on Christmas Eve.

"Everyone says we're very alike, so hopefully you'll like her." Rowan was peeling sprouts and throwing them into a pan.

"So, I don't need to worry about her taking over the conversation?" Tess smiled. This wasn't going to be the Christmas Day she'd expected, but Elsie had been delighted to hear about her invitation to the Russell family dinner. Archie had barely said anything on the phone, except to begrudgingly wish her a Happy Christmas for the following day, and she suspected Elsie had twisted his arm to even get that. It hurt deep inside, but she needed to wait for a suitable time to talk to him. At some point he was going to have to face up to who she was and that she had a life beyond being a mother.

"Oh, she's not quite as non-verbal as me. She was mostly brought up by my aunt, and she had three other kids.

Willow had to shout to make herself heard. They lived just down the road, but it made it easier for my dad to cope with bringing me up and running the business."

She put her knife down and wrapped herself around Rowan from behind. "You're not non-verbal love, you've got plenty to say." She nuzzled her neck. "You just like to think before you speak, that's all."

Rowan carried on with her chopping and didn't respond. Tess took the knife from her hand and put it down, forcing Rowan to turn and face her.

"What's going on in here?" She tapped the side of Rowan's head. "I can hear the little cogs whirring."

Rowan finally cracked a small, sad smile. "A couple of my relationships ended because I had nothing to say. My exes said I didn't make good company."

"I think people say those things so they feel less guilty about hurting someone. If that's what they truly thought, they must never have been listening. I find you fascinating." She reached up to pull Rowan's head down to her level and kissed her until Rowan pulled her to the bedroom, and the vegetables were left unprepared for a couple of hours more.

They arrived at the family home bright and early the following day, after Rowan surprised Tess with a breakfast in bed of smashed avocado on sourdough and smoked salmon and a glass of Buck's Fizz.

"I thought it'd probably been a long time since you weren't making breakfast for others on Christmas Day."

Tess had tucked in enthusiastically and then shown Rowan exactly what she thought of her thoughtful gesture.

Now they were getting the turkey in the oven so that when Willow arrived, they could relax and enjoy the company. Derek wanted to help too, but Rowan steered them both into the lounge, complaining that they were making the kitchen look untidy.

"Tess, would you pour Dad a glass of sherry please?"

Her beseeching look won Tess over, and she led Derek away from the chef's domain. "Come on, Derek, we know when we're not wanted. Let's get drunk."

She chatted to Derek about Christmases past and the most memorable mornings with the children. He even talked about the couple of years it had been the four of them before his wife had died.

"That first Christmas was the worst, Tess. Trying to keep things as normal as I could for Rowan. Willow's injuries were bad, but she was too young to know what was going on. But Rowan was so distraught. She blamed herself because she'd refused to go shopping with her mum so she could come to the rugby club with me. I spent so long trying to reassure and comfort her. And all the time I was dying inside too." His eyes went misty. "But you just have to get on with it, don't you, love? For the kids."

"You certainly do, Derek." She couldn't imagine the pain of losing your partner and having to carry on, but there had been a couple of times Pete had rocked up on Christmas morning, smelling of alcohol and someone else's perfume, and she'd had to put on her game face and sit smiling next to him, watching the children unwrap their presents.

She wondered how much baggage Rowan still carried from that traumatic time in her childhood. They both sat quietly, engrossed in their own thoughts.

"You're really rolling out the Christmas spirit there, Dad. Well done."

Rowan wore an apron and had a wooden spoon in her hand, and the sight made Tess want to kiss her.

"We're fine, love. Just reminiscing." The doorbell rang, and Derek hurried to answer it.

The couple who followed him into the room were smiling widely. Willow was very like her sister, with sandy hair that gave Tess a clue as to Rowan's natural colour. And she had the same light grey eyes that could skate over you or bore into your soul.

She manoeuvred her wheelchair around the furniture to get a long hug with her dad. "Merry Christmas to you all."

Her wife, Cara, was short, and bouncy, and noticeably pregnant, with a perfect Afro and dark brown eyes. "Pleased to meet you, Tess. We've heard so much about you."

Tess glanced at Rowan, surprised.

Cara must have noticed the look. "Oh, not from this one. We're lucky if we can get the basics out of her." She ruffled Rowan's hair. "No, it's the Tess fan club over there who's kept us up to date with developments."

Derek looked embarrassed. "I've just told you what's been going on with the business and everything."

Tess crossed the room and hugged him. "They're teasing you, Derek. But I'm very happy to have a fan club. You're my first member."

They made themselves comfortable, and Rowan went back to the kitchen, promising to return soon.

"You've must've had some fans when you played for your country, Tess?" Willow's question seemed genuine.

Rowan had said she was a keen rugby enthusiast and had played wheelchair rugby for a few years at college. Tess shrugged. "There were the diehard fans and the younger players who aspired to reach that standard, but it was over twenty years ago, Willow. The women's game had virtually no coverage. We would play our hearts out in some suburban venue, and the TV cameras would be focused on the empty stands at Twickenham or Murrayfield, while the pundits discussed the men's game later in the day. It didn't feel very prestigious."

"Things have improved now though, haven't they?"

"Yes, quite a lot." She smiled, not wanting to sound negative. "But there's still a way to go before the women's game has equity with the men's. I guess that's the case in most sports."

The conversation moved on comfortably to other subjects until Rowan joined them and announced dinner was right on schedule.

As they were clearing away plates later, Tess cornered Rowan in the kitchen. "I'm going to leave soon so you can catch up with your aunt and cousins."

"You don't to need to go. Aunty Mary said you were very welcome to join us."

"I know, and I appreciate that, but imposing me on your direct family is one thing. You should go and have proper family time now."

Rowan frowned, looking uncertain. "Are you sure you'll be okay on your own?"

"Are you kidding me? I'm going to put my feet up, eat a whole box of After Eights, and watch Christmas films without children bickering. Heaven!" She smiled to show Rowan she meant what she said. "You go and have a few drinks with your family and relax."

"I can't. I said I'd drive so Willow can have a drink. I need to get Dad back home after we visit my aunt, then I can chill."

Tess looked into Rowan's deceptively calm eyes and

knew she was overthinking something. She raised her eyebrows.

Rowan smiled uncertainty. "Dad'll be tucked up by ten. Maybe you want some help with those After Eights? And we didn't get time to open our gifts before we left this morning." She paused. "I understand if you'd rather not have me at the house. What with Archie being...you know. And you might just want some time to yourself."

Tess smiled widely. "Archie's not there, is he? And he can mind his own business, anyway. That would be delightful. I'll have a bottle of something special chilling." They kissed, only pulling apart when Derek came in and cleared his throat loudly.

Tess left soon after, and as she drove home, she smiled to herself. She had missed her kids like mad, especially this morning when there'd been no reason to get up and rush downstairs to open presents. But Rowan's company had made her day special in a different way, and she'd been happy to spend it with her family. Perhaps there was a life after kids if there was someone to share it with.

TWENTY-THREE

Rowan looked at her watch as she stacked the paper delivery alone. Tess should be here soon, and she'd be glad of the help. Keith was busy at the presses, and the boys were out on a delivery. The loading bay was icy cold and the sooner she got the boxes packed away, the sooner she could close the shutter and get warm again.

The new year had come and gone, and January had flown by in a busy routine at work. But it was outside of work that things had changed. Tess stayed over with Rowan whenever Archie was at his dad's, and Rowan visited the family house regularly for dinner, especially on a Sunday when she was picking Elsie up for a game. Occasionally she'd visit on a weekday evening, and they'd sit and watch TV together and chat about things that weren't work related. Elsie would often join them, but Archie tended to stay out of the way, making his excuses after dinner. He hadn't asked Rowan for any more help with his projects, and that made her sad. She wished they could get along, like they had before things had got more intimate with Tess. But she couldn't wish that hadn't happened. Being with Tess was the best thing that had ever happened to her.

Her thoughts stalled as Tess came rushing out though the loading bay door, a wide smile on her face. It faltered for a moment. "Wow, it's freezing out here. Come and have a cuppa, and I'll help you finish off when you've warmed up."

She led the way back inside and pressed the button to close the shutter door.

Tess's smile reappeared. "I think I've found the perfect house. Have you got time to view it with me after work?"

Tess had put her village house on the market and had an offer within days. She was now looking for a home in town, but house prices were higher, and she'd struggled to find anywhere big enough. Rowan wondered if they would get to spend more evenings together when they lived closer. She really hoped so, but she didn't want to pressure Tess. "It's not a training night, of course I've got time." She followed Tess into the break room and pushed her up against the worktop. "Where is it?" She kissed Tess gently. They hadn't seen each other alone for a couple of days, and she liked to make the most of the few moments of intimacy they could steal.

Tess wrapped her arms around her neck, clearly excited. She named a suburb Rowan wasn't that familiar with. "Oh, I thought you were aiming at something more central." Rowan stepped back, trying not to sound disappointed. She'd hoped Tess would be within walking distance of her flat.

"I know, I know. But this gives us more space. And it's three storeys, so I would have a really private bedroom with my own bathroom on the top floor." She winked.

Rowan chewed her lip. "If you think so. What about the kids getting home from the train?"

"Well, that part's not ideal, but they can jump on a bus from the station. And it'll only be for a few months. Next year they'll both be studying locally, and we'll get a lot of time back."

Rowan was looking forward to Tess's life revolving less around hours on the motorway. She knew the house move was all part of trying to find what was best for her, and she needed to accept that Tess had priorities too. They would make things work, wherever Tess ended up. She was going to have another look at those houses on Oak Lane anyway. Maybe she could find something cheaper, a fixer-upper she could help Tess make into a perfect home. She knew it wasn't really her business to interfere if Tess had found a place, but she couldn't shake her hopeful idea of Tess in a house that met her dreams.

Rowan swore and scuffed the snow-covered grass with the studs on her rugby boot. She hated to cancel a fixture, but the Haresby pitch was on high, exposed ground and if any pitch in the league was affected by icy conditions, it was always theirs. Underneath the light smattering of snow, the ground was frozen solid, meaning players wouldn't be able to get any purchase with their studs and that was particularly dangerous for the front row players during a scrum.

She swore again for good measure and looked at her watch. There were still a few hours until kick-off, and the pitch might thaw if the temperature rose. She looked up at the heavy white clouds and thought snow was more likely. The other team were travelling a long way, and Rowan had promised the referee and the opposition captain they'd give them as much notice as possible if a postponement was needed. She pulled her phone out from under the layers of clothes.

"Morning, Jack. I'm guessing it's bad news?" Hannah sounded as if she was still tucked up in bed.

Lucky her. As captain, it was her call to postpone, but she'd been happy to let Rowan make the early trip to the club to assess the pitch. Rowan quickly updated her and hung up, leaving Hannah to make the calls and let everyone know the situation. She'd take an early morning trip to the club over the phone calls any day. She stomped back towards the clubhouse and wondered what she was going to do with an unexpected free day. She'd started drawing a local scene, and she was keen to do more work on it. It was larger than the small sketches she usually did in her notebooks, but Tess had been encouraging her to challenge herself more, and she wanted to get it finished to see what Tess thought.

As she locked the car park, she heard a familiar bark and looked across the lane to see Becca and Digby approaching on the footpath that cut diagonally across the field opposite. Digby had spotted her and was yelping and woofing as he pulled at his harness. Becca was struggling to control him, and her muttered curses carried on the crisp air. Her feet slipped on the icy path a couple of times, and Rowan knew it was only a matter of time until she face-planted on the hard ground. "Let him go, Becs. I'll catch him." She crossed to the field gate as Becca released the lunging hound from his lead. He made a beeline for Rowan, and she caught him and held onto his harness as he thoroughly covered her face with dog slobber. She finally calmed him as Becca reached them, red faced from both the cold air and the wrestling match she'd just had.

"Cheers, Ro. He nearly broke my neck." She clipped the lead back in place.

"I noticed. You're not the steadiest on your feet at the best of times."

Becca swatted her. It was a running joke that she was a little accident prone. It was more that she was often trying to focus on too many things at once, but the teasing had been merciless during her rugby days, and Rowan had seen no reason to let up when she stopped playing.

Becca took off her gloves and pulled her phone from her pocket. "What the hell are you doing here at this time?" She waved her phone at Rowan. "You might as well just give up and move into the clubhouse."

"I needed to check the pitch. The game's cancelled anyway, so you'll be glad to hear I'm leaving."

"Yay. Does that mean we can do something? Ben wants to go sledging, but I think he's being overly optimistic." She kicked at the ground.

Rowan nodded towards the sky, where the snow clouds were gathering ominously. "I think he might be in luck later. Shall I come round to your house, and we'll make the call? If there's no snow, we'll distract him with the park instead."

"Are you sure you don't have anywhere else you want to be?" Becca raised her eyebrow and grinned.

"No. Now that Elsie can drive herself to games, Tess is trying to spend more time with Archie. He's still being a little shit." She shouldn't say that, but it was starting to annoy her how much Archie's behaviour upset Tess. "I think they're going out to fly the drone she got him for Christmas."

Becca waved as she tramped back across the field, and Rowan smiled to see her a bit more like her old self as she got into her car to go home. She would miss rugby, but a day with Becca and Ben was an unexpected bonus. If she hurried home, she could manage a couple of hours of drawing before she headed out. In truth, she'd much rather be spending the day with Tess, even with Archie's current behaviour. They should probably talk more about what was happening between them, but it was so good, she didn't want to spoil it. She'd long given up trying to fight how she felt, and it felt like Tess was as into their relationship as she was. Rowan's worries that Archie's behaviour would drive Tess away had been unfounded, much to her relief. She was doing her best not to put any expectations on what they were building, but some days it was hard because it felt so perfect.

Plump snowflakes began to land and quickly melt on her windscreen, and she smiled. Today's weather would make Ben happy.

TWENTY-FOUR

Tess wrapped her arms around herself, trying to stay warm. March had brought the start of spring to her garden, and the sight of green shoots and buds raised her spirits as they always did. The temperature had yet to show much sign of the new season though, and as she stood on the touchline, she could see her breath in the air in front of her. She'd got used to standing at this pitch freezing her brains out, but she'd be glad when it was less of an ordeal. To be fair, she hadn't been coming to games as often recently, due to her attempts to repair her relationship with Archie. Elsie had fed back from the few comments she'd managed to get from him that he'd been devastated that Elsie and his mother had found a new life in Haresby so easily. He'd felt as though he was being left behind. So Tess was going out of her way to find things for them to do together.

But it wasn't going well. He was still distant, and while he agreed to whatever activities she arranged, he didn't show much interest and took his phone out to chat to his friends whenever he could. It was emotionally exhausting, and Tess was starting to wonder if she should just leave him alone. He was under pressure with exams looming, and she didn't want to add to it.

He'd gone to his dad's today on a rare opportunity when Pete didn't have prior arrangements. She wasn't keen on him spending any more time there than was necessary. Pete would make sure to widen the rift in any way he could. But the kids needed to stay there until their exams were over, so this wasn't a good time to confront him about the things he said to Archie.

She returned her attention to the game. It was always a pleasure to watch Rowan in action, and Elsie's game was coming along so well, she made Tess proud. At half time, she had been moved to hooker, her favourite position, and she was playing well.

Jules wasn't around today. She'd bailed in favour of the spa, and Tess couldn't blame her. The familiar figures of Becca and Ben were on the other side of the pitch, throwing a ball for Digby. Becca had waved, but her focus appeared to be on exhausting her dog, so she could get a few minutes of socialising after the game.

Tess felt an unexpected vibration in her coat pocket and remembered she was looking after Rowan's phone. Cara's baby was due any day, and Rowan was determined to be at the birth, despite the three-hour journey to get there.

Tess saw Willow's name on the display and scrambled to answer. "Hey, Willow, it's Tess. Any news?"

"Yeah, she's in labour." Willow was slightly breathless. "The midwife says it's progressing quickly. Ro wanted to know."

"She's on the pitch." Tess looked up to see Rowan running with the ball. Two defending players were moving to intercept her, but she was faster. "I think she's about to score." She held her breath as Rowan sidestepped one player and outran the other to ground the ball between the posts. "Yes!"

"Well played, Rowan." Willow paused. "Tess, please tell her not to rush down the motorway. I know how much she wants to be here, but I was hoping to be able to give her a bit more notice. I don't want to be worrying about her too."

Tess knew she wouldn't be able to stop Rowan once she heard the news, so she didn't want to make assurances she couldn't keep. "I'll come with her, Willow, and I'll make sure she sticks to the speed limit."

"I'll text you the hospital address and send updates. Safe journey."

Tess looked up to see Rowan watching her as Hannah took the conversion. She waved the phone in what she hoped was a self-explanatory way and Rowan nodded. Hannah's kick was successful, and the two teams went back to their ends for the restart of the game. Rowan jogged over to Hannah and spoke quickly. Rowan was quickly replaced by one of the newer players, Tess wasn't sure of her name, and the game restarted. Rowan jogged over as Becca approached from the other direction.

"Willow says it could be quick. Are you sure you want to rush down there?"

Rowan nodded, her expression a mixture of excitement and nervousness. "Yeah, I always said I'd be there if I could."

"Okay, but I'm coming with you."

Rowan nodded, jogged off to the changing rooms and returned a couple of minutes later, having pulled on her training pants and top over her kit. "Sorry, we might need to drive with the windows open."

Tess turned to Becca, who'd wandered over to see what

was happening. She pulled out her car keys. "Becs, can you tell Elsie we've had the call?"

Becca nodded and took the keys. "Will do. Drive safe, you two."

Rowan got them through town quickly, and they were soon on the motorway. Tess played with the entertainment display until she found a cheesy playlist she could sing along to and settled in for the drive. Rowan looked at her affectionately as she got a little too optimistic with the high notes.

"I know, don't give up the day job." She grinned. Her enthusiasm for singing wasn't matched by her ability.

"Definitely don't do that." Rowan reached across and squeezed her hand.

Tess entertained them for a while longer until a song came on that she wasn't familiar with. She lowered the volume and turned to Rowan. "What were you talking about with Martin Wells last week? It looked serious." She'd overheard Rowan talking to the owner of a local publishing company who was a long-standing customer.

"Printing. That's what I talk to everyone about." Rowan didn't look at her.

"But as I was leaving, it sounded like he was asking about something else. You didn't mention anything afterwards." She thought she knew what they'd been talking about, but she wasn't sure if Rowan would appreciate her meddling.

Rowan's eyes flicked across to her and back to the road. Her face was expressionless. "He's looking for an illustrator for a children's book, and someone told him I might be able to help."

Tess sighed. "I'm sorry if I've overstepped the mark, Ro. I just think you're so talented, and you love drawing so much, you should try making a go of doing it for a living."

"I've got a job, Tess. You know the only thing that keeps Dad away every day is knowing I'm on top of things. I can't just walk away."

Tess ran her fingers across the back of Rowan's hand in what she hoped was a comforting gesture. "You don't need to walk away from anything. You could go part-time, and I could help pick up the slack."

Rowan loosened her grip and turned her hand to Tess's. "You already do far more than your fair share." She took her eyes off the road briefly, and her smile was warm. "I do appreciate your confidence in me. I just don't know if..."

Tess wished she could do more to help Rowan with her self-belief than reassure her. "Why don't you give it a go? Martin's not going to take any risks. He won't give you the job if he doesn't think your work's good enough."

Rowan was quiet for a while, and Tess didn't push it any further.

"Okay, I'll send him some of my work."

Tess couldn't stop the smile that spread across her face, but she didn't say anything else.

They made good time in getting to the hospital, and Rowan had been chattier than usual as she showed her excitement for the arrival of her new niece or nephew.

"You go. I'll find parking and come and join you as soon as I can," Tess said as Rowan pulled up at the doors to the hospital. Willow had called a few minutes before to say that if she was coming, she needed to get there now. Rowan kissed her and leapt out of the car. She took the steps into the hospital two at a time and quickly disappeared. Tess slipped across into the driver's seat and hoped Rowan would make it.

She finally got to the waiting room. It was unoccupied, so she made herself as comfortable as she could on the hard seats, tucking her legs up under her. She guessed she could be here a while, so she was determined to make the most of having no demands on her time. She pulled up a book on her phone that she'd been wanting to read for ages. She hoped everything was going well in the maternity suite, and she was grateful to be here for Rowan when she needed her. It felt important to be with her at such a special moment in her life, and with that thought came the realisation that she was no longer afraid of sharing her life with Rowan. It felt right, perfect even. She smiled and thought back to the births of her own children. She remembered the perfection of those tiny new people, with all their future and potential ahead of them. Her current relationship with Archie brought her back to reality and she sighed and opened her book, allowing herself to leave that particular problem behind for a while.

"Tess, how long have you been sitting here?" Willow wheeled alongside her. "Ro said she hadn't heard from you and thought you might be out here."

"I've no idea." She checked the time and realised she'd been reading for nearly two hours. "It's all good. I wanted to be here, and I was happy to wait. But now I need an update."

A wide smile broke across Willow's face. "Mother and baby are doing well, as they say. It was a quick labour with no complications."

"Congratulations." Tess jumped up and then regretted it as she realised her feet had gone to sleep. She hopped from foot to foot, wincing, which made Willow laugh. She hugged Willow, who quickly turned towards the coffee machine.

"Thank you, but caffeine is the priority now. How about you help me with coffee, and then you come in and meet Rowan's new nephew?"

Tess continued to stamp her feet to get some feeling back and then joined Willow at the coffee machine. She followed her through into the maternity suite and saw Rowan standing by Cara's bed holding a beautiful baby. She looked up as she saw Tess approach, her eyes shining. Tess could see she was already smitten.

Cara smiled up at her. "How does it feel to be Aunty Rowan?"

Rowan smiled broadly. "Wonderful. I'm going to be the best aunty ever." She turned so Tess could see the baby's face. "Isn't he the most perfect baby you've ever seen?"

Tess watched her as she played with the baby. She wanted to be with Rowan as she watched her nephew growing up. When had things changed from the thought of intertwining her life with anyone making her feel panicky to this sense of peace and being with the person she was meant to be with? It was reassuring and disconcerting all at the same time. The weeks since Christmas had been wonderful for her to really get to know Rowan, but had they fallen into a routine too quickly? Was she getting in too deep without really knowing Rowan well enough? All her instincts told her Rowan was good for her and would never do her harm, but the nagging voice in the back of her mind reminded her that her instincts had failed her before.

TWENTY-FIVE

"I don't know. It's a long time to leave Dad on his own. He's used to me popping in most nights." Rowan knew she was looking for excuses, and she didn't fully understand why she was so keen to resist finding out if her hobby could become more than that. Tess had found a residential drawing course that she was encouraging Rowan to attend, but it meant her being away from home for a week. She was considering her options as she sketched Tess, who was lying naked on the bed, eating pizza.

"I hope I'm not stuffing my face in that drawing." Tess was on her front, leaning on her elbows, and she reached across to pull the sketch book her way.

Rowan let go reluctantly. Allowing anyone else to see her work had always been hard for her, even Becca, who had always been so encouraging. But she wanted to let Tess into every aspect of her life. The tension eased from her shoulders as Tess's face softened.

"Ah, Rowan, you're so talented. You need to go on this course and find out if it's something you want to do more of." She passed the sketch book back and reached for the pizza box. "I can go and see your dad in the evenings before I go home. The kids are studying all the time now. They don't need me around."

Work had been relentless lately, and Tess had been taken up with Elsie and Archie's routine as their exams grew ever closer. They were now staying at their dad's house during exams and studying when they came home, so Tess's daily hours on the motorway had come to an end.

"Are you sure? You don't need more things to worry about."

Tess finished chewing and licked tomato sauce from the corner of her mouth. Rowan watched the movement of her tongue closely. She found Tess naked in her bed, even with added pizza, a distraction from any serious conversation.

"Honestly, I don't have the drive in the mornings now, and I can put something in the slow cooker for the kids when they're there. I'll go and have a cuppa and a chat with your dad and make sure he's got his dinner sorted. He's good company. It won't be a chore."

She threw her crust into the box, and Rowan retrieved it. She'd never understand why Tess would discard the best bit.

"Anyway, he seems pretty taken up with that bowls club now. Have you noticed? He's there most days. I doubt he's lonely."

Rowan nodded. She loved that Tess had such a close relationship with her dad, as if she'd known him for years. She couldn't think of any other excuses not to do this course and find out if she actually had any talent. "Okay, thank you. I'll book my place this afternoon."

Tess shoved the pizza box aside and make her way up Rowan's body. She smiled. "You'll blow their minds, Rowan Russell. You're an amazing artist."

Rowan enjoyed the sensation of Tess's body covering her own, but she wanted to talk about something else before they got caught up in other activities. She tipped Tess sideways and kissed her gently on the forehead. "Tell me about the house sale. You said the buyers may have pulled out." She knew how much moving closer to town meant to Tess. Whatever reservations she had about the area, it would still be an improvement from the hour-long round-trip Tess currently had to negotiate daily. She felt Tess's body tense against her own. Maybe that was too much of a change of mood, but she wanted to share so much more of Tess's life than just the pleasurable parts.

Tess lifted her head to look at her, her mouth crooked in a resigned smile. "Yup, that ship may have sailed. I'll need to withdraw my offer on the one I wanted, but there are plenty of similar properties around there. It'll work out."

Rowan ran her fingers through Tess's curls and rubbed the back of her neck. Tess pushed back against the pressure, and Rowan could feel the tension. "You had an offer within days, so there'll be more." She couldn't help feeling a little relieved that the mediocre house had fallen through. She was still doing her own search for a more attractive property, but she hadn't mentioned it since Tess had dismissed the idea so quickly last time.

"That's what the estate agent keeps promising me. We'll see." She brought her mouth close to Rowan's. "Why don't you find a way to take my mind off it?"

Rowan placed her sketch pad carefully out of the way and moved the pizza box onto the floor. She turned back to Tess and kissed her, pulling back to lick her lips. "Mm, more tempting than the pizza."

Tess laughed. "I will miss you like hell when you're

away. You'll have to spend the next month making it up to me." She placed her hand between Rowan's legs.

Rowan gasped. "I'm sure you'll think up a way for me to do that."

Tess started a rhythm and moved in to claim her lips. Before Rowan got completely caught up the moment, she wondered if Tess's faith in her abilities was justified, or if she would be disappointed when it turned out Rowan wasn't good enough. She pushed those thoughts out of her head. At this moment, Tess was happy to be in her company, and that's what she would focus on.

TWENTY-SIX

Tess strode into the office with a feeling of responsibility she hadn't experienced at work since she gave up nursing. She checked the inbox and made a few notes of important emails to reply to, then she went in search of Stefan and Charlie to make sure they were clear about their priorities for the day. She found them, as usual, in the break room, drinking tea.

Stef had the decency to look embarrassed when she opened the door. "Morning. Are you both on track for this morning? There's the RPC job to go out later and another couple of smaller orders this morning."

Stefan stood and drained his mug, but Charlie sat back and rested his feet on the table. "Don't you worry about us, Tess, we've been doing this job for years. As long as you get the paperwork right, we'll all be fine."

Tess gritted her teeth. He didn't have this kind of attitude around Rowan, but she guessed he was trying his luck.

"That's good, Charlie. I'll be back in a bit then. That

delivery needs to be out by eleven at the latest to allow time for the big job."

"We know, Tess. It's all written down." He waved at the list of jobs pinned to the notice board.

Tess marched back to the office before she said something she regretted. Rowan had made it very clear to the boys that Tess was completely in charge in her absence. Charlie's dig that she was just the office admin riled her, but she understood she was a new member of staff and didn't have the same relationship with them that Rowan and her dad had built over the years.

She pulled up the list of emails and got to work, hoping she'd go back to the warehouse to find the work completed on time.

The sound of the office phone ringing pulled her out of her work, and she looked up at the clock to see nearly two hours had passed since she sat down. She grabbed the phone. "DR Printing. Tess speaking."

"Morning, Tess. Derek here."

Tess smiled. Derek's voice was unmistakable, but he always introduced himself. "Good morning, Derek. How are you today?"

"I'm not feeling too good, but I don't want to leave you on your own there." His voice was downbeat.

"Don't bother about that, Derek. You know I've had the finest training at the hands of your very thorough daughter. You have a rest and if anything comes up that I can't handle, I'll give you a call."

"If you're sure, Tess? I might just wander down to the bowls club this afternoon to get some fresh air, so try my mobile if you need me." He suddenly sounded much perkier.

"Of course, Derek, you take care." She kept the laughter

out of her voice. For someone who had never had a good word to say about bowls, he was suddenly a big fan. There was more to his new interest than he was letting on.

She hung up and checked the time. The boys should be back from their deliveries now and starting to load the RPC job if the printing had gone to schedule. She headed first to the print room, where the sound of the printing machinery was oppressively loud. She stuck her head around the door. Keith was hard at work, his ear defenders in place. She gave up waving to get his attention and walked across the room.

He looked up and smiled, pulling the ear protection off his head. "Hi, Tess," he shouted.

She indicated his office, and they took refuge in the small sound-proofed space as she closed the door. "That's better. I don't know how you stand it all day."

"You get used to it. The RPC job is all done and ready to go out." He indicated the boxes covering the far wall. "I let Charlie know earlier, but they've not been in yet."

"Okay, thanks. I'll go and check their progress. Is everything else okay?"

"Yep, all running to plan." He gave her a double thumbs up and a cheerful grin and replaced his ear protection as they went back out into the noise.

The loading bay was silent in comparison...a little too silent. The van was nowhere to be seen, but she could hear muffled music coming from the break room. "Charlie!" She tried to keep her tone even, but the frustration at seeing him asleep in his chair with his feet up was the last straw. He jerked awake and scrambled to stand. His face went from startled to annoyed more quickly than she'd have expected.

"Bloody hell, Tess. That was unnecessary. I've been working hard all day."

"All day? It's not even lunchtime." She was trying to stay calm.

"Derek says it's fine to take a rest when we need one. It's hard work lugging boxes all day. You wouldn't know, sitting on your arse in that office most of the time."

She ignored the unfairness of that comment. "Charlie, what's going on? You were meant to be out with Stef on those first two deliveries so we could get the RPC job loaded before lunch break. That's a two-hour drive, and we've said it'll be there before three."

"Stefan said he was fine on his own. It's not my fault if he's late."

"Well, when he gets back, we're all going to have to work through lunch now to get it done." She looked at her watch. Even then, they'd be pushing it.

Charlie moved into her personal space, something she particularly disliked. He loomed over her. He wasn't more than average height, but most people could tower over her if they so desired.

"I'm not working through my lunch break. That's not allowed. I'll call my union."

She took a step back and let the distaste show in her expression. "You could say you've already taken a break, Charlie, what with you being asleep and all. You need to start pulling your weight. It's not fair on Stefan, leaving him to do everything."

"He's not said that, has he?"

Tess kept her face neutral.

"I didn't think so. So why do you have to come poking your nose in here? You know nothing about this business, and the minute Rowan's away, you're lording it over us." He pointed back at the office. "Get back in your place and leave us alone."

Tess took the deepest breath she could manage and let it out very slowly into Charlie's way too close, snarling face. "Just get the job loaded as soon as Stef is back. You can take your lunches when it's done. I'll do the delivery." She turned and left.

Back in the office, she collapsed into her chair and let all the tension escape. Why did Charlie have to be such an arse? She was sure he didn't give Rowan or Derek such a hard time or he wouldn't still be here. And whenever they were around, he was always vaguely polite to her. She got stuck back into the invoicing paperwork, knowing she'd need to get it done in record time to be able to get out on the delivery on time. Either that or she'd have to do another couple of hours when she returned. And Archie was due back from his dad's tonight, so she wanted to get home and make dinner for them all.

Tess dropped back into her seat five hours later, feeling so weary she didn't know how she'd deal with the drive home and feeding the kids. She just needed to finish the last few emails. She grimaced as her phone rang. "Hi, Derek, how are you feeling this evening?" She struggled with the positive tone, but she didn't want to add to his stress.

"Tess, love, is everything working out?" He sounded worried.

How could he know about her concerns? "It's all under control, Derek. Everything's out on time. Have you had a good day?"

"Oh, yes, thank you." He sounded distracted. "I think I'll come in tomorrow. Will you be around?"

"I should be in the office all day." *Unless Charlie's up to his tricks, and I have to do his job, too.*

"Righto. I'll see you first thing, then."

He hung up and Tess stared at the handset. Derek has sounded concerned, and she wondered what was wrong. She finally roused herself, finished the emails, and locked up. She wondered if she should stop at a supermarket for something for dinner but as she got into the car, her phone buzzed.

Got home early, so I've made spag bol.

She could hug her daughter. *Thanks, Elsie, that's great news.*

Busy day?

Yes, you could say that.

Drive home safely. Dinner will be ready x

Tess barely had the energy to eat dinner, but she did her best to engage the children in conversation. Elsie chatted away about her exams, but Archie barely said a word. "Have you got your revision planned out, Archie?" She knew he was nervous about his first maths exam next week. Maybe that's why he was so quiet.

He looked up at her for the first time. "I did my physics revision with Max. Can I go back to Dad's and do the same for maths?"

"Your dad let you go round to Max's house to study?" She wasn't sure if that was the best idea. Archie and Max were both conscientious students, but it was a lot of responsibility to put on them.

Archie jumped up. "Why are you so critical? Everything Dad does, you think you know better. He trusts me, and that's more than you'll ever do."

"Of course I trust you." She didn't have the energy for this.

"I want to go to Dad's. He treats me like an adult, not a baby."

She drummed up every ounce of patience she had left. "Sit down, Archie." Her tone was firm enough that he obeyed. She was determined not to lose her temper with him, but it was difficult. "I work really hard to make sure the two of you have everything you need. When you go to your dad's, he's usually not working and has more time for you. I'm trying my best, Archie."

"No, you're not. You're more interested in your girlfriend than you are in us."

"Shut up, Archie." Elsie hadn't stopped eating, but she was watching her brother with a frown on her face. "Mum never stops running around after you. Show a bit of gratitude."

"I don't *want* her running around after me. I *want* her to leave me alone."

"Go to your room, Archie. We'll talk when you've calmed down." Tess was so tired, she almost felt detached from what was happening. He marched out, pounded up the stairs, and slammed his bedroom door.

"If he rings your dad, I swear I'll kill him." She rested her head on her arms. She felt defeated, like the more she tried, the worse things got. She felt Elsie's hand on her shoulder and looked up, blinking to hold back the tears.

"Go and have a bath and get to bed. I'll clear up here."

She squeezed Elsie's hand. "That's not fair. You made dinner."

"I don't mind. It makes a change from studying. Go on."

Tess felt herself being pulled out of the chair and she complied, giving Elsie a kiss on the cheek as she went. "Thanks, kiddo. You're the best."

"I know."

She hauled herself up the stairs to the sound of plates clattering in the kitchen. She wasn't sure she'd make it through a bath. A shower would have to do for tonight. She knew Archie was stressed about his exams, and whenever he came back from staying at Pete's, he was always less respectful. He'd had nearly a full week of listening to his dad telling him what he thought of her, no wonder he was playing up. But it didn't hurt any less.

She knew Rowan was at dinner tonight on the final evening of her course, so she couldn't even ring her to complain. She'd said she would text when it was finished and check if Tess was still awake, but that was looking highly unlikely. Tess had missed her so much all week, and she knew that was part of the reason for her low mood. But Charlie's constant sniping, the volume of work, and now Archie playing up had left her feeling overwhelmed. She couldn't wait till Rowan returned, and they could get back to their normal routine. She sent a quick goodnight text and didn't wait for a reply before she was asleep.

TWENTY-SEVEN

Rowan tried to focus on the traffic as she drove back up the motorway, but her thoughts kept returning to the situation that faced her. The final day of the course involved a session with the tutor to assess the work she'd done over the week. She'd been looking forward to the feedback but then she'd had a call from her dad, who was freaking out about his two favourite employees. She'd thought leaving Tess in charge was a good move, meaning her dad didn't have to worry about anything. Tess had made it clear she had little time for Charlie, but Rowan was shocked she could take advantage of her new authority to punish him. Sure, Charlie needed a bit of a push now and then, but he was loyal, and he'd been a part of their team since the beginning. She wasn't entirely sure what had happened, but her dad had told her Tess had sent Charlie home.

When she entered the office Tess was working at her desk, and she looked up with a smile of joy.

"What the fuck, Tess?"

Tess's expression immediately turned to hurt at Rowan's outburst. Rowan felt a momentary pang of guilt, but her anger and her defensiveness of her dad and the business overwhelmed everything. She leaned across and gripped the desk.

Tess stood up and backed away, wrapping her arms around herself. "Ro, you left me in charge. Charlie's behaviour was putting contracts at risk. I even found him sleeping in the break room while he let Stef do everything. Every time I challenged him, he went running to your dad. I had to do something to make him take me seriously."

Her confidence in her actions just made Rowan even more annoyed. "I left you in charge so you could keep things ticking over in my absence, not make massive decisions about long-standing members of staff."

Tess threw her hands in the air. "I didn't make *any* massive decisions, Rowan. I dealt with an urgent situation. I gave Charlie two opportunities to pull it together and get on with work, and he just laughed at me. This morning he was extremely disruptive and personally offensive. I had to do something."

"You could've rung me or Dad. Asked us for advice. You decided to just do your own thing. I'm really surprised, Tess. I thought you were a team player." She felt deflated all of a sudden and sat back on the desk. "Now, Charlie's saying he doesn't want to come back if you're here, and Dad's really upset. I think you'd better go home until we decide what to do."

Tess was still standing with her back to the wall.

"We'll pay you, obviously."

Tess's eyes were shining now. "I thought you trusted me to do a good job. I didn't do anything I wasn't forced to. Speak to Stefan about how Charlie was behaving. He bore the brunt of it."

"Dad's spoken with him. He said they'd been working

full-on, but you were giving Charlie a hard time, lording it over him."

Tess's shoulders slumped. "Did he really?" Her smile was humourless. "And that sounds like something Stef would usually say, does it?" She turned away and pulled her coat from the hook. "Well, you're back now, and you can put everything right. So, why don't you just call me when you've decided what's going to happen?" She walked out of the door without another word.

Rowan couldn't think of anything to say either. When Tess was gone, she pulled herself onto the desk and let out a long breath. As her anger passed, she wondered at Tess's motivation. Petty vindictiveness wasn't her style, so was there something in what she was saying about Charlie's behaviour? He could be a little manipulative at times, but he'd never been outright disrespectful. And yet, Tess was always open and honest.

"Sorry, Rowan."

She jumped and turned as Keith poked his head in the door.

"I overheard some of that, but I didn't want to interrupt."

"No, *I'm* sorry, Keith." She waved him in. "I thought Tess was ready to take over for a bit, but she's only been with us a few months. I don't think she understands how we work yet."

"She did great." He sat in Tess's chair. "She kept everyone moving and picked up anything that needed doing. She's a machine."

"But she was a bit over the top with Charlie?"

He tipped his head to the side. "Maybe you should have a chat with Stef when Charlie's not around. Get him to relax and be honest."

Rowan didn't hide her surprise. "Really? You think there's a problem in the warehouse?"

"I think there's been a problem for a while, and Tess picked up on it. Charlie didn't like that, and to be honest, he was a dick." He stood and made his way to the door. "Speak to Stef." He closed the door quietly as he left.

Rowan rubbed her neck as the tension there moved up into the base of her skull. She looked around at the perfectly organised office. Tess had proven her worth long ago, and Rowan had just pulled apart what they'd built together in moments. She'd messed things up, as always. She focused on the day's orders and sent Stef a message asking him to meet her at the pub at lunchtime. The morning flew by, and she went to the pub ready to find answers.

Stefan looked up from his pint. "What do you want to talk to me about, Rowan?"

Rowan bit her lip. This wasn't her strong suit. "I just thought it would be good to have a chat about how things are working."

"We never do that." He sipped his beer and licked the foam from his top lip.

"And maybe that should change. I'm always interested to know how you're getting on. You've been with the company for nearly fifteen years now."

"I have, Rowan, and I'm very grateful for the opportunity. When I started here, my English wasn't so good, but your dad gave me a chance, and now Kasia and I have the children and our house. We have a good life." He smiled broadly.

"I'm glad, Stef. Dad and I both really value the work you put into the company."

"I'm sorry there have been mistakes recently." His smile faded.

"Everyone makes mistakes. What about overall? Do you think things work well? Is everything okay with Charlie?"

"Yes. He's my mate." His eyes widened.

"And the issues with Tess?" She left it there. If he wanted to speak up, she wasn't going to lead him.

"She's a good worker." He looked away. "But she likes to lord it over Charlie, and he doesn't like that."

That phrase again. "What do you mean by lording it over him, Stef? What does that look like?"

He frowned. "I'm not too sure. But Charlie doesn't like it, and he says she doesn't know her place."

Rowan felt the anger rise. "And what is her place, Stef?"

His eyes drifted away again. "I don't... He says women shouldn't be working in printing." He looked up. "Not you, Rowan. It's your business and you've worked your way up, but Charlie says Tess thinks she can just walk in and take over, and that's not fair." He took a long drink.

"Stef, you know that's up to me and Dad, right? Not Charlie."

His head bobbed. "Yes, of course. Charlie has opinions on a lot of things. He says that I can do most of the work because I'm so young and strong, so it's only fair."

Rowan rubbed her face. How had she never noticed this going on? But Tess had, and she'd paid for it. "Does that happen a lot?"

He nodded but kept his eyes on his beer. "It's why I've made a few mistakes. I don't have time to check properly, because I need to get the work finished." He paused and looked up. "And when Charlie messes up, he says it was me. But I try my best, Rowan. I don't like to make mistakes."

"I know, Stef. You're a good worker. And were things worse this week?"

"Oh, yes. Charlie said we had to do as little as possible

to make Tess look bad. Then you wouldn't leave her in charge again. But I couldn't do that, so he left me to work on my own. And then when she asked him to help Keith with a job because I was busy, he got really angry and was very rude to her. She sent him home and said you would deal with him when you returned."

She gritted her teeth. She'd had no idea Charlie could be so underhanded. "Thank you for being honest with me, Stef. I might need to talk to you about this again with Dad."

His eyes widened.

"Your job's safe. You're a great asset to this company. But we need to make sure people are treated fairly. Charlie gets paid the same as you. He should be doing his share of the work, and I won't have anyone mistreating their colleagues in our company." She finished her Coke. "You get back to work, and we'll talk later, okay?"

He nodded, drained his glass, and stood. "Thank you, Rowan." He hesitated. "I don't want to get Charlie in trouble. But...I didn't like how he was behaving. It didn't make me feel good."

She watched him leave and lowered her head to the table. What a mess. And she'd put all the blame on Tess, showing no confidence or trust in her at all. She let out a long groan before she picked herself up and headed back to speak to her dad. She found him in the office and quickly updated him on what Stef had told her.

"Yes, loyalty is important, Dad. But risking contracts to make a colleague look bad doesn't show much company loyalty, does it?"

"We don't know he did that, love."

He looked pale, and she hated having to burden him with this, but if Charlie was taking advantage of his friendship with her dad, she needed to address it.

"They've got a delivery this afternoon. Why don't I go out with Charlie, and you can have a chat with Stef? And maybe ask Keith what he's picked up on."

Her dad scratched his head. "I'll do it if you think it's necessary. But can't we just take everyone to the pub and get them to make up?"

"No, Dad, we need to get to the bottom of this. Tess is sitting at home, waiting to hear whether she's got a job or not."

"Oh, bless her. Should I ring her?"

"And tell her what? Let's get things sorted out here, and we'll talk to her then. I told her we'd pay her until things were sorted. We'll fix this together, Dad, okay?"

He nodded, and she left him in the office. She found Stef in the loading bay, stacking boxes into the van. She thought back to the first time she and Tess had kissed in the back of that van and how their relationship had developed since then. Had she blown it all by getting too protective about her dad and the business? The business she didn't even want to run. How could she explain to Tess that she'd messed up? She dragged her thoughts back to the present and smiled at Stef. "Afternoon, Stef. Are you able to stay and help Dad with something, please? I'll do the delivery." She took the boxes from him, and he nodded wordlessly and made his escape. She heard the cab door open, and Charlie appeared from the side of the van, sausage roll in hand.

"Hi, Charlie. Hard at it, I see."

He stuffed the rest of the pastry into his mouth and wiped his hands on his overalls before hurriedly picking up the last box. "We started early. I was just having a quick break."

"How early? Keith texted this morning to say he was going to be late unlocking the door. How did you get in?"

229

"Well, not early as such, but we got a lot done today."

"That's great, Charlie. Let's get going then."

He turned from the back of the van. "Where's Stef?"

"He's helping Dad with something, so you're stuck with me."

"Ah, that's good."

She closed the van and headed for the passenger door. Charlie was already there. "You can drive, Charlie. I've had a long week." She turned her nose up in distaste as she swept the mounds of food wrappers and coffee cups off the dashboard and into the footwell. Charlie settled himself in the driver's seat. "And do me a favour, Charlie, don't go home until you've cleaned this van. It's disgusting."

"That's Stef's fault. He's a right slob. I've told him, but he doesn't listen." He pulled out onto the road. "But it's been hectic here, Rowan. It's not the same without you organising everything."

"Is that right?" She didn't have the energy for small talk, and she certainly didn't want to hear his opinions on Tess's management skills, so the journey was a quiet one. When they arrived at the client's business, a small flower shop on the edge of town, Charlie jumped down and went into the front of the shop to announce their arrival. Rowan opened up the back of the van and lifted out the first couple of boxes.

The side door of the shop opened and Doreen, the florist, stepped out. She was a long-standing customer, and her face lit up when she saw Rowan.

"Good to see you, Rowan."

She took the boxes and headed back in. Rowan picked up a couple more and followed her. Charlie was inside the back of the shop and took the boxes from Doreen at the last moment and hefted them onto a shelf. He followed Rowan back out and picked up a single box before hurrying back in. He was good at looking busy without doing much.

When they'd finished unloading, Doreen counted the boxes and frowned. "I thought I'd ordered two thousand brochures this time. That's only a thousand."

"I don't think so, love. We've delivered what you've ordered." Charlie stood close to the diminutive customer, and she stepped back.

Rowan had her phone ready to sign off the delivery, so she quickly checked the details. "You're right, Doreen. I'm so sorry. We'll get the rest of the order to you tomorrow morning." She glared at Charlie. He was working late to get this fixed, and she wasn't accepting any excuses. The ride back was silent, and she could see his jaw clenching in her peripheral vision, as though he was biting back whatever he wanted to say. She didn't want to hear it.

When she arrived back, Rowan went straight to the office. Her dad was nursing a mug of tea. He looked up. "Where's Charlie?" His frown suggested he hadn't had glowing reports from Charlie's co-workers.

"He's in the break room. What did Stefan and Keith say?" She sat down and her dad pushed a pack of sandwiches across the desk.

"I guessed you might be hungry."

"Thanks, Dad." She tore them open. "So?"

He sighed. "They confirmed everything you told me. I think Charlie convinced Stef that he'd lose his job if he complained, so he's just been getting on with it." He ran his hand through his thin hair. "I'm so disappointed, Ro. He's worked for me since the beginning. I thought we were friends."

Rowan squeezed his hand. "I wouldn't take it too personally, Dad. He's not evil, just lazy, and a bit of a bully.

He won't have thought about the impact this would have on you."

Her dad turned his hand over and squeezed hers back. "You're such a good daughter, Ro." He reached out with his other hand, and she dropped her sandwich and clasped hands.

"I think I'm going to retire. Properly, I mean. Sign the whole business over to you."

Rowan knew her smile wasn't as wide as her dad would have expected, but she was struggling to smile at all. A year ago, this news would have pleased her. To know her dad would rest, and she'd be in full control of the business would have been a good outcome. But this past week, she'd really come to terms with how much she enjoyed drawing, and her tutor had assured her she was good enough to make a career from it. By the end of the week, she'd been seriously considering talking to her dad about going part-time and making Tess general manager. Then her dad had called in a panic, and now that idea was in tatters.

She found herself nodding to something she didn't want. Same old Rowan, waiting for life to happen to her. "Let's decide what we're going to do with Charlie, then I'll go and talk to Tess."

She was resigned to running the business. It had always been her destiny. She'd just allowed herself to dream a little lately. She'd have to focus on work and see if she had any chance of patching things up with Tess. *Trust me to mess things up.*

TWENTY-EIGHT

Tess drove home, rubbing away the tears running down her face. She couldn't stop replaying the events over and over in her head, but she couldn't see where she could have done anything differently. This morning's clash with Charlie had been the worst. He'd refused to help Keith pack an order of posters, and then he'd whispered to her that she'd only got the job because the boss was stupid enough to sleep with her. When she'd sent him home, Derek had tried to intervene, and she'd reminded him Rowan had put her in charge. He must've rung Rowan immediately.

The injustice of everything stung so hard, and she couldn't believe Rowan had thought the worst of her. Their last few months had been so perfect, she should've known better. Good things like that never happened to her.

She felt weary to the bone as she unlocked the front door. Elsie was sitting at the dining table, studying on her laptop, and she looked up with a start as Tess entered the hallway. "Hi, Elsie. Early finish." She couldn't face explaining.

Elsie was wearing a strange expression. "Mum, come and sit down."

"Why, what's wrong?" An icy wave of fear travelled down her body.

"Nothing. Nothing terrible, anyway. I just need to talk to you."

She sat and looked across the table at Elsie. "What's going on?"

"I'm sorry, Mum." She pushed her hair out of her face. "I got home and Dad was here, picking Archie up."

"What? He's meant to be here till Tuesday."

"I know. Archie called him and said he wasn't happy here. You know what Dad's like. He was up the motorway like a shot."

"What? Why isn't he happy? We just had a row." She was struggling to make sense of anything in her already scrambled brain.

Elsie looked more closely at her. "You look awful. Are you ill? Is that why you're home so early?"

"No, I'm just exhausted, Elsie." She sank into a chair. "Trying to please everyone and making no one happy. I'm sick of it all." She rested her head on her arms and felt Elsie's fingers rubbing her shoulders.

"You make *me* happy, Mum. Did something happen at work?"

"I suspended Charlie. Derek and Rowan disagreed with my decision. She sent me home." Tess kept her head down, not wanting Elsie to see the tears that were brimming over again.

"Mum, they're lucky to have you. Jack will sort it out, I'm sure."

Elsie's touch on her shoulders was relaxing, but she just wanted to cry.

"Why don't you go and run yourself a bath? That'll make you feel better. I'll make you a cuppa and bring it up to you."

Tess forced herself to stand, but she couldn't stop the tears from falling.

"Oh, Mum, don't cry. It'll be okay." Elsie pulled some tissues from a nearby box.

Tess did her best to pull herself together. She blew her nose. "Sorry, Elsie, I didn't want to bother you with all of this."

"Go on." Elsie pushed her towards the stairs. "I'll bring you a drink."

Tess hauled herself up the stairs. Elsie was right. A bath would make her feel more human, and she'd decide what to do about Archie when she could think straight.

Almost an hour later, Elsie's knock on the door roused her from her now cooling bath.

"Mum, are you okay?"

"Yeah, I'll be out in a minute." She stood and grasped her towel, drying off quickly as she started to shiver. Maybe she was starting to come down with something, and that's why she felt so unable to cope. Once she was dressed in her warmest pyjamas with a steaming mug of coffee in her hand, she felt a little better. "Thanks, Elsie. Pass me my phone, will you?" She didn't want a row with Archie, but she needed to talk to him about his disappearance. He couldn't just march off if things didn't go his way. His phone went to voicemail. "Archie, call me, please." She hung up.

"He'll be too terrified to speak to you." Elsie snuggled up next to her on the sofa. "Why don't you leave him alone for a couple of days?"

"He doesn't just get to change plans without talking to me, Elsie. He's in the middle of his exams." She typed out a text to Pete. *It's not very supportive for you to pick Archie up the moment he's got a problem. He should've talked things through with me.* She didn't wait for a reply before she sent another. *If you're with Archie, could you ask him to pick up, please? I need to speak to him.* She tried calling again, but it went straight to voicemail this time. She swore and rang Pete.

He picked up immediately. "Leave him alone. He doesn't want to speak to you."

"I'm his mother, Pete, and he's still a child. He doesn't get to choose when to speak to me."

"He's sixteen. That's grown up enough to know what he wants. He says you've got no time for him anymore, so I don't know why you're even bothering."

It was pointless arguing with Pete, as he'd do everything he could to make things difficult for her. "Just ask him to call me, please." She hung up and turned to Elsie, who was watching her as she sipped her coffee.

"He'll calm down, Mum, and he'll start missing you. I'll speak to him when I go back on Sunday. He'll apologise, I know he will."

She rested her head back on the arm of the chair. "Is it bedtime yet? I just want this day to be over."

"It's six thirty, sorry. What do you fancy for dinner?"

Tess roused herself. Elsie had exams next week. She didn't need to be running around after her dramatic mother. "I'll sort it. Jacket potatoes?"

"Ooh, yeah. You can't beat a bit of comfort food."

Tess propelled herself off the chair with as much energy as she could muster. "Find us a good film to watch, and our Friday night's sorted."

As she was preparing dinner, the doorbell rang. She

wasn't expecting any deliveries, but she heard Elsie's voice and another lower response.

"Mum." Elsie was at the door. "Jack's here to talk to you."

She stepped aside, and Tess was confronted with Rowan, standing in the doorway, her hands shoved in her pockets and her teeth gripping her bottom lip. For once, her heart didn't lift at the sight of Rowan. She was so disappointed in her, and she didn't have the energy to deal with it tonight. She stood silently watching Rowan as she shuffled her feet.

Elsie took over. "Mum, go on into the room with Jack. I'll finish dinner." She took the block of cheese out of Tess's hands and propelled her towards the door. "Just hear what she's got to say," Elsie muttered.

Tess shrugged. "Fair enough. Come on in, Rowan." She led the way into the lounge and sat in her favourite chair.

Rowan sat opposite, perched on the very edge of the sofa, her large hands hanging loosely between her knees. "I'm sorry, Tess. You were bang on about Charlie. We should have listened to you immediately and not assumed the worst."

"And what was 'the worst,' Rowan? That I was some sort of power-crazed dictator?"

Rowan's mouth opened wide as she struggled to respond. "No, of course not, never." She rubbed her hands together. "I thought I'd given you too much responsibility, too soon, and you'd struggled. But I should've known better. You're better at running that business that Dad or I ever were. Please come back?"

The question was asked with such desperation Tess realised she actually had some power for once. She wasn't sure if she cared. "Of course I'll come back. I need the job. And what about Charlie?"

"He's had a written warning, and we'll set him some clear goals for the next three months. If he meets them, he can stay." Rowan's silver eyes flickered across her face. "Is that...okay with you?"

She waved a hand. "Of course. All I ever wanted was for him to pull his weight and treat me with a little respect."

Rowan smiled hesitantly. "So we're all good then?"

Tess shrugged. She needed to say how she felt. "I think we should take a break from seeing each other."

Rowan's head shot up, her eyes wide. "What?"

"I'm spreading myself too thin, Rowan. My kids need me these next couple of months. Archie's moved to his dad's and won't come back because he feels like I don't care anymore. I need to focus on them." She considered her next words. "And you really hurt me, Rowan. You didn't give me a chance to explain. You didn't trust me, you just assumed the worst. I've had enough of being treated unfairly and getting shouted at."

Rowan stood. "It was a mistake, Tess. I'm sorry. But what we've got is wonderful and worth fighting for. You'll work things out with Archie, but you can't give up on us. You just can't."

Tess felt her defences kick in. Rowan was standing over her and telling her what she could or couldn't do with her life. She was never going back there. She summoned the last of her energy and stood. "I can do anything I want with my own life, Rowan. You need to leave. I'll see you at work on Monday." She strode to the door and held it open. Rowan stared at her in disbelief, but she didn't budge. "Bye, Rowan." She wasn't proud of the coldness in her voice, but she needed to take back some control of her life, and this was a good place to start.

Rowan continued to stare, as if she was trying to think of something to say. Then she moved, as quickly as she could, towards the door.

Elsie emerged from the kitchen behind her. "Night, Jack. See you on Sunday for the big game!"

Rowan didn't turn. She didn't even look at Tess as she marched out and got into her car. Tess closed the door to the sound of her reversing out of the drive at speed. She felt empty.

Elsie was standing there watching, oven gloves in hand. "What the hell was that about?"

She threw her hands up in frustration. "Leave it, Elsie, I haven't got the energy."

Their meal was subdued, and as soon as she had cleaned up afterwards, Tess excused herself and headed for bed.

"Night night, Mum. Things will seem better tomorrow."

Tess smiled as enthusiastically as she could muster. She doubted that. A night of sleep wouldn't remove the memory of Rowan's face when she'd said they were over. That was etched into her brain as if Rowan had drawn it herself. She welcomed the few hours of oblivion ahead before she had to start all over again tomorrow.

TWENTY-NINE

Cara opened the door, baby Eli in her arms. "Rowan, what's wrong? Is it your dad?"

Rowan saw the look of alarm on her face and realised she should have let Willow know she was coming. What an idiot she was, so tied up with her own misery she hadn't thought about how her arrival would look. "Oh God, Cara, I'm sorry. I should've rung or something. No, Dad's fine. I'm fine. I just needed a change of scenery." She trudged inside as Cara held the door for her, peering at her closely as she passed.

"Are you sure? You look worse than I do, and I've not slept for a month."

Rowan knew she must look terrible. Her eyes were gritty from the tears that had flowed intermittently on her journey down the motorway, her head was throbbing from the effort of trying to drive through the tears, and her bottom lip felt as though she'd chewed her way through it. "I, um, just need to think a few things through, and I was hoping you'd be able to put me up for a few nights. I'm so sorry I didn't call first." She was seriously considering running out of the house and sleeping in her car to avoid Cara's keen observation. What had she expected, that Cara and Will would just give her a place to stay with no questions asked?

Cara sighed. "You can stay as long as you need, honey. It's the box room now, I'm afraid. The guest room's the nursery these days."

"Of course, yeah. I can make the bed. I'm sorry, Cara, I wasn't thinking straight. The last thing you two need is me causing disruption. You must be knackered."

Cara shifted the sleeping baby onto her hip and pulled Rowan into half an embrace. "I meant it. You're always welcome here. Go and get yourself settled, and I'll put the kettle on. Willow's out at a quiz night, but she should be home soon."

Rowan straightened and hoisted her rucksack onto her shoulder. "I'll put this upstairs then I'll make the tea. You go and sit down." The last thing she wanted was to sit and have a cup of tea and a chat, but she'd imposed herself on her sister-in-law so the least she could do was be polite.

When she carried two mugs of tea into the lounge ten minutes later, Cara was half asleep on the sofa and baby Eli was just starting to stir, making small, cute noises. She put the mugs safely out of the way and leaned down to take him from his exhausted mother, who muttered her thanks and curled up on the chair. Cradling his head gently, Rowan pulled him close and inhaled the unforgettable baby smell as her body relaxed. She lowered herself slowly onto the sofa and propped her legs up so she could look down at her tiny nephew while he rested against her knees. He stared up at her with huge brown eyes. She stared back and wished everything made her as happy as looking at this perfect little person, so unaffected by anything that was happening around him. They stayed like that for a while until Eli started to fidget and grizzle. Rowan looked around for entertainment within arm's reach and found a cloth toy that made different sounds. She waved it in front of Eli's face and rustled it. His eyes followed it, transfixed. If only she was as easily pleased. The front door opened, and she heard Willow manoeuvring herself into the hallway. She would've seen Rowan's car in the driveway, so she waited for her while Eli grabbed at the toy.

Willow entered the room and wheeled herself around in front of her. She glanced at her wife, asleep on the sofa. "What's wrong, big sis? You've not come down here just to see your nephew, have you?"

Her expression was so full of concern that Rowan felt a rush of gratitude that she had people in her life who loved her. To her horror, she felt her eyes fill up, and she couldn't stop the tears that fell down her cheeks.

Willow reached for the baby and expertly scooped him onto her lap, where Eli gurgled and grabbed at her fingers. She indicated a box of tissues on the side table. "I don't think I ever remember seeing you cry. This has got to be bad. I know you'd have let me know if Dad was ill, so I'm assuming this is about Tess?"

Rowan blew her nose as quietly as she could without waking Cara. "I'm sorry. I'm being self-indulgent. Tess and I broke up, and it hit me harder than I expected. I didn't know what to do, so I just got in the car and drove."

"Oh, Ro, I'm so sorry to hear that." Willow moved closer and squeezed Rowan's hand. "You'll get a proper cuddle when this little fella is in his cot. Tess was good for you, and last time I saw you both, she seemed pretty smitten. What changed?"

"Working together got a bit stressful, and I made a bad

decision, as I always do. I shouted at her and made her feel like I didn't trust her. And her son started playing up during his exams. I guess she had to decide what was most important to her, and I lost." She hated the self-pity she could hear in her voice. It was her own fault Tess had dumped her. She'd let her down.

"That sounds like the sort of stuff all couples have to deal with, Rowan. Are you sure it's over? Did you talk it through when things were less emotional?"

No, because I ran away and turned my phone off. "I don't think Tess wanted to talk about it. She made her feelings very clear."

"If there's one thing I've learned recently, it's that kids make you irrationally sensitive, Ro. Maybe after Tess calmed down, she thought about how important you are in her life. Did you apologise for what you'd done?"

"Not really. I tried to, but then she talked about us splitting up, and I got angry again and told her what she should do. I should've known that would upset her."

Cara stirred on the chair and sat up suddenly. "Shit, how long was I out? Oh, hi, honey, you're back." She stood and stretched, leaning down for a kiss with Willow. "I'll take sleeping beauty and get him settled for the night. Don't keep that one up too long, she looks wrecked." She took Eli from her wife and gave her another kiss, blew one at Rowan, and left the room.

"Night, Cara, and thanks," Rowan called softly after her. Her head dropped involuntarily back onto the cushions.

"I'm not going to keep you up at all, sis, you need to get some rest. Fancy a morning dip in the sea tomorrow?"

Rowan raised her head to look at her. "It's May. Won't the sea still be pretty cold?"

"I go once a week, there's a whole bunch of us. There's an all-terrain wheelchair so I can get in easily. We've kept it up all winter, so I'm acclimatised." She grinned. "There's a wetsuit available for wimps though, if you're interested." She tipped her head to one side. "You used to love going for a swim."

"I do love the sea, in warm weather." Swimming had always been the one activity they'd been able to do together as kids. They'd spent as much time in the water as they could, mostly at their local pool as they lived so far from the sea. And on summer trips to the seaside, their dad had struggled to get them on dry land at all. "I don't know. Let me see how I feel in the morning."

"Go to bed. I'll lock up down here. You might want to use earplugs if you've got them. Our nights tend to be quite noisy."

As Rowan trudged up the stairs, she doubted anything would wake her tonight. Her emotional exhaustion was matched by the physical. It had been a long day in so many ways. Willow was right about Tess. She must have felt so hurt by Archie's moving out, as well as guilty for making him think he wasn't a priority. Then Rowan had come marching in making demands. No wonder she'd reacted so badly. And Rowan hadn't tried to put it right; she'd just walked away. Run away, in fact. She'd told Tess their relationship was worth fighting for and then walked away from it all. And after how long Tess had spent being told she was worthless, that must have felt devastating for her. She didn't need someone like Rowan letting her down. And Rowan knew she'd lost something that could have been real, and true. As always, she'd messed up.

Rowan had been moping around the house for a couple of days, staring out the window at the unseasonably bad weather. Today she felt particularly low, knowing she was missing the game. She sat in the bay window seat, watching the raindrops slide down the windowpane. She followed one with her finger, until it joined with all the others and became indistinguishable. She sighed and hoped the weather back home was better. Today was such an important fixture, but she could never have faced everyone, especially with Tess there. It was better she just stayed out of the way.

She'd tried to stay out of Willow's way too. She didn't need any more lectures about how she could have handled things better. She was under no illusions that she was in this position because of her own stupidity, but that only reinforced the feeling that she was bound to screw up any relationship she was in, and Tess had been right to end it.

Willow and Cara had gone out for the day to visit friends. Last night, as she sat silently between them, pretending to watch TV, Cara had pleaded with her to come with them.

"You need to get out of the house, take your mind off things. Our friends have got two-year-old twins. They're guaranteed to distract you from everything."

Rowan had fobbed her off, saying she'd decide tomorrow, but this morning she'd stayed in bed until she heard them leave, knowing they'd be disappointed with her but unable to do anything else. Calling her dad and Becca the day before had been painful, but she couldn't just disappear without telling people not to worry. Willow had rung her dad when she arrived, but he deserved a proper explanation. She'd told him she messed it up with Tess, and she needed some time away. He'd clearly been worried about her, but he'd told her to relax and take a few days out. He offered to step back up and run things at work, but Rowan had reassured him Tess was more than capable of running the business in her absence, and it might be better if he left her to it. Tess didn't need to be micromanaged on top of everything else. She hoped Charlie was behaving. He'd be out on his ear when she got back if he wasn't. When she got back. What did that even mean now? Could she work with Tess now she'd messed things up so badly? The thought of being around her and no longer having what they'd shared was unbearable.

She leaned her head against the cold glass of the window and let out a moan. She couldn't put Tess's job at risk. Maybe this was the time to step back completely and make Tess general manager. That would make everyone except Charlie happy, and he could leave if he didn't like it.

Becca had been more difficult to placate. She wanted to help, as she always did. She'd even offered to drive down and spend a few days with Rowan. Knowing how much Becca had to deal with already made Rowan feel even more wretched about how self-centred she was being. She'd promised Becca she'd be back soon and apologised for leaving her to explain to her teammates why she wouldn't be there today. Poor Becca. She hadn't been part of the team for years, but she'd kept turning up to support Rowan. Why couldn't Rowan be more supportive, instead of obsessing about her own petty problems and being a drain on Becca's energy? Now she was even messing up her friendships.

Eventually she dragged herself back to bed before Willow and Cara returned. It was so much easier than facing up to people. It felt like there was no way forward anymore.

THIRTY

Tess stood on the touchline, stamping her feet to try and keep them warm. How was it still so cold in May? She'd barely noticed what a miserable spring they were experiencing this year when she'd been happily spending time with Rowan. Now the poor weather seemed to reflect her mood as an icy wind cut through her coat.

She looked around. There were very few Haresby spectators who'd made the two-hour trip today. It was a shame because the girls needed all the support they could get. They'd finished their pre-match warm up and had gone back inside before kick-off, but they'd been visibly unsettled. Although Rowan wasn't the team captain, she rarely missed a game, and her absence was keenly felt. By Tess, too, if she was being honest. She realised she'd never watched the team play without Rowan, and she was looking forward to it much less enthusiastically. That made her feel guilty. She was meant to be here for Elsie, and that just compounded the feeling that she'd made the right choice. Rowan distracted her from her family, and that wasn't right.

When Derek had rung her yesterday morning and

asked if she could manage the business for the next week, she hadn't been surprised. It wasn't in Rowan's nature to confront problems and talk them through. Tess knew that, but it still pissed her off. But she'd been surprised Rowan would choose to miss this game. It was a key one for their league standing, and they would need every strong player.

"What brings you to a cold field in the middle of nowhere?"

She looked up from her musing and smiled as she saw Jules approaching. She'd often made it to home games this season but rarely made the long journeys to away games. "I sacrificed enough weekends in my playing days," she'd explained to Tess once. "My Sundays are now about relaxing, eating, and drinking wine."

"I'm supporting my teenage daughter. What's your excuse?"

"I thought you might need a bit of company." Jules pulled her close. "How are you feeling?"

"Pretty miserable, to be honest. How did you know?"

"Becca called me. She's worried about Rowan, but Derek has assured me she's just gone away to visit her sister." She paused. "Two days before one of the hardest away fixtures in the calendar. Tell me what happened."

Tess leaned into Jules, making the most of her body heat. She'd spent the weekend trying not to think too much about it. She'd resisted the urge to drive to Pete's and haul Archie back home. Instead, she'd taken herself out for a long walk yesterday and tried to clear her mind. Going back to work with Charlie this week wasn't going to be an easy ride. And thinking about Rowan hurt too much. But maybe talking it through would help her process what had happened. "It's complicated. We had some trouble at work, and Rowan decided it was all my fault without even discussing it with me or waiting to hear my side of what was happening. I've put a lot into that business over the last few months, and I thought I'd proven my worth. But she treated me like I was no one."

Jules tightened her hug.

"Archie started playing up at the same time, and I didn't have the energy to deal with it all. I told her we should stop seeing each other, and then she tried to tell me what to do. So I told her to get out. I assume she ran away to Brighton, because now I've got to run the show single-handed again this week."

"Sounds like she struck a nerve. Do you want to fix it?"

"I don't know. After I had a good night's sleep, it hit me how much it hurt to end things. It still hurts, but I don't want to be treated like that."

Jules took her by her shoulders and pulled her around to face her. "Defeat does not become you, Tess. You're all about the sunny disposition and endless optimism."

"Well maybe there's an end to it after all." She sighed. "I don't want to be with someone who doesn't value me. I've been there. It's not pleasant." She knew she was being unfair. Until the problems at work, Rowan had always made her feel valued. In fact, she'd made her feel things she'd been waiting her whole life for.

"When she gets back, you two really need to talk. What you had was too good to throw away over one row."

"For fuck's sake, Julia, have you tried getting her to talk? It's like squeezing blood from a stone." She lowered her voice when people turned at her outburst. "I'm tired of everything, Jules. I don't know if something that's such hard work is good for me."

The girls ran out onto the pitch and the game was soon underway, stalling their conversation for now. The game started with a strong attack from the home team. Jai had been moved to centre from the wing, while a less experienced player covered her position, and it soon became clear none of them could cope with the attack of the stronger team. Hannah did her best to rally them, but they ended the first half twenty points down. Their performance picked up slightly in the second half, but they didn't manage to claw back the points, and the final score was a reflection of how much the team had missed Rowan's quiet, steady presence in the backs.

"Well played, Hares. Unlucky." They patted the disconsolate players on their muddy backs as they passed. Tess gave Elsie a brief hug while trying not to get too dirty herself.

"Rowan's needed more than she thinks," Jules muttered.

Tess knew that was true, and not just by her team. But could they find a way to talk their issues through, and if they did, what was to stop Rowan behaving in the same way again?

THIRTY-ONE

The chill of the water seeped through the rash vest and into Rowan's flesh. After days of nagging from Willow, she'd finally agreed to go for a swim. She'd sat on the towering bank of pebbles and stared into the murky water unenthusiastically. But she was there to appease her sister and saying yes had been easier than trying to find yet another excuse, so she'd got in as quickly as she could so as not to prolong the agony. Now that she was in, Willow was messing about with her friends closer to shore, and she was beginning to wish she hadn't bothered. She turned and looked out to sea. It was a grey morning, and the sky blended with the sea on the horizon, matching her mood perfectly. She took a deep breath, knowing that submerging her head for the first time would be a shock, and it was, for a moment. Then she struck out, enjoying the sensation of moving through the water with powerful strokes. After a minute or two, she didn't feel cold any longer, and the water soothed her body and her mind. She swam for a while longer towards the grey horizon, emptying her mind of her problems.

When she turned to get her bearings, she was surprised at how far she'd come. She could just about make out the other swimmers, their hats and tow floats dots of colour near the beach. A couple of more serious swimmers were further out but parallel to the beach, nowhere as far from the shore as she was. It probably wasn't the best idea to just strike out for France on her own, there were currents out here that she had no knowledge of, and Willow would start to worry. But she was reluctant to give up the solitude yet, so she lay back in the water for a few minutes, making the most of the peace. All she could hear was the wind and the occasional cry of a gull.

Eventually, without any activity, the cold started to seep into her bones, so she flipped herself around and headed back, correcting her path to compensate for the current. It had driven her further along the beach but not too far to worry about. Her strokes were less frantic now that she'd burned off some of her nervous energy, but she still made good headway. Her mind drifted back to Tess as she neared the shore, but whether it was the cold water or the silence, for once her thoughts were calm and not full of the internal voices that told her she would never do the right thing.

She'd really messed it up, she knew that. Tess had been frantic that day, in part due to Rowan's own behaviour about the work issues. Now, in the tranquillity of the open sea, she accepted how her behaviour had pushed Tess's buttons and forced her to defend herself like she'd been doing for years.

But Tess was worth putting up a fight for. She was so strong and had been through so much, she deserved someone who could be strong for her too. But could Rowan really be that person? If she put aside all her own insecurities, Rowan knew in her heart that she had to be.

She wasn't the lost, guilty child she'd been when her mother had died, and she needed to understand and accept that, if she was going to become the person she wanted to be, for herself and for Tess.

And if she lost Tess now, she would never be the same again. She thought about what it was that Tess needed as she swam back toward the shore. She recalled Tess's body language when she'd been angry about Charlie. Rowan had stood over her and shouted. How many times had that happened in Tess's life before? But instead of her usual pattern of beating herself up about her actions, Rowan felt the need to be better for Tess. She needed to work out her issues; Tess deserved that, and she had to make it happen. And, maybe, not just for Tess. She had a life to live, and if she wanted something better, then she needed to stand up for it. Tess made her feel visible and appreciated and interesting, and she needed to do the same for Tess to show her how loved she was.

Loved? Rowan choked on a mouthful of seawater. She retched and lifted her head out of the water for a moment, treading water as she regained her breath. Was that what this was? Who was she kidding? She was so in love with Tess it made her life before look like a half-drawn sketch, scribbled with a blunt pencil. Being with Tess was a beautiful full-colour illustration of life.

She swam back with a new sense of purpose and was soon within a safe distance of shore.

Willow swam towards her. "Rowan, what the hell were you thinking? You haven't even got a tow float. There's boats and all sorts out there."

Rowan looked back at the grey expanse and smiled. "I didn't see a soul. It was amazing." She turned back to her sister, who opened her mouth, then closed it again, and smiled back.

"I'm glad you enjoyed it. Nothing can beat a good sea swim."

"Do you want to swim for a bit longer?" Rowan hoped the sense of resolve wouldn't leave her when she was back on dry land but just in case, she wanted to extend her dip as long as she could.

Willow checked her watch. "We've been in nearly an hour." She looked back at Rowan. "Go on then. It's not often I get to swim with my big sis these days." She launched herself away from Rowan. "Race you to the pier."

Rowan swam after her, laughing. She didn't know if she could make things right with Tess, but she knew she'd spent too much of her life not acting. If she didn't succeed it wouldn't be because she'd been too afraid to try. Those days were over.

THIRTY-TWO

Tess poured herself a generous measure of whisky, then doubled it. She took her glass and dropped heavily into her chair by the fire. The week had been hell so far. Charlie had sullenly done what was asked of him and no more, and Derek had barely been in the office. She was glad he was taking it easy, but it felt as though he was avoiding her since Rowan had left. She wasn't sure how much he knew about what had happened, but the fact he'd had to tell her Rowan had gone to stay with her sister must have told him all he needed to know. But he hadn't asked any questions. In fact, apart from sticking his head in the door a couple of times, he'd stayed clear. Tess had been working until way into the evenings to get all the orders packed.

She kicked off her shoes and rested her weary feet on the sofa, then took a long swig of her whisky, enjoying the burn as it made its way down her throat. She took a second gulp and rested her head back on the cushion of the chair, hating the silence in the house. Elsie would be staying at her dad's much more over the next few weeks while she got through the bulk of her exams. It had been agreed before they moved but now, with Archie gone as well, Tess thought the solitude might be the end of her. She tried to still her mind and relax, but as she took a long breath, the buzz of her phone startled her.

Hey, Mum, have you heard from Archie tonight?

Tess didn't really hear from Archie at all at the moment, unless she called him. When she'd dropped Elsie off last week, he'd been polite but subdued. She knew she needed to do something to fix their relationship, but she didn't want to cause any drama just before his exams. When they were over, she'd have a long talk with him about her having her own life to live and ask if he really wanted to spend the next couple of years living with his dad full-time. What would she do if he said yes? She didn't know how she would bear it, but he was old enough to make up his own mind. She only hoped Pete was serious about having him there. The novelty of getting one over on Tess would wear off eventually, and she wondered how much support he could offer to their sometimes-vulnerable son.

Not at all today, why? And how is your studying going?
Her phone lit up with a call from Elsie a moment later. "What's up? Is Archie okay?"

"I don't know." Elsie's voice was hesitant. "I don't want to get him in trouble, Mum."

"Just tell me, Elsie." A cold feeling started to well up inside her.

"He's probably fine, but he went out to a party with Max. That girl he likes was going to be there, Milly. Dad's been teasing him about talking to her all week."

"What's he doing going to a party on a school night? Where's your father?"

Elsie cleared her throat. "Erm, he's staying over at Lucy's the rest of the week. He says it's too busy here with us in the house all the time."

Tess felt the dread joined by anger. "He's left you to it in the house? All week?"

"He says I'm an adult, and we're old enough to be trusted, and there's plenty of food in the fridge. And that would be fine, but Archie doesn't really listen to me."

Tess switched her phone to speaker and threw it onto the seat next to her. She rubbed her forehead, trying to calm herself. "Elsie, he's supposed to be looking after you both, making sure you've got everything you need while you're doing your exams. Not..." She stopped herself. She needed to deal with the current situation instead of flying off the handle with Pete. "Where was Archie when you last heard from him?"

"Max texted me to say he'd left the party, and now he's not picking up."

"Left the party?" She guessed there was more to it than that.

"Max said he was talking to Milly, and her boyfriend turned up. I think he embarrassed Archie, and Max said he ran out of the house, and he didn't know where he was going."

"Anything else?" Tess pulled her shoes on as she spoke. The journey would be quick at this time of night, and she couldn't just sit here waiting to hear if Archie got home safe.

"He took a bottle of vodka from the party, Max said." Elsie's voice was subdued. "I texted Dad to ask if he's heard anything, and I've called, but he's not picking up."

"Fuck. Fuck. Fuck." She pulled herself together. "Sorry, Elsie. Do you have any idea where he might go?"

"No, not at all. He barely leaves the house. It's not like he's got a favourite place to be." Elsie paused again. "The party was on the edge of town, near the cemetery. If he's wandered off into the countryside, he might be hard to find. I've tried the location app, but he must've turned it off."

At least the weather had warmed up a little, and there were no open bodies of water nearby. Tess tried to reassure herself Archie would probably be fine, but her protective instincts made her desperate to be there and keep him safe. She looked at her watch. It was nearly nine thirty. "I'll be there by eleven at the latest. You stay at home and keep trying to call him. Let me know if you hear anything."

"Will do, Mum. Drive safely."

"And Elsie? Try and get some studying done. Please?"

She hung up and stood to grab her coat. As she turned to look for her car keys, her eyes drifted over the almost empty whisky glass on the table. *Shit.* She picked it up and swirled the dregs as she tried to remember how full it had been. Had she had a double? More? Since she'd had the children, Tess had maintained a very strict rule that she never had a drink if she was driving. Not even a taste of champagne or a half pint. She'd never broken that rule but now here she was, unsure of how much she'd even had. Suddenly the chance of killing someone else outweighed her instincts to protect her child no matter what. She put the glass down and sank onto the sofa. While she'd had a purpose ahead of her, she'd managed to keep it together. But the awfulness of everything bore down on her, and she started to sob. Pete's interfering in her parenting had brought this about. Why could Archie not understand she always had his best interests at heart? She put her face in her hands and let it all come out, the disappointment in herself, the unfairness of the situation at work, and Rowan. How had things gone so wrong? She'd thought she'd finally found some happiness, and it had just blown away on the first strong wind. Why couldn't she be happy *and* look after her family? Other people managed both.

She wrapped her arms around herself and collapsed into the cushions of the sofa, allowing the sobs to rock her body. She didn't have the strength to stop them anymore. Eventually, her head started to ache from all the crying. She forced her breathing to slow, and the sobs subsided. She sat up and wiped her face on her sleeve. What was she going to do about the immediate problem? She racked her brains for someone she could beg to drive her, but it was a big ask to take her nearly a hundred miles down the motorway at almost ten on a Wednesday evening. The only person she would have considered asking was Jules, but she was away at a conference. She'd have to tell Elsie she wasn't going to make it. She could call the police, but she didn't think they'd do much about a sixteen-year-old who'd left a party. They'd have to keep trying his mobile and hope he'd pick up eventually.

She dragged herself into the hallway bathroom and splashed water onto her hot face. She looked into the mirror and groaned. Her face was red and blotchy, and her eyes were so bloodshot they had a pink hue. But as she couldn't leave the house anyway, it didn't matter, did it?

The sound of the doorbell made her jump. Who could possibly be at the door at this time of night? She went cold. Surely not the police? She dashed to the front door and swung it open but instead of a police officer, Rowan stood there.

"What the fuck are you doing here, Rowan?" She couldn't help herself. Rowan was the last person she needed

IONA KANE

to see, reminding her of what she'd lost and how alone she was.

Rowan's mouth dropped open. "I'm sorry. I didn't realise the time." She looked down at her watch and frowned. "I was driving back from Brighton, and I wanted to talk to you as soon as possible." She cleared her throat. "But it's late, I wasn't thinking. I'll call you tomorrow." She started to turn and then swung back. "Are you okay, Tess? You don't look..."

"There's nothing for you to be concerned about, Rowan. I'll be at work on time tomorrow." She started to close the door, disgusted with her own coldness but desperate to get out of Rowan's presence.

Rowan stepped forward and put her hand on the door. "You know that wasn't what I was asking. Is something wrong?"

She was so close now, the need to bury her face in Rowan's chest and sob was overwhelming, but it was being with Rowan that had got her where she was now. That was the last thing she needed. She pushed the door, but Rowan pushed back more firmly.

"I'm not leaving you here like this, Tess. Please tell me what's wrong."

She looked up. If Rowan wasn't going to leave her in peace, she might as well make use of her. "Will you drive me to Pete's?"

Rowan's eyes widened. "If you need to get there, yes, of course. But you have to tell me what's going on."

Tess let go of the door and sat on the bottom stair as Rowan closed the door behind her. "Pete's left the kids to fend for themselves, and Archie's gone to a house party that went wrong, and now no one knows where he is."

"And you need to go and look for him?" Rowan nodded. "I'll take you, but we may need to stop for coffee."

Tess jumped up with a new sense of purpose. "I can do better than that." She went to brew some to take with them, while Rowan stood in the kitchen doorway. Tess chose to ignore her and finally thrust a travel mug into her hand. "It's the way you like it. I've made more for the journey." She held out a flask, and Rowan took that too and led her outside to her car. Rowan's Audi would be a much more comfortable ride than her own old wreck. But she was more concerned about the company than the transport. What would she and Rowan talk about for the next hour and a half? Maybe this hadn't been such good idea. But finding Archie was her priority.

As Rowan reversed the car out of the drive, Tess sighed and rested her head back against the plush leather upholstery.

Rowan glanced over. "I'm sorry I left you to run things without any notice. Have you had a long day?"

"I've had a long week, Rowan. One person can't run that business alone. You're going to need to think about what happens in the future when you're not around." She glanced at her as they pulled out. "Why are you back so soon? Your dad said you'd be away until the weekend." She couldn't see Rowan's face clearly in the darkness, but she kept her eyes on the road.

"I came back to talk to you." She shuffled in her seat. "But this isn't the time or place. Can we talk when we know Archie's safe?"

"It's going to be a long journey if we sit in silence."

Rowan didn't respond.

"Okay, I'm going to call Elsie and let her know what's happening. There's no way we're driving back tonight. I'm going to look for a hotel. Is that okay with you? Can you ask Keith to open up in the morning?"

"Yes, of course. And...I'm sorry if any of the problems with Archie are because of what happened with us."

As she made the call Tess wondered what Rowan wanted to talk to her about that couldn't wait until work on Monday. Elsie picked up and was pleased to hear Tess was travelling with Rowan.

"He's still not answering. I've sent him dozens of texts. Maybe you should try."

Tess hung up and sent Archie the sort of text that would usually receive an immediate response. But she got nothing back. She did a search for hotel room vacancies near Pete's house. No way was she spending another night in that house, whether Pete was there or not. She looked up from her phone.

"I've found a room at the Premier Inn, but they've only got one left. A twin. Will that be okay?"

Rowan glanced at her quickly, her face in shadows. "That's fine. I'm pretty tired. I'm sure I could sleep anywhere."

Tess felt vaguely guilty Rowan had just made a long journey home, and she'd asked her to turn around and get back on the motorway. "How was your visit to Brighton?"

"It was good to spend a bit of time with Willow."

She let it go. She didn't have the energy to keep up one end of the conversation for the entire journey.

"I'm sorry I ran away. I should've tried to get you to talk it through." Rowan took a deep breath. "I messed up, Tess, and I can't stand not being with you. I'm so sorry for everything."

Every inch of Tess's being wanted to touch her, to reassure her, and make all the hurt go away. But what if it happened again? She couldn't take the chance. "What do you want, Rowan?"

"I don't want to let you down." Her voice cracked and a tear glinted on her cheek in the light from passing headlights.

Tess reached over and wiped away the tear. Rowan grasped her hand and kissed her fingers. She pulled away. "You're right, this isn't the time. You need to keep your attention on the road."

Rowan nodded and rubbed her face briskly. "Why don't you try and get a bit of sleep. You look terrible."

"No, you must be knackered too. I'll try and stay awake to keep you company. Let's listen to some music." She went to turn on the radio but was confronted by a screen with too many options.

Rowan chuckled and pressed the screen a couple of times. "There you go. You can choose the station."

"There's more choice than I know what to do with. In my car, it's three stations or one of the tapes kicking about on the floor."

"Seriously, your car has a cassette player? And I thought it was bad enough you couldn't pick up calls."

Tess was so embarrassed about her heap of a car that she'd always been relieved when Rowan was so quick to offer to drive. She figured she was doing them both a favour not to have to travel in the dilapidated Volvo. "Nothing wrong with that. They were built to last, not like today's fancy gear." She waved at the display and laughed. "It's official; I've turned into my dad."

Rowan laughed again and laid her hand on Tess's leg.

Warmth spread through her body.

"Rest, I'll be fine with the music, honestly."

Tess tried to keep her eyes open, but between the

alcohol she'd consumed and the toll of the last couple of weeks, she felt her eyelids getting heavier. Her last thoughts were that everything would be okay. Rowan was by her side and between them, they'd find Archie and make things right.

THIRTY-THREE

Rowan rubbed her eyes and tried to ignore the gritty feeling in them. She really needed to pull over soon, but she understood how urgently Tess needed to find Archie. They weren't far away now, and she wondered what the plan would be when they got there if no one had heard from Archie. As if on cue, Tess's phone buzzed. It was on her lap with the screen facing down but it continued to vibrate, so Rowan assumed it was a call. Tess must be truly exhausted for it not to wake her. Rowan put her hand on her shoulder and shook her gently. "Hey, Tess." She shook again a little more insistently.

"What?" Tess shook her head, evidently unsure of where she was.

"Tess, you've got a call. It might be Archie."

Tess sat up straight and grabbed at her phone. She peered at the screen and picked up. "Archie, are you okay? Where are you?"

Her brow furrowed as Rowan heard an indistinct answer on the other end.

Tess switched to speaker. "I can't hear you, Archie."

"I'm sorry. Am I in trouble?"

Rowan thought that was what he said. His speech was slurred to the extent it was difficult to know for sure.

"It's okay, Archie. We just need to get you home safe. Do you know where you are?"

Tess's voice was calm and reassuring, showing no trace she'd been asleep moments before. He said something garbled about trees. Rowan didn't think it was going to help much.

"Right, Archie, just switch your phone location back on. Do you remember how to do that?"

Archie muttered something.

"I'll talk you through it, Arch. Go to settings."

Rowan was impressed with how well Tess was handling the situation, but she'd always had a cool head in emergencies. Archie muttered a couple more sentences Rowan couldn't make out, and Tess fiddled with her phone.

"That's it, Archie, good boy. I've found you. Now, sit tight and don't move from that spot. I'll ring you back in five minutes." She hung up and let out a long breath of relief.

"Send me the location, and we'll get it on the sat nav." Rowan flicked the screen to navigation.

When Tess's message appeared on the screen, she copied the coordinates from her message into the mapping app. "I guess this new-fangled technology has its uses."

Rowan smiled, despite the stressful situation, as the location came up on the map. She knew Tess was enthusiastic about technology. She didn't have a tape deck in her car to be retro, she just had a very old car. She often wished she could help Tess financially. She had more money than she needed. She owned a decent car, and her flat was paid off. What more did she need? She and Becca enjoyed holidays in the sun, but it was difficult for Becca to leave Ben for long, so they were more often than not long weekends away and were few and far between.

Perhaps if she stepped back from the business and they made Tess general manager, they could pay her a salary that would sort her financial problems. But kids were expensive, especially when they went to university, and she suspected Tess's money problems were far from over. They were less than twenty minutes away from Archie, which was a relief. She didn't know how much further she could safely drive. It felt like a lifetime since she'd got up this morning to go for a swim with Willow.

Tess made a quick call to Elsie and asked her to let Max know Archie had been found. Then she called Archie back. "We're nearly there. Can you see any houses or anything?"

Rowan looked at the screen. "Looks like he's near a leisure centre. I'll head for the car park."

"Can you see a leisure centre, Archie?"

Rowan suspected in his condition he would struggle to remember what a leisure centre was.

"It's okay, just stay where you are. We'll be there soon."

Tess continued to talk to her son as they got closer. Rowan guessed she didn't want him to forget they were coming and wander off. She flicked her eyes to the map. He appeared to be in a recreation ground of some sort. She tried to remember if her Maglite was still in the boot. She was sure it was. That would make things easier than trying to find him with the light of their phones.

She pulled into the deserted car park a few minutes later. The security lights must be on a timer as the whole place was in darkness. The car headlights lit their way to the far side of the car park, the nearest to Archie's signal. Beyond the low fence, Rowan could see football pitches. "He's out there somewhere."

They got out of the warm car into the chilly air, and Rowan saw Tess shiver. She was only wearing her DR Printing polo shirt. Rowan went to the boot of her car and rummaged for the flashlight, pleased when she located it. "Here." She pulled out her warm post-training top. "Sorry, it may not smell too fresh."

Tess shrugged it on then pulled up the inside for a sniff. "It smells of outdoors, and grass, and you."

Her smile was warm, and Rowan wished the circumstances were different, so she could finally tell Tess what she came to say. Instead, she ducked back into the boot and found an old fleece that didn't look too muddy. She pulled it on, glad of the extra layer as they headed to the playing fields.

"How many trees, Archie? A wood or just a row of trees?"

Rowan shone the torch ahead at the far end of the field.

"Can you see the torchlight, Archie?" Tess listened to the reply. "Are you sure? Try standing up and looking around."

They peered into the darkness. The torchlight lit up a figure momentarily, and Rowan swung the beam back to illuminate a staggering Archie, making his way towards them. Tess took off at a sprint, and Rowan jogged along behind.

Tess enveloped Archie in her arms. "I was so worried, Archie. What were you thinking?"

He started to sob. "I'm sorry, Mum. I didn't mean to do it."

He sobbed some more words into her shoulder as she hugged him. Rowan slipped the nearly empty bottle of vodka from his hand and hid it from Tess's view. It was enough for her to know he was drunk. She didn't need visual proof to add to her worry.

"Let's get you back home."

Rowan lit their way back with the torch. She unlocked the car and opened the back door, helping Tess to lower Archie onto the leather seat.

Tess looked at the plush upholstery and back at Rowan. "I'm worried he'll be sick."

"It doesn't matter, Tess. It's just a car, it'll clean up."

"Have you ever tried getting the smell of vomit out of a car seat? Have you got a bag or anything? I'll sit in the back with him."

Rowan pulled off her old fleece jacket. "This might work but really, it doesn't matter."

Tess threw her a grateful look and climbed into the back seat. Archie slumped against her, and she laid him down, his head on her knee. Rowan closed the door, got back into the driver's seat, and typed in the address Tess had given her. "We'll soon have you home, Archie." She turned to see Tess stroking the hair off Archie's face, and their eyes met. The moment, as stressful as it was, gave her hope.

Ten minutes later they arrived at a large, detached house with a green door.

"Pull onto the drive," Tess said.

Rowan did as instructed and between them, they managed to get Archie out of the car and up the steps.

A worried-looking Elsie opened the door. "Oh, thank God. Is he okay?"

"He'll be fine when he's slept it off," Tess said as they manhandled him up the stairs.

She kicked the door open to his room. For a skinny looking kid, Archie was a heavy dead weight, and Rowan was relieved when they finally lowered him onto his bed. Unfortunately, he immediately rolled over and threw up.

Tess shrugged. "It's not my rug." She rolled it up and carried it out of the room. "Just keep an eye on him for a minute, will you?" She returned quickly with a glass of water and a wet towel. "I was probably a bit optimistic about the hotel room. I'm going to need to sit with him or I won't be able to sleep, worrying he's choking on vomit." She sat on the bed and wiped Archie's face. "Why don't you head to the hotel and get some sleep?"

Rowan couldn't think of anything she'd rather do. Her eyelids felt like they were made of lead. But she didn't want to leave Tess here in what felt like enemy territory. "I can sleep on the sofa and drive you back in the morning. It's not a problem."

Tess scratched her chin. "Well, it might be. Elsie's been texting her dad all night in case he'd heard from Archie. If he comes charging back to play the hero..."

She didn't need to say anything else. Neither of them wanted Pete to turn up and find Rowan asleep in his house. She rubbed her face. "How will you get to the hotel?"

"As soon as I'm happy Archie's sober enough to stay alive, I'll get a cab. I don't want to be here any longer than I need to."

Close up, Tess looked even more exhausted. Her eyes were still bloodshot, and she was paler than Rowan had ever seen her. "Are you sure?" She wanted to take Tess in her arms and kiss her and tell her what an amazing parent she was. But she'd messed that up, and now she didn't know where she stood.

Tess nodded and turned back to Archie. "Yeah, I'll see you later."

Rowan turned to leave.

"Rowan?"

She looked back.

"Thank you so much for driving me here. I don't know what I'd have done without you."

Her tired eyes were full of gratitude.

"You're very welcome. I'm always here if you need me." She left them alone and went in search of Elsie, who was making coffee in the kitchen. "Don't make your mum's too strong. She's been surviving on caffeine for far too long today."

"Don't worry, I'll look after her, and I'll send her back to you as soon as possible."

She grinned cheekily at Rowan, who wondered if she knew she and Tess were no longer together. Rowan decided she could leave that for another day and just nodded. "Night, Elsie. Get some sleep."

She trudged to her car, relieved the hotel was only five minutes away. When she arrived and checked in, she went straight to the room and resisted the urge to collapse onto the bed. She had her bag from her trip to Brighton, so she could brush her teeth. She finally slipped between the covers with a sigh. The single bed was narrow, and she was accustomed to sprawling across her own king-size bed, but she wouldn't be awake for long. Her last conscious thoughts were about Tess. She hoped she would get some rest and that she wouldn't be subjected to any nonsense from Pete. This evening had been tiring and stressful, but she couldn't help feeling grateful she'd got to spend it with Tess.

The door opening quietly woke Rowan in the early hours, and she turned on a side light.

"Sorry," Tess murmured as she kicked off her shoes and headed for the bathroom.

"Is Archie okay?"

Tess emerged with Rowan's toothbrush. "He's sleeping, but Pete turned up and said he'd watch him the rest of the night." She disappeared again.

"Is that all he said?"

"It doesn't matter, Rowan. I'll tell you in the morning. Go back to sleep."

Rowan lay awake until Tess came back. "Are you okay?"

"I'll be better for some sleep." Tess headed to the other bed and then turned. "Is there room in there for me? I could really do with a cuddle."

Rowan threw back the covers and shifted as far back in the bed as she could. As Tess got in and switched off the light, she wondered how she would get any sleep at all with Tess's warm body backed up against her.

"Thank you," Tess said.

Rowan gave in to the urge to wrap her arm around her and pull her in even closer. She inhaled the familiar smell of Tess's coconut shampoo and found herself drifting straight back to sleep.

THIRTY-FOUR

Tess awoke to find herself alone in the bed. She quickly looked at the other bed, wondering if she'd driven Rowan away with her need for intimacy, but it hadn't been slept in. She felt surprisingly refreshed, considering how tired she'd been and the—she checked the time—four hours of sleep she'd managed. She lay thinking about the last twelve hours and how Rowan had been there for her unquestioningly. She'd pushed her away and said she needed to prioritise her children, but the moment she'd needed support, Rowan had been there. Could she really rely on her to be there always? Her feelings for Rowan were much stronger than she'd ever admitted, even to herself, so why was she so afraid to feel them? Because she needed to be in control, not controlled, whether that was by a person or by feelings so strong they scared her. She and Rowan could be friends, lovers even, but she couldn't let things get out of hand again, could she?

She finally got up to use the bathroom and rummaged through Rowan's bag to look for spare clothes. She found a clean T-shirt and a pair of boxers and smiled at the thought of borrowing Rowan's clothes. She headed for the bathroom. A shower had never seemed so attractive.

When she emerged, wrapped in a towel, Rowan was coming in the door, holding coffee cups and a couple of brown bags adorned with promising grease stains. It was the perfect sight, and Tess smiled warmly. "Oh, my brave hunter-gatherer, what have you brought me?"

"I know you can't stand instant." Rowan tipped her head towards the kettle. "So I nipped out for these."

"Thank you." She relieved Rowan of her burden, checked out the contents of the bags, and was happy to find a pain au chocolate. "Mm-mm. My favourite." She took a bite.

"I know."

Rowan watched her as she savoured the flaky pastry. She pushed the bag towards Rowan, who continued to stare. Tess looked away while she took a mouthful of her coffee, and when she looked back, Rowan's gaze had slipped to below the bottom of her too-short towel. Tess felt her bare skin tingle. How did Rowan have that effect just by looking at her? She needed to know where they stood, because Rowan made her feel more alive than she'd ever done in her life. She couldn't let that go. "Why don't you freshen up and then we can talk." She walked across to the bed as Rowan's eyes flickered from her to the bathroom door, as if wondering if she should undress here. Tess resolved the issue by dropping her towel. She slipped into Rowan's spare boxers and T-shirt. "I borrowed some clothes from your bag. I hope that's okay?"

Rowan nodded wordlessly, still staring.

Tess laughed. "Go on, I'll be waiting."

Rowan grabbed some clothes from her bag and did as she was told. Tess busied herself with drying her hair and thought about what she wanted to say to Rowan. She also remembered to send Archie a text, asking to talk before she headed back.

When Rowan emerged, half-dressed and with her hair tousled from towel drying, Tess dropped her phone onto the bed and smiled. "I wanted to be all business-like, but it appears the very sight of you is enough to make me go mushy inside. I miss you, Ro."

Rowan bit the skin of her thumb. "I've only been gone a few days."

She looked so uncomfortable, and it made Tess sad that she could make Rowan feel that way. "I meant I miss the old Rowan who used to tell me what was going on in her head and who made me feel special." Tess patted the bed next to her. "Come and sit down."

Rowan moved over and tucked her legs up under her. "I'm so sorry I didn't stay and try to talk things through with you. I knew how frazzled you were." She hung her head. "I behaved badly, Tess, and I can see how it must have made you feel. I promise that I'll be better in the future. I think you're the most incredible woman I've ever known, and I hate that I made you feel like anything less. I'm sorry."

Tess caressed her chin and lifted it gently until Rowan had no choice but to look into her eyes. "And I'm sorry for what I said to you. You've only ever supported me and helped the kids, and I must've made you feel like you were a burden." She looked up into Rowan's shining eyes. "I love being with you, Rowan. You make everything feel better, and I want to spend time with you. But we need to talk about what we're able to give to each other."

Rowan bit her lip again but Tess waited, giving her the time she needed.

"I ran because I thought we were over, and I didn't

know what that meant for me. It hurt so much, I couldn't think, and I didn't know what to do." She ran her fingers through her hair. "I love you, and I want to be with you, whatever that looks like. If you need me to stay away when your kids are at home, I can do that. I'll do whatever it takes to make you happy and to earn your trust to let me love you." She looked up with clouded eyes. "But at this moment, I just want to make love to you."

Tess moved back on the bed, slipped off her T-shirt, and pulled Rowan down close to her, until they were touching from hip to chest. Rowan's declaration of love was unsettling. She had to think about what that meant, and if she wanted to get in that deep. But right now, her priority was the immediate and physical connection she'd been missing for too long.

Too many layers of clothing separated them, and Tess tugged at Rowan's T-shirt until she raised her body enough to allow it to be pulled over her head. When she lowered herself back, her breasts touched Tess's, and Tess smiled at the shudder that went through Rowan's body, knowing how sensitive her nipples were. She moved her hand up to cup Rowan's smaller breast. "Do you like that?" She played with the nipple and ran it over her own hardening peak.

Rowan gasped. "Oh. Yes."

"Good." She tweaked the nipple a little harder, watching Rowan's reaction with fascination, and moved her other hand for a similar move on the other breast. Then she lifted her head and kissed Rowan hard, breathing in her gasps as she continued the attention on her nipples.

Rowan moved restlessly and slid her hands down to where the layers of clothing between them denied her the contact she clearly desired.

Tess pulled back. "Take your shorts off."

As Rowan lifted her weight to follow the command, Tess used the opportunity to roll Rowan onto her back. She plunged her tongue deep into her mouth, and Rowan groaned again. Tess pulled back and forced Rowan to look at her. "Tell me what you need."

Rowan's eyes were unfocused, and she shook her head. "Um..."

Tess tweaked her nipple to get her attention. "Don't think about it. What do you need?"

Rowan's whole body shook. "I need you inside me. I want you to fuck me."

Tess nipped her ear with her teeth. "Good."

She spread Rowan's legs even wider with her knees and moved her hand lower to run her fingers lightly down the soft skin, drawing patterns as she went. She kissed Rowan deeply as she slid her fingers through her soaking folds. She groaned. "Oh yes, you do need this, don't you?"

"Please, Tess. You're killing me." Rowan moaned.

Tess laughed as she thrust two fingers deep inside and started to move in a steady rhythm. She kept it up, enjoying the sensations, until Rowan moved more insistently against her.

"More," Rowan gasped.

"What was that?" Tess whispered.

"I need more of you."

"My pleasure." Tess added another finger and felt Rowan stretch to accommodate her. The feeling was so exquisite, it almost hurt. She could feel herself getting wetter by the moment. She increased the speed of her movements, and Rowan's hips bucked until her body went rigid and her head tipped far back. Tess took advantage and nipped her exposed neck, causing Rowan to let out a moan that almost became a scream as she climaxed. Tess watched in wonder as her climax seemed to be never-ending. As Rowan relaxed, Tess lowered herself onto her damp chest and listened as her breathing gradually slowed.

Tess stroked her hair and pulled the duvet up to cover her sweaty body. "For such a quiet person, you can really make some noise when you want to." She pulled Rowan as close as she could and watched her eyes flicker as she fell into a doze. She kissed Rowan's forehead and rested her face against her hair. She had surprised herself with her need to take Rowan so urgently. As always, their connection made for an intense experience. Unfortunately, she had worn out an already exhausted Rowan, who appeared to be sleeping quite deeply. Her own need was still very much an issue, and her borrowed boxers were a couple of sizes too small and were pressing down on her clit, which felt so swollen it should be showing through the sheets.

She slid her hand down and wondered if she could give herself some relief without disturbing Rowan. She slipped a couple of fingers into the warm wetness she had known would be waiting. She bit her lip in concentration to stop her hips from bucking and waking Rowan. It felt so good, and she was *so* ready.

The slow groan she let out was involuntary, and Rowan began to stir. She stilled her hand as Rowan opened her eyes. As she realised where she was, she smiled sleepily.

"Hey, there. I'm sorry, did I doze off?"

"Yeah, I think I wore you out."

"How very rude of me." Rowan pulled the duvet aside and looked down to where Tess's hand disappeared into her boxers. "Oh, I see you've been taking matters into your own hands." She smirked.

Tess felt her cheeks colour. "Well, no one else was

available, and I was left in a state of great need." She pulled her hand up, holding her fingers out for inspection.

Rowan licked at her fingers. She nodded approvingly and took the full length of Tess's finger into her mouth and sucked hard. Tess groaned and felt her centre pulse. Rowan lifted herself up on one elbow and made room on the bed for Tess to lie down fully. She relaxed onto her back, trusting Rowan with all her heart to treat her gently. Rowan smiled down at her and wrapped one arm around her waist, tipping her hips upwards. Tess let her knees drop outwards and opened for Rowan, who gazed down with a look of appreciation. She ran her fingers gently down the length of Tess, skating over the sensitive tissues with a teasing lack of pressure. She pushed her hips up to increase the pressure, but Rowan pushed her back down.

She looked up into Rowan's eyes and realised revenge for her earlier teasing might be on the cards. She let out a groan. "Please, Rowan. I've waited so long."

Rowan's touch returned, with more pressure this time, and she skated around her aching clit before dipping to her centre and back out, making the same circuit of all her most needy parts.

She kept eye contact, wanting to convey to Rowan what she was feeling, not just the physical sensation but how deeply she felt their connection. Rowan's fingers moved faster, but Tess needed more. She moved her hand down to Rowan's and directed it firmly towards her centre. Rowan's eyes opened slightly as she slipped inside Tess. Tess let out a gasp. "Oh, yes, that's where I need you."

Rowan started to build the rhythm as Tess rocked her hips rock against her, her climax building quickly. She moved her fingers back to circle her own clit and held Rowan's gaze. The emotion she saw there was doing as much to bring her closer to her release as their physical connection.

She panted as Rowan increased the pace even more, her own breathing speeding up as she watched Tess reach her climax. Tess let out a moan and arched her body towards Rowan as she came. Rowan's groan almost equalled it as she held her steady until her body relaxed, and she covered her in kisses.

As the haze of her orgasm faded, Tess looked up at Rowan, holding her so tenderly, and she knew she never needed to worry about Rowan controlling her or pushing her in directions she didn't want to go. Rowan loved her, and she would always be safe with her.

THIRTY-FIVE

Rowan walked up the steps to her dad's house with mixed feelings. She knew what she had to do, and the thought of being free of the responsibility of running the business filled her with a sense of lightness, as if she could finally be free of the weight of a responsibility she'd taken on so many years ago. There had been good times there as well, and she'd loved spending so much time with her dad when she was younger. But those days were gone now anyway. Her dad had stepped back from the business, and it was time for her to do the same. She knew they'd found in Tess someone who had a passion for running the firm and would continue to make it a success. She'd done her bit, and now it was time to do what she really wanted to do.

She rang the doorbell and let herself in. Her dad was always saying she didn't need do that, but it was respectful to announce her arrival. He wasn't in the lounge. She hoped she hadn't disturbed him having an afternoon nap. "Dad? It's me," she shouted up the stairs.

"Rowan? I wasn't expecting you. Get the kettle on, and I'll be down in a minute."

Her dad sounded a little flustered. Weird, he was usually thrilled to see her. She went into the kitchen and flicked the kettle switch. She pulled down the chipped mug he'd used since she'd painted it for him as a small child. The painted words had faded over the years, but it still declared "World's Best Daddy" in childish scrawl. She remembered so vividly sitting with her mum and focusing so hard on getting the letters straight. The curved surface had made it difficult. Finally, her mum had taken her paintbrush and calmed her. She'd wiped away her frustrated tears and reassured her that her daddy would love it because she'd made it.

And he had. Its survival for nearly thirty years proved it.

She'd attributed so many of her issues to the trauma her mother's death, but she'd been an uptight child long before. Her mum had always told her to be kind to herself, and she'd never understood what she meant until recently. She didn't have to spend her whole life punishing herself. She was allowed to be happy.

"Afternoon, love."

Her dad nearly caused her to spill the boiling water she was pouring. Served her right for daydreaming. "Hi, Dad." She turned to see him running his finger through his uncharacteristically tousled hair. "Everything okay?" She hoped he wasn't neglecting himself now that he didn't have to make the effort to come into work. She shouldn't have left him for nearly a week with no proper explanation.

He beamed back at her. "Everything's grand, duck. You're back sooner than expected." He took the mug she held out. "How are Willow and Cara? And my beautiful grandson?"

"They're all good. I had a lovely time." She blew on her

tea while she thought about what she was going to say next. "Are we going to sit down?"

He looked over his shoulder at the door and pulled out a chair at the table. "If you want, love. Are you staying long?"

She didn't get it. It was usually a struggle to get away, but he seemed keen to get rid of her. She dropped into the chair opposite him. "Look, Dad, if I annoyed you going away at short notice, I'm really sorry. It felt like the only thing I could do at the time, but it was irresponsible, I know."

Her dad took a long swig of his tea. "Nonsense, you can take a break if you need to, Ro. Tess managed brilliantly on her own, but I think it was hard for her. If you're going to make a habit of it, you might need to get her some extra help."

Her jaw dropped. She needed to seize her moment. "That was what I wanted to talk to you about, as it happens." She put her mug down and clasped her hands, hoping she'd come up with the right words. "I've loved the years we've worked together, Dad. You know that, don't you?"

"Of course, Rowan. You were the best daughter I could've hoped for, dropping your career plans and everything to help me out when I got ill." He squeezed her hands. "I just thought it would be for a few months to begin with. But I loved working with you so much, I didn't want to push you to leave. And you seemed happy enough."

"Oh, I was. Always." She could say that truthfully. She'd never been unhappy, just unfulfilled and hoping that one day she could do something different.

"And now?" He looked at her with shining eyes.

She wasn't sure if the emotion showing on his face was regret or pride. "Now I want to go and see if I can make a living from my drawing. We've found the perfect general manager in Tess. She's better at the business side of things than we ever were."

Her dad nodded. "And the salary would help her out." He sighed. "Oh, Ro, it's the end of an era."

She turned their hands around and looked down at his worn and callused fingers. "It is. But does that mean I have your blessing to leave?"

"Rowan," he said sharply. "You've never been under any obligation to work there. It was your choice, and I hope you've always known you were free to leave at any time."

"Of course I know that, Dad." That part wasn't entirely true. She'd always been aware it would have been her mum's business too, as she and her sister grew up, and that had made her feel she had a duty to fill her place.

"But if you want to know if I'm confident in Tess's ability to keep the place running, then yes, I have no concerns about you leaving. It's just a little final."

She got up, relief mixed with sadness, and knelt by her dad's chair to wrap him in a warm hug. "I'm not going anywhere, Dad, not like that feckless younger daughter of yours."

His shoulders shook, and she joined him in his laughter. As she stood, she heard the sound of a creak on the stairs, followed by footsteps. She turned to look at her dad. He stared back wide-eyed, like a little boy who'd been caught stealing biscuits.

"Has she..."

Rowan turned towards the voice and saw an older woman wearing her dad's dressing gown appear around the door.

"Oh, sorry. I didn't hear any voices for a while." The

woman turned a shade of crimson as she ran her hand over her hair.

Rowan looked back at her dad. No wonder he'd been eager for her to leave earlier. She fought to keep the grin off her face. She remembered the conversation they'd had before her first sleepover as a teenager. Let him squirm a little.

"Rowan, meet Sandra." He stood and moved himself between Rowan and the poor woman in the doorway, as if she might do her harm.

She stifled a laugh, but her smile broke through. "I'm very pleased to meet you, Sandra." She held out her hand.

Sandra stepped around her dad and shook her hand, smiling nervously. "And you, Rowan. I've heard so much about you."

"Really? Unfortunately, Dad's not mentioned you at all." She turned to grin at her dad. "Why's that, Dad?"

"Ah, well, I didn't know how you would feel about me seeing someone." He looked away.

Rowan took pity on him. "Dad, Mum's been gone for over twenty-five years. You've been there for everyone. It's time to start living life for yourself." She laughed to herself. Who was she to be giving that particular piece of advice? "Whatever you've got with Sandra," She turned and smiled at her, "make the most of it and enjoy."

Her dad's face broke into a wide smile. "That's all good then. Let's get the kettle on and you two can get to know each other."

———

"He never was!" As she roared with laughter, Tess threw her head back so far, her short ponytail dipped into the bubbles that surrounded them. "Damn, I was trying to keep it dry. It'll go all frizzy now." She wiped the bubbles off as best she could.

They were sitting face to face in Tess's bath, and Rowan was trying to ignore the taps digging into the middle of her back. Tess's bath was nowhere near big enough for both of them, but she'd turned up to share the news of her dad's newfound love life just as Tess had run a bath. It would have been rude to refuse the invitation to join her. So now she sat, knees tucked up around her chin, impaling herself on the plumbing as she regaled Tess with the story. It still felt wonderful to have regained their intimacy, but she wished it was in a more comfortable setting. "I'm so happy for him." She smiled. "I may not have let it show immediately because it's good to keep him on his toes. But I couldn't be more pleased."

"Me too. Derek deserves to be happy." Tess was still trying to wring out her sopping hair.

Rowan took pity on her. "I think it's too late to save it. Why don't you turn around and lean back, and I'll wash it for you?"

Tess shot her a grin. "Sounds erotic."

Probably not in this ridiculous-sized bath, but she'd give it a try. Several careful manoeuvres later, they achieved their desired positions without the bathwater slopping out. Tess slid down and soaked her hair fully, her body slipping between Rowan's spread knees. She really hadn't thought this through. The sensation was exquisite, but this was definitely not the bath to be having full-blown sex in. Tess slid back up, repeating the contact with Rowan as she did. Was she doing it on purpose? Rowan resolved to finish the bath as soon as possible and take this somewhere more comfortable. She reached for the shampoo and tipped a copious amount into her hand. Tess's hair was thicker than anything she'd ever known, and there was no such thing as too much shampoo.

She began to massage it through Tess's hair, which was curlier when it was wet, and Rowan loved how the copper hues shone. She ran her hands through it more than was strictly necessary, knowing by the moans coming from Tess that she was appreciating the experience. She reached for the shower head, before Tess could do any more moves on her tender parts. "Is that water all right for you?" she asked, mimicking the voice of their local hairdresser.

Tess elbowed her. "Get on with it, and I'll make sure your tip is worthwhile."

"I'm just going to put your conditioner on now." Rowan continued playing the role. She applied plenty of the creamy liquid and then began to massage Tess's scalp.

The groans reached a whole new level. "You can never stop. That's just too good."

"Not even to tell you Dad and I have decided we want to you to take over running the business?" She'd wanted to wait to tell Tess face to face, but she was so relaxed and happy, even if Rowan had lost the feeling in her legs. It seemed like a good time.

Unfortunately, Tess's reaction was to turn fully around and plant a kiss on her lips. The ensuing tidal wave poured over the top of the bath and landed with a splash on the bathroom floor.

Tess leapt up with a shriek. "Shit, shit, shit. The surveyor is coming tomorrow. I can't have water leaking through the ceiling."

She jumped out and grabbed all the towels she could lay her hands on, to mop up the mess. Rowan chuckled as she jumped out after her. They could talk about the future when this particular problem was addressed.

As they crawled around naked trying to mop up the deluge before it soaked through the floor, Tess turned to her. "And what does that mean for you?"

"I'm thinking of trying to make a go of my drawing. I might need to do all kinds of things until I can get a portfolio built up." She ducked her head to reach the puddle under the sink. When she re-emerged Tess was right in front of her, her eyes soft.

"Oh, Ro, that's wonderful. You're going to be successful. People will love your work." She wrapped her arms around Rowan's neck.

"Thanks for the vote of confidence, but I think you may be a little biased." Still, she couldn't help the grin she felt spreading across her face.

Tess stood and Rowan remained where she was, looking at the woman she'd admired for so long and now had a future with. As Tess pulled her to her feet and towards the bedroom, her only concern was what that future might look like. She needed to talk about the house situation, but she couldn't bear to ruin the moment. Tess had put an offer on another less-than-ideal house in the suburbs and if she left it much longer, they'd have to make the best of it. She wanted more than that for Tess. For both of them.

THIRTY-SIX

Tess grabbed her jacket and reached on the worktop for the keys to her car. Rowan slid them out of the way and held out her own car keys. "I put you on the insurance for the Audi. It's bad enough you're driving down there on your own. You might as well have a bit of comfort."

"Oh, Rowan, that's so sweet." She took the keys and reached up on tiptoes to give Rowan a kiss on the cheek. Rowan turned her head and kissed her firmly on the mouth, her arm snaking around Tess's back to keep her close. Tess melted into the kiss and wished she could just stay and enjoy Rowan's warm mouth all day. She forced herself to pull away. "And you know I need to do this on my own. If Archie's going to come home, I need to talk to him and Pete. Your presence would just give Pete more ammunition." She stroked Rowan's cheek tenderly. "And you can't miss another game. They struggled without you last week."

"I know, but I don't have to like it," Rowan muttered.

Tess moved away from the temptation of her arms. "Look, Archie isn't going to come home today. He's got his last exam tomorrow afternoon. But I'm hoping he'll agree to come back after that." She slung on her jacket. "I'll be home by the time you get back from the game. Why don't you book us into that French restaurant for eight? I'll come over to yours when I'm sorted, and I'll stay the night if you want me to."

Rowan looked up with such joy as she nodded, Tess was glad she'd suggested it. The next few weeks of the kids being home all the time and hopefully a summer house move meant they'd be unlikely to have much time to themselves. They should make the most of what they could get. And she needed more intimacy with Rowan. Their short breakup had left her feeling bruised, and she still felt a tenderness that could only be healed by spending time in Rowan's arms.

"I'll see you later." She treated herself to one final kiss before she headed out to the shiny car awaiting her.

She pulled up outside Pete's house for the third time in a week. She'd texted both Pete and Archie to say she was coming. She'd had a subdued message back from Archie saying he would be in, but Pete hadn't bothered to reply. She checked the time and saw she was quite early, having made the journey in record time in Rowan's sporty little car. She relaxed back into the plush leather seat and wished Rowan was her with her now. Was that a good thing? How quickly had she gone from independent woman, determined never to rely on anyone else again, to wishing she could spend every minute with Rowan? Should she still worry she would lose herself in Rowan? Rowan was the most caring, loyal person she had ever met. If she wasn't safe loving her, she didn't know who she would be safe with.

There, she'd finally said it, even if just in her head. She loved Rowan. And she wasn't going to let her go just because she was a little scared of commitment. Now she needed to make sure Rowan knew that.

She opened the car door reluctantly. This was something she needed to do before she could think about her own relationship. She might as well get it over with. Pete's car was on the drive, and she hoped he would be reasonable.

"Hi, Mum."

Archie swung the door open before she'd even got to it and stood behind it, as if for protection. She stepped inside and waited for him to close it before wrapping him in her arms. "How are you feeling, Arch? All set for tomorrow?" To her surprise, he hugged back. She pulled back to look at his face.

He didn't quite meet her eyes. "I'm fine, Mum." He shuffled his feet. "I'm really sorry about last week. I shouldn't have gone to the party."

"You shouldn't have been allowed to go, Archie. I don't know what your dad was thinking, leaving you on your own." She led him into the kitchen and switched on the kettle. "Will you make me a coffee? I'm parched from the journey." She had always tried to avoid criticising Pete to the children, but Archie needed to know it wasn't acceptable that Pete hadn't taken his responsibilities seriously.

"Dad said you'd blame him." Archie was facing away as he pulled down the cafetière from a shelf. "He says the only mistake he made was thinking I was grown up enough to handle myself at a party."

His shoulders shook, and Tess jumped up and pulled him towards her. His eyes were wet, and he was trying to hold in a sob. "Oh, Archie, you're a teenager full of exam stress and hormones. You're supposed to make bad decisions. And parents are meant to protect you from them. Or try to, anyway. You acted irresponsibly, but your dad has responsibility for your care. Can you see that?" She handed him a tissue from her pocket, and he blew his nose as he nodded. "When your exams are over, I want you to come home and help get the house packed up. I want us to settle in Haresby, Archie. I want it to be your new home as well."

He nodded. "I want that too."

She took him by his shoulders. "But if you live in my house, you need to obey my rules, Archie. We can discuss things if you think I'm being unfair. But no more running off to your dad without talking, okay?"

He sniffed. "I promise. But will the new house have room for my friends to come and stay?"

"We'll make room. It might not be as big as we want, but you'll be able to walk into town to go bowling or meet your new friends when you make some at college." That was a little optimistic. "I know it's hard to be moving house again, but I promise this one will be for good." She knew now that she meant it. Her old plans to up sticks as soon as her kids had flown the nest had long faded. She wanted to be in Haresby with Rowan, as long as Rowan wanted her. She sat back down and waited for Archie to finish making the coffee. There was another conversation they needed to have. He placed the mugs on the table and sat down.

"When you come home, Archie, Rowan will still be around. Is that going to be a problem?"

Archie's cheeks flushed, and he shook his lowered head. "Of course not. Sorry I was such an idiot."

"Is it because she's a woman?" She didn't want to ask,

didn't want to open herself up to knowing if her own son was ashamed of who she was. But she had to know.

His head shot up, and his mouth opened wide. "No! Why would it be? Elsie's a lesbian. Max is gay. He fancies a guy in Sixth Form who doesn't even know he exists." He scratched his head. "I'm sorry if that's what you thought."

She put aside the relief that washed over her. "So why the drama and all the nasty comments? It hurt, Archie."

He lowered his gaze to his hands. "I'm sorry. I was just feeling really alone. I like Rowan. She's fun, and she knows about cool stuff. But when I saw you together, I thought I'd lost you *and* my new friend, and it felt like everyone had someone except me."

Tess hugged him close. "I'm always here for you. Talk to me if you're worried about anything, okay?"

"Okay."

"Where's your dad? He was supposed to be here."

"He went out early this morning on his motorbike."

Tess stopped herself from rolling her eyes. "How long has he had a motorbike?"

"A few months. It's his new hobby. Lucy has a bike, so he got one too."

Tess had no idea who Lucy was, but she didn't have the enthusiasm to ask. "Ah, that's nice for him. Did he say when he'd be back?" Hopefully not accompanied by his new, leather-clad girlfriend.

Archie approached with the coffee. "I was still in bed when he left, but he left a note for me and Elsie, asking us to make lunch for around one."

Tess took her mug and looked around, not seeing much sign of food preparation.

"I didn't really get around to anything yet. I was in the middle of something."

295

Tess suspected the "something" wasn't revision but trusted her smart son to have done enough preparation for his final exam. "Where's Elsie? She's got an exam tomorrow too."

He looked up guiltily. "She's gone into town."

"For anything in particular?" She suspected it was more of an *anyone.*

"Um, I think she said Jai was coming down on the train for the day. I can't really remember."

Archie had never been a good liar and for that, she was grateful. "I'll be having words with your sister later." She looked around the kitchen, so familiar and yet so alien. The flashbacks she used to dread when she came into this house had subsided, but she wasn't keen on spending any more time here than she needed. She turned back to Archie. "How about we go out for lunch? You can choose where. We'll let your dad know, and he can join us if he wishes. If he does, we can talk to him together about you coming home, okay?"

Archie smiled widely. "Is pizza an acceptable Sunday lunch choice?"

"Absolutely not, but let's do it anyway." She ruffled his hair and reached for her car keys. "Let's go."

Tess was in an extremely good mood as she dressed for dinner. Pete had shown his face at the pizza restaurant for long enough for Tess to explain that she felt it was better for Archie to be at home with her while he worked towards his A-levels. He'd just stood over them, glaring. But for once, Tess didn't feel threatened. He had no power over her, and Archie knew which parent had his best interests at heart.

"Is that what you want, Archie, or has she twisted your arm?"

Archie had looked up at his dad with wide eyes, but his voice had been steady. "I'd like to make a new start in Haresby for Sixth Form. But I'll come and stay at weekends, Dad. We can still do stuff."

Pete had shrugged. "If that's what you want, son. You know where I am."

Tess wasn't sure if she imagined it, but after all her years of having to guess his emotions, she got the distinct impression he was relieved. As he walked out of the restaurant and Archie turned and returned her smile, a weight lifted from her shoulders.

Now she was getting ready to spend the evening with Rowan, and she searched for the new clothes she'd splurged out on a couple of months ago but had never had an occasion to wear. The silk shirt was a green that she knew Rowan loved to see on her. When she was ready, she looked at herself in the mirror, and decided she approved.

She got out of the car at Rowan's flat and looked up. Rowan was smiling down from her kitchen window. They were going to the French restaurant Rowan had taken her to on their first date. Tess had spent her journey thinking about how much had changed since then. Her life felt so much more manageable now that the kids were only going to school for exams. There were still a couple more stressful exam weeks to get through but once it was over, she could fully embrace their new life in this little Midlands town she had grown to love. She had always believed she would end up back in Yorkshire, but now she couldn't imagine being anywhere else. She had a job that she loved, and she wanted to be close to Rowan. The next house she bought would hopefully be her home for a long time to come.

Her offer on the semi in the suburbs hadn't yet been accepted, but she was reassured by the estate agent it soon would be. It wasn't ideal in many ways, but it was still better than being isolated in a village, and she'd make the best of it.

Rowan waited just inside the door, her coat already on, and after a long kiss, she slipped her hand in Tess's as they started their walk into town.

"Talk me through the game. Was it an easy win?"

Rowan squeezed her hand. "Rugby can wait. Tell me how you got on with Archie."

Their meal was just as delicious as the first time and with a similar level of sexual tension. They were seated at the table they'd been at four months before, when Tess had spent the whole meal anticipating how the evening would end. "One day, can we come here and just enjoy the food instead of me wanting to shovel it down my face and take you home to bed?"

Rowan raised her eyebrow. "Are you only interested in getting me into bed? How shallow."

Tess laughed. "Not just into bed, no. Alone will do. Kitchen table, stairs, anywhere that takes your fancy." She grinned.

Rowan cleared her throat. "Well, before you drag me away to sate your desires, I wanted to talk to you about something."

"Ooh, sounds serious." She placed her elbows on the table and propped her chin.

"Promise you'll let me finish before you react?"

"You've got my full attention." She wiggled her eyebrows and grinned.

Rowan didn't smile back but bit her lip. "So, I know you quite like the house you've put the offer on." She pulled a brochure out of her back pocket and flattened it out in front of Tess. "But this looks so much more like your kind of house. Period features and more central."

Tess looked at the brochure in disbelief. "Of course this is more my kind of thing, Rowan. It's gorgeous. We've talked about this before." She ran her hand over her face as she flicked through the images of a beautiful Edwardian terraced house. She paused to look at the beautiful period fireplace that had been modernised with a log-burning stove. Why was Rowan torturing her with houses that were out of her reach? "Trouble is, it's way out of my price bracket. I've got two kids to get through university. I can't afford to mortgage myself up to the eyeballs." She wasn't trying to sound whiny, but she was surprised at Rowan's lack of sensitivity. To be able to live in a house like this, within walking distance of work, Archie's college, and Elsie's campus would be a dream come true. It was a beautiful area of town, but she had ruled it out from the beginning of her house-hunting, because she knew she couldn't afford anything big enough for them all. She pulled herself out of her thoughts and realised Rowan had gone quiet. She looked up after admiring the photo of a beautifully tiled hallway.

"I thought you said you'd let me speak first."

Oh bugger, I need to try harder not to talk over her. "I'm sorry, I just don't think there's much to say. But go ahead."

"I know you've not long come out of a relationship that didn't make you happy, so I doubt big commitments are on your to-do list." Rowan let out a breath. "But I love you, and I'd really like to buy this house with you, Tess."

She hadn't seen that coming. "Rowan—"

Rowan held up her hand. "Wait. I'm not trying to rush anything. I can stay in the flat. I have savings that are sitting in low interest accounts, so it makes sense to invest them. I can stay over as much as you want me to and give you space when you need it. You can always buy me out later if you want to. In the meantime, you and the kids get to live in a house that gives you a good quality of life, and I get to keep you close by. And there's enough room for me too if that's what you want later." She sat back and chewed the side of her nail, her eyes still on Tess. "Please say yes."

Tess took the hand Rowan was biting and pulled it to the table with their fingers entwined. She looked into her eyes. "I love you too, Rowan Russell." She leaned across the table and planted a kiss on Rowan's gorgeous lips, which widened into a wondrous smile. Tess did feel a little overwhelmed. It was a wonderful, generous gesture, and she believed Rowan when she said she had no expectations. But she knew she didn't want a life without Rowan in it. If they were going to do this, they might as well go into it wholeheartedly.

"Is that a yes then?" Rowan's eyes shone.

"Yes. I would love to buy this wonderful house with you, Rowan, and I want us to live together. I don't want to spend another night without you. Now let's pay the bill and get out of here, so I can show you exactly how much I want to share with you."

As they walked home hand in hand, she knew she was finally safe to look forward to a life of being happy and loved.

THIRTY-SEVEN

Tess packed the last few kitchen items into a box and folded the flaps closed. Through the front window, she could see Rowan and Becca wrestling the sofa into the back of the rented van. She should've got a removal company in, but Rowan had insisted they could manage. Rowan had spent the previous day, with Becca's assistance, moving her own belongings into the new house, and Tess envied their energy on a second day of furniture-hauling.

They'd roped everyone in to help today. Jules had gone ahead with a car full of breakables, along with her new girlfriend, Natalia, who she'd met at the spa. They'd been seeing each other for a few weeks and were taking it slow, but Jules had a new bounce in her step that warmed Tess's heart.

Archie and Ben had helped load the van, and Becca was going to drive the van with the boys to the house while Tess and Rowan gave everything a last clean before following them in the work van.

Elsie appeared at the door, a large poster frame in her

arms. "I think that's it. Are you sure you'll be okay cleaning up here?"

"Of course we will." She held out the box. "Ensure coffee is prepared for our arrival."

Elsie gave her a peck on the cheek as she balanced the box alongside the frame. "See you soon. Are you excited?"

Tess rubbed her face, feeling the grime. "At the moment I'm slightly overwhelmed and exhausted. Ask me again when I've got my feet up."

Elsie nodded. "See you later." She all but ran out of the door to Jai's car, which was packed to the roof with her belongings.

Tess waited at the door while Rowan locked up the back of the van and went to speak to Becca in the cab. Becca started the engine, and the van rolled away slowly. Archie leaned out of the window and waved. She waved back as Rowan came to join her. She was glad of Rowan's arm around her waist.

"You okay?" Rowan watched her closely.

She felt her eyes prick with tears, and she turned back to the house. Rowan pulled her back. She leaned into Rowan's strong arms. "I'm sorry. It's nothing really."

Rowan held her, and she let a few tears soak into Rowan's dusty T-shirt.

She pulled back. "I'm okay, let's get cleaning."

Rowan took her hand and led her through the house and out the back door. All the pots and garden furniture were long gone, but there was still an old wooden bench built into the wall. She sat and Rowan sat next to her, watching.

"Someone once told me it's better to talk about what's going on in here." Rowan tapped the side of Tess's head.

Tess chuckled and ran her hands through her hair,

trying to put her feelings into words. "When I came back here, less than a year ago, I thought it was a chance at freedom. All those years of yearning to be able to do what I wanted, see who I wanted. Just being on my own was all I was aiming for. Then I met you again, and as I got to know you, I realised that there was so much more to being with someone than giving up control. You don't take anything away from me, Rowan. You make me more than I ever thought I could be." She pulled Rowan close. "So, the reason I'm feeling a little emotional is because I'm overwhelmed with how my life has changed in ways that I could never have imagined, in a few short months. I love you, Rowan, and I'm never letting you go."

Rowan kissed her tenderly and pulled away. "That's good, because I love you too, and I'm not going anywhere."

Tess stood and pulled Rowan back into the house. "Let's get out of here and start our new life together." She looked around at the house, so full of old memories, and she knew that none of them mattered. She was going to build all the memories she needed with Rowan.

ACKNOWLEDGMENTS

I didn't want this to be just a rugby story. Not everyone enjoys sport, and my friends would happily tell you I don't know enough about rugby anyway. But the bonds that grow out of playing on a team together are special, and that's what I wanted to write about.

So my biggest thanks have to be to my Gate teammates, and particularly those who've remained my dearest friends long after we hung up our boots and packed away our scrum caps in case we ever need them for fancy dress (that might just be me). Age, time and geography don't matter. We'll always be there for each other.

To Niki (sorry the coin toss didn't make the cut) and Oisín, for technical advice.

And to Vix, who taught me so much with her unique brand of compassion, humour and brutality.

Thanks again to Global Wordsmiths for helping me further along the road of becoming a writer. I will understand commas one day!

Louise, always, for endless patience and support.

And finally thank you to all the readers who bought and enjoyed Sleepless Nights. Without your wonderful comments and reviews this book would definitely never have existed.